"Sedgwick weaves science and the imagination into a melancholic yet magical tale. . . . Readers would do well to suspend disbelief and open their hearts to the romance, the lush prose, and the mystery of Sedgwick's original and inventive debut."

—*Library Journal*

"Helen Sedgwick has written a first novel of remarkable grace, beauty, and insight, in which a careful love of language meets an immense storytelling talent. I was moved and inspired by this book." —Joseph O'Connor, author of *Star of the Sea*

"In her ambitious . . . debut novel, journalist, editor, and former research physicist Sedgwick leaps through time, from 1066 to the present, following the trajectories of her characters' lives as various comets surge gloriously through the night skies."

—*Kirkus Reviews*

"*The Comet Seekers* is a brave and tender debut from one of the brightest new stars of the literary world. It's one of the most vivid, original, and magical books I've read in years."

—Kirsty Logan, author of *The Gracekeepers*

"Inspired by the mysteries of the Bayeux Tapestry, a work of art nearly a millennium old, *The Comet Seekers* weaves an exquisite tale of love and fate, impermanence and infinity, the pull of the sky and the bonds of earth. Helen Sedgwick charts the paths of the cosmos and the human heart with unnerving intelligence and grace. This is a novel about the universe, yes, but also about spaces small and secret—the homes we make for ourselves: how we build them, why we leave, and what it means to stay. A luminous debut." —Leslie Parry, author of *Church of Marvels*

"A spellbinding tale of love and loss, aglimmer with passion and melancholy." —*Sunday Express* (London)

THE COMET SEEKERS

The Comet Seekers

A Novel

Helen Sedgwick

HARPER

NEW YORK ■ LONDON ■ TORONTO ■ SYDNEY

First U.S. hardcover edition published in 2016 by HarperCollins Publishers.

HarperCollins books may be purchased for educational, business, or sales promotional use. For information, please email the Special Markets Department at SPsales@harpercollins.com.

Originally published in Great Britain in 2016 by Harvill Secker.

FIRST HARPER PAPERBACK EDITION PUBLISHED IN 2017.

The Library of Congress has catalogued the hardcover edition as follows:

Names: Sedgwick, Helen, 1978- author.
Title: The comet seekers : a novel / Helen Sedgwick.
Description: First edition. | New York : Harper, 2016. | "Originally
    published in Great Britain in 2016 by Harvill Secker"—Verso title page.
Identifiers: LCCN 2016008606| ISBN 9780062448767 (hardback) | ISBN
    9780062448781 (ebook)
Subjects: LCSH: Astronomers—Fiction. | Comets—Fiction. | Giacobini-Zinner
    comet—Fiction. | Antarctica—Fiction. | Psychological fiction. | BISAC:
    FICTION / Literary. | FICTION / Sagas. | GSAFD: Love stories.
Classification: LCC PR6119.E37 C66 2016 | DDC 813/.6—dc23 LC record
available at https://lccn.loc.gov/2016008606

ISBN 978-0-06-244877-4 (pbk.)

17 18 19 20 21   OFF / LSC   10 9 8 7 6 5 4 3 2

For my family

THE COMET SEEKERS

Comet Giacobini

THEY ARRIVE ON THE SNOW during the last endless day of summer. Forty-eight hours of light and then, they gather outside to watch their first sunset of the South. The ice shelf they're standing on is floating, slowly, towards the coast – will one day melt into the sea. There is nothing permanent about this never-ending white.

Róisín stamps her feet, watches the sky for the full twenty minutes of night, not that it ever gets dark. Dusk is the most she can hope for, this week at least; everything turning a golden red, the sun's rays like torchlight through the curved walls of a child's tent, the full moon opposite. It shines like a second sun but fainter, its reflected light a ghost of the star below the horizon.

During the day, some people run a marathon around the base – eight laps of the research station at minus ten degrees.

Róisín joins them on their final lap. Her legs feel heavy; gulps of air chill her lungs. The winner is lying flat on the snow at the finish line. When he sees her looking he smiles up at her, says: You should try it.

Maybe next time, she says.

His name is François.

He holds his hand over his eyes, trying to shield the glare.

He looks so young.

One hour, forty minutes of darkness, and someone is behind her. Five days she has been here, five days she has searched the sky alone. Róisín turns around.

What are you looking for?

François is here, wanting to see what she's doing, to join in. She's not sure how she feels about that; she did not come here to make friends. Róisín thinks about telling him so, asking him to leave, but for some reason she decides to let him stay. Beside her, François looks at the sky and exhales.

There's a comet predicted, she says. It's going to be very bright. But it's too early. I mean, we're too soon.

Because it's not dark enough yet?

Yes. Well, that and other things.

It's beautiful, isn't it?

Above them, colours swirl like sea mist.

François stays where he is, doesn't ask any more questions. He doesn't take his eyes from the sky.

Róisín finds she has walked into the kitchen. She says she wants to help – it doesn't feel right with François in there on his own, cooking for sixteen, even though he's the chef. She offers to slice onions and retrieve diced meat from the freezer, watches his hands as he works. The smell is of roasting tomatoes and rosemary.

This was one of my favourites, he says, when I was a child.

Abbey Road is playing on the tape deck.

Róisín thinks of soft-boiled eggs and soldiers. The sun is setting again.

Three hours, twenty minutes of darkness. The night is increasing by twenty minutes each day. It is building up to 21 March, when things will be perfectly balanced and there will be twelve hours of light and twelve hours of dark.

Every day, Róisín marks the calendar with a cross. Turning over the page – a photo of lights, traffic, people, noise, the cityscape a world away. She checks the footnote. It is Cape Town, and underneath Cape Town a day, three weeks away, is circled in blue.

She stands outside and listens through the muffled layer of her hood to the absolute silence of snow and ice dust and rock. Sometimes François comes outside to stand with her, but she never asks what they will be cooking the next day for dinner.

They hear on the radio that a group of sea lions have been spotted off the coast. The research team goes to investigate, Róisín and some of the others, taking cameras with long lenses, notebooks and food enough for two days. They're not far from the coast but it still feels like a hike from the base; four hours' walk in snow boots, pulling the sleigh, is not easy. There was training for this job, a series of tests you had to pass: physical, survival, psychological.

As they approach the coast they can see kelp gulls circling; something must have died. On arrival they see that something has. One of the sea lions has been killed in a fight, over territory or perhaps a female. They take photographs, look for any tags from other research teams, keep their distance. The red of its blood seems like the most vivid, most deeply coloured thing Róisín has seen for years.

There is a building by the coast, a square, basic sort of place, where they can sleep, or at least rest, before making the hike home tomorrow. Lying down, Róisín turns to face the wall and cannot see the concrete two inches from her eyes in the dark.

She's alone. She's walking towards the dead sea lion even though she knows it's wrong; they are not allowed to get too close, not allowed to touch or interfere, but she sees the blood and has no choice – how did this happen? she asks the sea lion corpse, how did this happen? She tries to pick him up, but his skin is like whale blubber and she is repulsed.

She wakes, sick and longing, and full of guilt.

When they get back to the base she sees François in the kitchen. He turns, sees her; there is a look of wonder in his eyes that she wishes she understood, that she wants to share.

The door is only half closed and Róisín's eyes only half shut when she hears a quiet tap tap at the window before sunrise. A rope has come loose from the sleigh they were using, snaking in the wind.

I heard it too, François whispers from the doorway, hardly making a sound. He is wearing thermal underwear and indoor boots, bobble hat and knitted gloves. She would have laughed, if her throat hadn't been so dry.

He lies next to her on the bed and together they listen to the whip of the rope on glass, through snow. As the light dawns, she pulls off his hat.

SOMETIMES, LATE AT NIGHT, FRANÇOIS writes to Severine, notepaper balanced on bent knees, head propped up on pillows. He describes the white, the snow, the sky so open he can see it curve around the Brunt ice shelf and meet the horizon in a swirl of frozen blue.

He describes the Halley VI research station, each module standing self-sufficient on legs that keep it elevated above the floating ice, a strange caterpillar of research labs and sleeping quarters with a central red hub where they all meet to talk and wait for snowstorms to pass. As the days edge closer to winter the pages of his letter take on a chill. He asks her how she is, if the sun is warm in Bayeux.

He pulls the cover over his legs, rubs the scar on his thumb and looks down at red fading to silver; the two colours of this world.

I hope it's peaceful there, Mama, he writes.

It is peaceful here, but I think a storm might be brewing.

What am I supposed to see? he asks, taking the binoculars from his eyes.

Róisín smiles.

Well, at this magnification, all you can make out is the comet's nucleus, which is the bright bit at the front...

He puts the binoculars back to his eyes, thinks about telling her he is not so young as she imagines.

...and the tail, which is the stream of dust and ice that gets blown out behind as it accelerates towards the sun.

So, it's ice?

Ice and rock and maybe some bits of molecules, you know, the interplanetary junk that gets picked up along the way.

It's not junk, he says, it's extraordinary.

You remind me of someone from a long time ago.

He turns to look at her; she hasn't mentioned her past before, and he doesn't know if he should ask her questions about it now.

I used to watch the comets when I was a child, he says, with my mother.

She was a scientist?

No, he laughs, no. She just loved them. Do you think it's strange to love something you don't understand?

Róisín shakes her head. Just human, she says.

Why is next Monday circled on the calendar?

The comet will be at its brightest.

Is that all?

He puts the binoculars down. His tone changes.

Róisín?

François leaves his room and goes in search of something to dull his restlessness. They are playing cards in the central hub; he lingers by the door then retreats back the way he came. He doesn't know why he's behaving like this. He has been knocked off balance; and worse, he didn't notice it happening.

When he looks back at his letter to Severine, the smudges of the words make it look as if he's been crying on the page. It doesn't matter. Of course it will not be sent, not any time soon – there is no airlifted postal service here. The next delivery is six months away. But even so, he describes the comet he has been watching, with Róisín, in the sky. I have seen its nucleus, he writes; I could make out its tail. It is a different colour to the stars, isn't that miraculous? I feel so close to home today, and so far away.

He folds his letter, written over weeks, and seals the envelope. Presses a first-class stamp to his tongue. The taste lingers long after the letter has been safely stowed at the bottom of his case. He heads outside; he needs to sleep under the stars tonight.

- - - - - - - -

RÓISÍN OPENS THE ZIP TO François's tent slowly, not wanting to wake him if he is asleep. She's not sure what he's doing out here, but she saw the red tent in the starlight and knew that she had to join him.

Are you sleeping? she whispers.

Yes, he replies.

That's good, she smiles, though it's so dark she knows he won't be able to see that. I'll just talk, and you can sleep, she says, and we'll both feel better for it.

She talks about Liam, because she feels now that she has to speak about it, if she has any chance of letting it go.

And she suspects that François might have lost somebody too.

There is a gust of wind that makes the taut fabric of the tent resonate like a string; ripple with harmonics.

He closes his fingers around hers, but there is only a second of this closeness before she pulls away again.

I think I need to say goodbye, she says. I'm sorry.

He follows her outside as she leaves, but not back to the base – he has his own past to remember, or to forget. Instead he turns away and starts packing up the tent by the light of the morning stars, under the glow of the comet.

The next night François dreams there is a strange woman sitting on his bed, with a voice he knows but has never heard before.

So you found me, then, he says. I knew you were coming.

It's cold, she replies. You're on the wrong continent.

Could you take it easy on me, please? he says. I know why you're here.

He opens his eyes to an empty, watery room. He blinks; the water in his eyes clears for a second, and then returns.

He is surprised by the conviction of it – it is not logical, but undeniable nonetheless. He's been waiting for news even though the news couldn't reach him. He doesn't know what else he can do so he drinks, and cries, and lets his heart break because he knows – somehow he knows – that tonight, a world away, his mother has died.

Róisín hikes through the night, now and then stopping to take out her notebook from the side pocket of her jacket, mark with pencil where the comet is relative to the stars. She keeps walking until the base is no longer visible – she doesn't want any signs of humanity on the horizon. There is only one person she wants to see tonight. The wind is starting to get strong, biting at her skin even through her layers of protection – it is incredible, the way wind can do that. Soon it will be too dangerous to continue; she can see the swirls of ice ahead, where the wind is so strong it can lift the top layer of the ground.

Róisín chooses her spot carefully: a cave of sorts, an overhang of rock and ice that will provide some shelter from the wind. She looks up at the comet – still visible, still daring her on – then looks more precisely through her binoculars and marks it again on her map before starting to unpack the shelter.

Her highest marks in the Antarctic Survey were in the survival test. She has seen worse than this.

The shelter is red, bright red, the colour of something that can't be missed, should anyone look for it. Inside, by the light of the torch, everything is rosy and golden; tent torchlight is beautiful. The storm is getting louder though. She steps outside and is almost knocked off her feet, but she struggles to stand upright, facing the wind, and watches the comet on this, its brightest night. No storm will stop her.

Some say that comets seed life on lifeless planets. She finds that hard to believe. The comet is ice, it is burning with wind; wild, inhospitable, stunning. It is not unlike where she is standing. This is, perhaps, the closest a human being can get to travelling on a comet as it approaches perihelion. Clinging on for life.

The first time she wakes, she thinks something is trying to get inside; a big shape – a bear? – is pressing against her tent. It takes her a moment to realise it is the snow piling up outside, and that there are no bears here. Perhaps there is nothing here.

The next time she is back on soft, dandelioned grass; she is wearing pyjamas and lying in the open air. Liam is beside her. No, this can't be right. There is no grass on the comet. Wait.

She finds the torch, turns on the light. It helps. She wonders if the sun will rise soon. Perhaps François will come in the morning and unbury her from all this snow. Perhaps the snow itself will melt as they hurtle through space, towards the heat of the sun. Perhaps Liam will come home from wherever he wanted to go; he will have seen enough light, and she enough snow, and together they will lie on the farm grass and look up to the comets overhead and pretend like they don't need to breathe; and in secret, they will breathe.

Comet West

RÓISÍN KEEPS LOOKING OUT OF the window as they eat their boiled eggs. Liam knows why; sundown is coming and she wants to be out before dark. Every night this week it has been the same; the comet was predicted, but still it hasn't arrived. There's only two days and a weekend left of the half-term holidays, and then she'll have to go home.

If he knew how, Liam would stop the time from moving forwards and stay in this week – this exact one – for all his life. He looks at the clock on the kitchen wall and Róisín looks at the dusk beyond the window, out to the red tent that is pitched up in the field.

The red tent was a present from his mum the year before she died. Liam knows it was from her because his dad would never have chosen something red, although it had both of their names on the label. His mum wore red; yellow and gold and red and purple, all the colours of the rainbow. She never seemed quite in the right place on their farm, so far from everywhere. Maybe that's why she left it so early. Inside the red tent, the light is different to anywhere else in the world; it is like being inside a balloon that is flying up into the sun.

Can I bring Bobby with me tonight?

Róisín rolls her eyes.

Liam's not really this young – he'll be seven later this year – and most nights he forgets about Bobby altogether, but if he's going to try to stay in this week forever, without time moving forwards, he'd quite like to keep Bobby with him.

Pandas don't live in tents.

Bobby does. He likes the red. Anyway, pandas don't live in Ireland either.

Róisín made Bobby stay in the house last night because of the risk of rain, although it didn't rain in the end and there was no comet either, so it was a bit of a waste. Liam thinks that maybe Bobby will be a good omen for them tonight.

If you like you can bring an omen too, he says.

I don't need one – Róisín zips up his coat by the back door and puts Bobby in his big coat pocket – I've got you.

While Liam arranges everything in the tent in the field, Róisín starts work on her maps. She's been drawing them every night. Maps of the night-time sky, so that she can see how each thing moves, how near and far from each other they get. It was one of the first things she learnt to draw when she was little, and she still think it's the best. Why draw a square house with a triangular roof when you can draw the patterns in the stars? Liam thinks her maps look a bit like join-the-dots – that if he just knew how to read them properly something extraordinary would appear. Maybe the comet will help, like the code key he has in his colouring books. Yesterday he did a tractor.

Liam!

He puts Bobby in his sleeping bag and unzips the tent. The dark comes quickly; he's noticed that this past week.

I think it's come.

The comet?

Of course!

That's grand.

Róisín doesn't look at him the whole time; her eyes are fixed on the sky.

The comet is more like a blur really. Like someone has dropped a silver pen on a page of black paper and then smudged it with their thumb.

Is that it? Liam says. Why's it so small?

Because it's far away. But what you mean is why is it so faint. And that's because it's far away too, but it's moving towards us so it's going to get brighter.

When?

Maybe later tonight.

Are you sure?

Maybe tomorrow.

So what are we going to do tonight?

He's getting cold already, out here in the dark, what with it not even being spring yet, not for a few weeks anyway.

Tonight we're going to watch it move, Róisín says, as she pulls her sleeping bag from inside the tent. If we lie here, we'll be able to see the sky all night long.

Liam crawls inside the tent. He's cold. He thinks that Róisín will follow him in, but he knows that's a stupid thing to think – she's never followed him anywhere. It's always the other way round.

He takes Bobby out of the sleeping bag, brushes away at the bits of grass on the floor of the tent and sits him up in the corner instead.

But it's not fun being in the tent on his own, even with Bobby, so he forces himself to count to one hundred and then he unzips the door again and looks out. Róisín is lying on her back in the sleeping bag.

He drags his sleeping bag out of the tent, lays it along the grass next to Róisín and wriggles inside.

I'm back, he says, although she doesn't reply and even if she did all she'd say is that he is stating the obvious. He always seems to be doing that.

Hold your breath and count, she says. If you count long enough, and hold your breath long enough, you'll be able to see it move. Because it's flying.

No it's not.

Yes it is. It's flying so fast and so far away it can change the whole sky in the time you can hold your breath for. It's the fastest thing in the solar system. You just have to hold on, and then you'll see.

Liam lies as still as he's ever been and watches, and waits, and holds on. The grass bristles against his skin, the night breeze blows his hair into his eyes but he doesn't move to brush it away. His face gets hotter the longer he goes without breathing; his lips purse into a tight wiggly line, eyes wide and gleaming, his hand grasping onto his cousin's.

Can you see it? she asks.

You breathed!

Liam lets out his breath, gasps in more night-time air – it's the kind of air that smells of ice and fresh grass and pyjamas.

Róisín's hand is clutching his, and they look at each other and breathe in unison, a big open-mouthed breath to sustain them for another thirty seconds, or sixty, as they turn their eyes back to the sky.

Nothing moves.

They both know what they want to be when they grow up. Liam is going to be a farmer like his dad and Róisín is going to move far away and become an astrophysicist. She knows the names of all the constellations, and the different shapes of the moon, and the order of the planets, and she knows when the comets are going to be in the sky. That's why she persuaded Liam to camp out in the field with her tonight, the night when it will be at its brightest. She stares up at the sky and then, still lying on the grass, holds the notebook high over her face and starts drawing.

What are you doing? He wants to understand.

Astronomy, she says. I'm mapping the sky. I have to mark where the comet is now in relation to the stars. So that we can see how far it moves. Otherwise we might forget.

It's *not* moving.

But it will. Have patience.

Liam rolls his eyes. This astronomy takes too long.

Look. She shows him her map. See those stars? I've marked them here. And the comet is in between those two right now. See?

He nods, reluctantly.

You can go inside if you really want.

I don't want.

She tears off a blank sheet of paper and gives it to him, along with one of the spare pencils from her pencil case. She takes it with her everywhere, so she can always map the sky.

What should I draw?

Whatever you want to draw.

She always talks to him like this, as if she's the grown-up, even though she's only two years older than he is.

He frowns in concentration; he's not going to ask her any more questions tonight. His pencil hovers over the page.

Liam falls asleep while the comet is still between the two stars overhead, buried deep into his sleeping bag with the zip done up to way over his head.

On the dew-damp grass in the early hours of the morning his drawing blends into indecipherable marks. The farm, the field, his house, the cows and sheep, his dad, the lack of his mum, and Róisín staring up at the sky: dots and lines that have been smudged out of context by a careless thumb until their meaning is lost.

- - - - - - - -

YES, OF COURSE I WENT to the priest. You're a nosy old man, you know that? I went on account of the dirty books I've been reading.

Severine's granny has walked into the room, mid-sentence, un-invited; she has started talking to her ghosts again.

I said to him, in the confession, now, Father, there's no point in you telling me to stop reading them because I'm not going to stop reading them and that's that.

People say that Severine's granny is mad in the head. Severine can see they're thinking it now, in the way they look at her mother as if she should do something about it this time.

They're my books now, I told him, they were given to me by my dead husband – God rest his soul – and I like reading them.

The ladies from the village sip silently at their tea and let their china cups rattle in their saucers.

Severine's granny has finished saying what she wanted to say and is now turning her back, but before she leaves the room she looks at Severine with a wink and a nod of her head.

Severine understands. She waits five minutes then follows her granny upstairs, so she can talk to the ghosts as well, and maybe get a read of her granny's books. She's not sure why her mother seemed so embarrassed but she's fairly sure that means the books would be worth a look.

Who's here today, Granny?

Announce yourselves.

Her granny is not theatrical; her delivery is dry. A quick swipe of her hand in the air shows her impatience with the ghosts. Come on then, who's here?

She stops still for a moment, listening, then begins the register in a voice not entirely unlike Severine's schoolteacher. Severine is in quatrième but already the middle school feels too small, she can't wait to start at the lycée.

We've got your uncle Antoine – hello, pet – Henri from the 1750s and the sisters in lace dresses, then there's Ælfgifu, her soldier boy, and your great-grandpa Paul-François of course. And Brigitte. Over in the corner.

Hello ghosts, Severine says and curtsies to the room. She's fourteen now and wants to make a good impression, behave like a grown-up; not like the last time they were here, when she was a child and ran around the room trying to catch them like moths in her palm.

Tell me about Mama, from before I was born.

Severine talks to Antoine, and her granny tells her his reply:

Your mother used to lead him into trouble, so he says, she says.

Severine can't imagine her mother leading anyone into trouble, not ever. Her mama's not fun like that.

Was Mama clever?

She was the cleverest, he says. But he thinks you knew that already— Oh! Do be quiet, you daft old man.

What? Granny! Tell me what he said!

He says they were best friends. That they used to camp out in the field past the stream, stay awake all night and watch the stars.

But what did Great-Grandpa Paul-François say? When you told him to be quiet?

He'll tell you himself when he's good and ready.

It's not fair; her granny knows that Severine can't hear the ghosts, and Severine doesn't really believe she'll ever be able to.

Maybe in their next visit, her granny softens, speaks kindly.

But that could be years from now.

Severine purses her lips, listens as hard as she can. Tries to believe.

What Antoine can't believe is how old she's got; the last time he saw her she was skipping between the grown-ups' outstretched arms. But now: almost a woman. And so like her mother, who still refuses to see him.

What would he say to her, if she could hear?

He doesn't know the answer but he wishes this comet would stay for longer. He can feel himself being pulled away already, feel the earth slipping beneath his feet.

Severine!

Her mother is calling her from downstairs. Maybe she wants her to go and play the piano for the ladies.

Severine!

I'd better go, Severine says to the room. Please excuse me for a moment.

She quietly shuts the door behind her and heads back down the stairs.

Her mama wants to know if she's done her piano practice yet, tells her she should be doing that instead of encouraging her granny's nonsense.

Ten minutes later, Mozart morphs into 'Mr Moonlight' and her mother doesn't even notice. She finishes with a flourish and leaves the piano. There are more important things to do today.

Severine passes the bookcases and looks out of the window, steps closer to peer up at the sky and measures the length of the comet's tail between a thumb and forefinger held up close to her eyes.

Her granny says the ghosts will only stay for as long as she can see it in the sky. The brighter it is, the more they have to say. It's already bright this evening, and it's not even completely dark yet, so she still has time. She has to learn to hear them, if they do exist – she wants to know the truth, and her granny says they don't come often, the ghosts and their comets. What would ghosts really talk about? she wonders.

But when Severine gets back upstairs, her granny is having her afternoon nap and the ghosts, so far as she can tell, are resting in the corners of the upstairs study; Great-Grandpa Paul-François's ghost is probably curled up under the desk like a tabby cat.

Severine thinks about waking them, but her granny is always talking about her aching bones and she thinks maybe she should let her sleep, for a little while at least.

At school in needlework they are making a tapestry; well, really it's more of a quilt. Everyone in her year has to embroider a square, stitching in colours and people, sewing on sequins and beads and small patches of fabric. The theme is Bayeux. It is their home.

Some of her classmates have stitched outlines of their houses, family members looking out from windows or standing in front gardens, wool and thread dyed especially for their hair. Others are making the countryside, with blue chiffon for a river, red beads hanging from cherry trees. Severine's is full of faces – her granny in the middle, sitting on a chair that looks more like a throne, the room around her hidden behind all the faces of all the ghosts (at least the ones she knows about); there is Great-Grandpa Paul-François with cotton wool for his beard, Uncle Antoine who died when he was only a boy, Henri from the 1750s standing in between the sisters with lace dresses, Great-Great-Grandma Bélanger (she thinks that's her granny's granny), and behind them are others whose names she can't remember, but whose stories she has heard; there's the woman who originally built their house in Bayeux – Brigitte, she remembers, and looks out some orange fabric for flames.

Ça alors, you must have a big family, the teacher says, looking over her shoulder. How many of you are there, in your house?

It's me, my mama, and my granny, Severine replies, needle in hand, lips pursed again in concentration as soon as she has spoken. There is a scattering of laughter from along the row but Severine ignores that. Behind her, the teacher frowns to herself but says nothing; moves on to the next girl embroidering the next version of a family.

Now – the teacher claps her hands to get their attention – how many of you have visited the real Bayeux Tapestry?

Granny, why do the ghosts come to visit? Severine asks, as she watches her granny beat the soft dough for the brioche.

Because they like to be seen – pass me the butter.

How am I supposed to see them if you won't tell me how?

Her granny smiles, scrapes the dough from the sides of the bowl. Not everything is about you, sweetheart.

Severine goes quiet, but her granny doesn't.

Now tell me, what are you learning about at school?

The Bayeux Tapestry.

Her granny's eyebrows rise and fall; she looks to the corner of the room and smiles.

That's good.

Severine runs to the corner of the kitchen and smacks her hands into the wall, leaving palm-prints of flour.

Are they here? she asks, spinning around. She's getting impatient – who cares about school when there are ghosts to talk to?

They're misbehaving today. No place for young ladies.

Granny.

The dough has to rise now. You know for how long?

Ninety minutes, says Severine. Maybe two hours.

Good, says her mother from the door. That means you can do your homework while you wait.

Severine looks up at her granny, who winks and nods. We'll try getting some sense out of these crazy ghosts later, chouchou.

Her mother beckons her from the door, and reluctantly she leaves the kitchen and the ghosts, and her granny.

But why does Antoine come to visit? Severine asks later, as they spread the warm brioche with butter and redcurrant jam.

Her granny smiles. I think my son is here for me. Or perhaps your mother.

Mama? Severine asks, surprised, but her granny doesn't respond.

And why does Brigitte always stand on her own?

Later. Stern, but softening again. I'll tell you later, Severine. Have patience. If you want to see the ghosts, you have to be able to wait.

Severine does not finish her assignment about the Bayeux Tapestry; she spends the evening going through the old photo albums she's found in the bookcase in the piano room. There are only a few of her mama from when she was really young – one when she was a baby and her granny had curly dark hair and a knowing smile.

Then a family holiday – with the only photo she knows of Great-Grandpa Paul-François. They're on the beach with bucket and spade,

Granny, Great-Grandpa Paul-François, and her mama and Antoine, in swimming costumes that go down almost to their knees.

There's the one with her mother and father together, smiling at the fifties as they slipped into the sixties and everything was soon to change.

And then the final page: on top is a wedding photo, her mama in a white lacy dress that her granny had made by hand, and her dad in a suit, with the best man beside him.

Below that, the last in the album: a hospital photo, her mama smiling at newborn Severine, her father beside the bed. He was smiling too, maybe, but he is blurred and out of focus and her mother's eyes are looking up, out of the room, straight out of the photo, as if searching for something hidden behind the camera's lens.

WAKE UP!

Liam's on a dark beach, full of crashing waves and salt that stings his eyes; he's trying to shout but he can't, trying to run but he falls and the rocks scrape away at his skin. He scrambles up from his knees, there is only fear and panic and the ground dissolving beneath his feet and he has to find his mother.

Come on. Róisín pulls the sleeping bag down despite his hands clutching it up above his head. You have to see this.

Is it daytime?

It's morning, but it's amazing now, it's so bright.

What?

Wake up! I don't know how much time we have!

Two countries, two channels away, Severine stands in front of a tapestry, the laughter of the others from her school all around her. The tapestry is behind glass – if it wasn't she might have reached out to touch it. Instead, she just stares and stares.

In the corner of the panel, embroidered in shining thread, is what looks like a shooting star, all yellow and gold, like a child's drawing of a comet-chariot, powered by the sun and the wind.

And there's something she's trying to remember, one of her granny's stories from years ago; there was a girl who was in love with a soldier, a boy who died on a battlefield. And their names, she was told their names once, strange-sounding names; not French, nor English – something else. And there's something pulling at her mind, at her heart, that dissolves when a boy from school pulls on her ponytail.

Hurry up, he says. The teacher told me to get you. Everyone's leaving. You're out of time.

As it turns out, there's all the time in the world for Liam and Róisín, that morning. The sky is orange peel and baled hay; clouds are gathering over towards the hills but the air is fresh as lemon juice. They are lying side by side on opened sleeping bags on the damp grass and staring at the comet that can be seen in the day-time sky.

It's so rare, Róisín says, but she doesn't need to explain, not really. Liam might not know so much about the stars but he knows that there is something special in what they are seeing. A comet so bright it can be seen in the daytime sky; that has to mean something. That has to be something worth watching.

How are you going to mark it on your maps?

I don't know.

She sounds despairing.

You could draw it next to the farm. Between Dad's shed there and the fence around the cows' field?

Liam can see how that would work – when he imagines the world it is always somehow relative to the farm.

It's not about the farm, says Róisín, a little stroppily.

He can't answer that.

But it was a nice idea, she says, softening.

He looks from the comet to his cousin and back again.

The comet gets dimmer as the morning passes. Liam's dad trudges around the farm, feeding, checking, clearing, talking to himself, or sometimes to the memory of his wife beside him.

Don't you want to leave here? Róisín whispers.

No.

How could Liam leave his dad, when it's just the two of them?

Not now, obviously, I get that . . . You're still a kid. But when you're a grown-up?

You're still a kid too.

But there's nothing left to explore on the farm.

I don't want to go away.

But you can come on an adventure. With me.

Maybe one day.

Liam doesn't like lying to Róisín, but he doesn't know how to make her understand.

Well, I'm going to explore the universe, she says.

Liam knows that they should go in soon, for breakfast. His dad will be waiting for them. It seems like his dad spends all his time waiting for people to come home, though most of them have gone for good.

That's what astronomers do, says Róisín; they go and explore the universe.

Liam looks up at his cousin – she is spinning round and round now with her arms spread wide – and he forgets about his dad.

I know, he says, with a cheeky smile – he doesn't usually talk back to her – you've already told me about the universe.

She stops spinning and looks surprised for a second, then pulls his bobble hat down over his eyes.

Glad you were paying attention, she says, before grabbing the sleeping bag from the ground and running inside.

That afternoon, Liam's dad drives them to the village fete – Róisín stares out of the truck window at the sheep watching them pass, then into the woods where the trees hide weasels and badgers. As they wind through the outskirts of the village she waves at her house, even though she knows her mum is still away.

You OK, pet? asks her uncle.

Did you know that there are 100 billion stars in our galaxy?

Look, he smiles, we've arrived.

Róisín is up and out of the car, waiting impatiently for Liam to undo his seat belt.

There are stalls lined up along the high street; sweets and candy-floss, wooden figurines painted in bright colours, soft rugs of sheepskin that Róisín can't help but touch, knitted dolls and, on the green, an assortment of engines and tractor parts that have arrived on a huge truck.

Róisín grabs Liam's hand – come on – and leads her cousin, running, up to the toffee-apple stall.

Can we have one? she asks, fishing in her bag for this week's pocket money. The coins spread out on her palm when she shakes her hand, a jangle of silver and copper, pennies and a ten-pence piece. We'll share.

She passes it to Liam and smiles at Mr Toffeeapple (actually it's Mr Morris that runs the toffee-apple stall) and they go to the green and sit on one of the benches by the trees.

He's my Latin teacher, Róisín says, nodding at Mr Morris.

Róisín is in a different school to Liam, though when they're older they'll go to the same school in the town, because that's where everyone goes.

Do you want to know Latin? she asks.

He doesn't answer; he is preoccupied with the toffee apple, so Róisín starts reciting for him anyway, or maybe for herself.

Amo, amas, amat, she says.

Ama-mus, ama-tis, am-ant.

Lego, legas, legat. Lega-mus, lega-tis, leg-ant.

The textbooks they use in her Latin class tell stories, and actually Róisín likes the stories more than she likes amo amas amat. There is a Roman man called Caecilius who lives in Pompeii, and he has a wife called Metella, a son Quintus and a dog Cerberus.

She knows that Vesuvius will erupt by the end of the year, but the whole family will refuse to leave their home. She's flicked forward in the book and read the final chapters; she likes to know how things will turn out, but she doesn't like the fact that they stayed in Pompeii. They should have run away when the ash started to fall. For now, Caecilius is going to do business in the agora and his son is playing with the dog in the garden. They are quite rich Romans; they used to have a slave but soon Caecilius is going to make him a freedman. It's a very moral textbook.

We could run away, she says. We'll go on an adventure.

Liam takes a bite of the toffee apple, smudges caramel on his chin.

Down to the river, how about that? We can make a secret hut where no one will find us and we can explore all the country and you can bring Bobby.

I don't need to bring Bobby, he says, momentarily sounding older than he is; he can't always be the baby.

But we can build the secret hut?

She takes a bite of the toffee apple, still clutched in his hand.

Liam's dad is looking at the tractor pieces on the green, but every now and then he turns round to check on the kids. They're like brother and sister, those two, he thinks; it is good for Liam not to be on his own all the time. The last year has been hard, on them both.

The toffee-apple stick is thrown in the bin and Róisín's on her feet again.

Right, let's go.

It's starting to get dark.

But she's pulling him along beside the green and heading for the river that runs by the village, through the woods.

Then Liam's dad is beside them, and he's saying, where are you two off to?

Just playing, Uncle Aedan.

Time to go home, he says, taking Róisín's hand and trusting Liam to follow along. Your mum asked me to look after you while she's away, he says to her, and that's what I'm doing.

He's not normally strict, Liam's dad, he's too preoccupied, and Róisín is surprised that he even noticed they were running away.

So, he says, fish fingers for tea?

Can we watch the comet again later?

Liam's dad looks up; he can't see anything so unusual about the sky. She's a funny girl, Róisín. Head in the clouds. And always staring at the stars, just like his brother, searching for something – not that that's any excuse for running off the way he did. Taking Róisín in for the week was the least he could do.

Of course you can, pet, he says kindly, wondering how a father could ever leave his child.

At dusk, the stars begin to appear around the comet one by one.

Tonight's the night, Róisín says; she seems more excited than ever. They're back out by the tent and she's arranging the sleeping bag for them to sit on.

But I've already seen it.

That's not the point. It's not enough to just see it. You have to see it fly. You have to see it change.

All right then. Liam looks up but her hands are suddenly clasped over his eyes. Not now. Not like this. Wait.

She starts digging around for her maps and a sigh escapes his lips.

She's insisting he pays attention to the dots and lines on her sketch pad; some constellations are named, and they are the ones she points out to him.

See this shape?

Yes.

OK, good, now remember that. And see here? That's where the comet was last night. OK?

Yes, yes, yes.

Grand. I think you're ready. And it's nearly time.

Her ponytail has come loose in the breeze and a strip of hair is caught in her mouth. He reaches to her face and brushes it away.

Of course I'm ready, he says, and she looks at him as if she's pleased.

Liam wonders how his cousin got to be so bossy. He likes it though, in secret. It's not often someone tells him what to do; it's not often that someone even notices him. He once heard his dad talking about the farm to one of his great-aunts that came to visit from Dublin. It was just after the funeral, on the day everyone came for cake. He said that the world didn't need the farm, but that his heart wouldn't let him leave.

When Liam remembers that, he wonders if it was really the farm his dad was talking about.

Now, I'm going to prove to you that the comet is flying faster than anything else in the sky.

But it's *still* not moving.

She puts her notebook down on the grass and squeezes his hand tight.

I'll help you.

How are you going to help?

Don't look up, look here. Remember?

She puts her map on his lap and he stares at it, trying to memorise the shapes, biting onto his bottom lip in the expression that he's had when concentrating since he was learning to read and write; learning to build a farm with wooden blocks.

This is exactly what the sky looked like last night, at exactly this time. Now close your eyes.

But I'll miss it moving if I do that.

You won't miss it moving, you'll notice that it has moved, and that's different.

OK, Liam says with a bit of trust, and a bit of uncertainty, and a bit of something else that he's not able to describe.

Go on, she insists. Close your eyes. For me. Please?

This time Liam closes his eyes.

He feels Róisín moving, but keeping hold of his hand. He can tell she's sitting up. Next, he feels the air get warmer, his shivers stop, the breeze dies down. And then she plants a kiss on his lips. It is the swift, soft kiss of children, of cousins and best friends; of someone who has known you since the day you were born. She lies back down and the breeze picks up, the smells of the farm brush over his skin. His lips feel tingly. He keeps his eyes closed as he listens to the sound of her lying back down on the grass, and listens for the sound of the comet flying overhead. What kind of sound would that make? The sound of running out past the horses' shelter, past the stream that winds along the bottom of the field and up the hill, up to the highest point of the village, to look back at things that are small and big and that make up everything he has known in his life.

OK. You can open your eyes now.

Liam opens his eyes.

At first he can't find it. He looks back to the bright star it had been next to, then sideways to Róisín. He looks for the constellations, but the comet's not where it should be. Róisín has her hair in a sideways ponytail so she can lay her head flat on the ground, and she's grinning at him like she knows a secret she's not quite decided to share.

It's there now, she points.

And it's true. The comet has moved on. It really must be the fastest thing in the whole of the sky. It has passed by stars and through the transparent scattering of clouds and even though it looks like everything is completely still overhead now, even though he hasn't actually seen the comet moving, he knows that it has moved. Róisín's hand is still holding his.

He doesn't want to take his eyes off the sky. He doesn't want to move. He watches the comet for a long time – longer than ever before. They lie side by side and stare at the sky and Liam wonders if staying perfectly still is the way to live in one week, in one moment, for the rest of his life.

But when he looks back down to the farm everything has moved. He can feel the rush of the wind as the Earth races around the sun. He feels like he needs to cling on, or he will go flying off into space. Things shifted while he wasn't looking at the ground and now the world is different; everything is beautiful, and wild, and precarious, because now he knows how the sky can change.

Halley's Comet

In Bayeux, two sisters in lace dresses read to one another as their husbands play cards and drink cognac. The family home was once deserted, so the story goes, burned down to its stone foundations, but it was rescued by twin sisters, like them, and now it is filled with books and flowers and laughter. They read in the paper about the naming of a comet after an astronomer who did not live to see it arrive, but they are not saddened by this. They know that their house is filled with more than children – sometimes, when a comet flies through the sky, they see generations past and know that their family is tied to the skies and to their home and they are glad.

That evening as the sun starts to dip they look for it in the sky, Halley's comet – it is flying low, over the sea to the north. So the sisters take the carriage out past Saint-Laurent-sur-Mer, with their three daughters and Henri, the youngest, the only son. He loves the beach, Henri; he runs along the coast exploring the caves and collecting sea-urchin shells. Don't stray too far, his mother calls, and he turns back and waves before racing on – his mother likes to stay near Bayeux, he knows, but Henri wants to go to sea.

The sisters watch the sky as the night falls and the stars begin to shine from the dark, but they don't notice that the wind is building up and the waves are crashing closer to the shore. They point out constellations to their daughters and teach them to read the skies, to follow the patterns of light in the dark and watch how the comet moves between them. But then they look down.

Where is Henri? A question at first, changing to a shout, his name called by his mama and aunt and sisters, but Henri doesn't hear – he is trapped by the waves along the coast, the ground sinking beneath his feet as tides pull him further out to sea. He tries to gasp in air, to shout, but his mouth fills with water and his eyes sting with salt; he can't see through the dark, through the crash of the waves, but then a hand is holding his, an arm pulled around his waist, and he is lying, coughing on the rough sand of the beach.

Mama? he says, as soon as he is able, with his eyes still scrunched up from the salt and his sisters running to him.

He forces his eyes open, sees the whites of the waves crashing on the rocks beyond the sand. His sisters are crying and his aunt is running deeper into the sea – why is she in the sea now? Her lace dress is ghostly as it catches the light of the stars, disappears beneath the waves, and reappears again. As she walks, falls, crawls back to the beach, her hair is soaked and sticking to her face like seaweed. She wants to collapse, but doesn't.

Mama?

She shakes her head, looks down.

Henri rushes towards the sea but his sister grabs his hand and his aunt pulls him into her arms, holding him through his cries.

Overhead the comet continues on its journey, speeding towards the sun before circling round to race away. It travels from light to dark, from intense heat to the frozen edge of the solar system, until reaching its limit half a century later and turning, again, towards the warmth.

Halley's Comet

THE FAIR ARRIVES OVERNIGHT; TRUCKS and lorries and motorbikes moving snake-like through the high street, a multi-parted centipede of bright red and yellow, sparkling silver and plastic creatures and scenes of snow and forest and the Wild West.

They set up during the day, the carousel, the twirly thing with swings that Róisín doesn't know the name of, the rotor that spins so fast you can stay suspended against the walls after the ground disappears from below your feet.

And that evening they open, and all the town arrives, and suddenly there are more people on the green than there have ever been. Róisín's there with girls from school, all short skirts and coloured tights and trainers, jumpers that stop at their midriffs and hair blowing crazy wild in the wind. Róisín's in skintight jeans, DM boots, silver hoop earrings that jangle down to her shoulders and catch the moonlight when she scoops back her dark hair.

Is your cousin coming? they ask, all giggles; Liam has become the boy they want to impress.

Róisín shrugs as if she thinks their latest crush is absurd, as if she couldn't care less, but she scans the crowds as they move through the rides, past stalls, as they take turns to form a protective circle so one by one they can sip cider from the bottle concealed in her friend's bag. And at the same time, she is somewhere else, she is above the clouds, waiting for Halley's comet to get closer; and for Liam to find her.

From the big wheel there's a view over the trees, past the school, over fields and woodland and all the way to the farm; she thinks she can make out the sheds and stalls even in the dark, even with the fairground lights casting the rest of the world in shadow. Some kids in the carriage behind are swinging as hard as they can, screaming as they nearly overturn, almost make a full three sixty. Róisín doesn't do that. She lets the carriage rock slowly in the wind and enjoys the world getting smaller beneath her.

As she gets down she nearly trips on the metallic slats they use for steps but Liam catches her arm, steadies her.

Didn't think you were going to come, she says.

His hand stays on her elbow for a moment.

We all make sacrifices.

His face is serious but his eyes dance.

Want to go on the rotor?

She steps closer, lets her hand brush against his leather jacket, enjoys the way he is so much taller than her now; and without taking his hand she leads him through the queues to the only ride she really wants to go on, the only ride she thinks he might enjoy.

Just this one, she says, then we can get out of here.

A smile is playing about his lips; they know each other so well.

He hands two tokens to the girl by the entrance and they step inside.

There are ten of them in the circular room painted red and silver. She recognises another boy from the year below at school, smiles at how young he looks compared to Liam, how Liam already seems too old for this scene. Then at the last minute Rachel comes in as well, waves at Róisín from the opposite side of the circle, although it's Liam she's staring at – trying to get him to notice her – but then they all go quiet and wait for the room to move and the floor to drop.

It starts slowly; someone laughs to break the silence but not Liam or Róisín, they are both waiting for the world to spin. They put their hands flat against the curved wall behind them, close to one another but not touching. Liam looks at the ground beneath their feet. It's getting faster. He keeps his hand perfectly still but Róisín doesn't, she moves it a few centimetres closer until her little finger touches his. It's getting faster. And now the walls are starting to blur; red seeping into silver until they see flashes of light rather than stripes of colour, and they are pressed back hard into the wall and the floor starts to move. She can feel it sinking below her feet but she doesn't sink with it, she stays suspended, weightless, needing nothing to stand on, closing her eyes so she can feel like she is able to fly and her hand moves again, presses over Liam's and she doesn't even hear the screaming and laughing of the others in the circle with them; she is soaring over the world.

Beside her, Liam keeps his eyes open, although he wants to close them; he is afraid that if he did he would forget there are people watching. He can feel each one of her fingers over his own and as they spin faster the palm of her hand is pressed harder into the back of his and he moves his thumb in closer, holding her there, and he wants to do more than that and at the same time he likes this feeling, wants to stay in this moment of being together in a blurred world of colour and light.

When the floor rises up to meet them he feels too heavy; it is difficult to lift his feet and walk to the exit. Everyone else has gone and they are the last, alone, in this circle of faded paint but her hand is still in his, until she steps away, reaches out for the wall to steady herself and glances back at him, over her shoulder. Her eyes are not smiling; they're saying something else now. It's time to move on from the rotor. He stumbles, makes it look like he is dizzy from the ride, not that the contact of her hand on his hand is still enough to make him feel like he could fall.

Behind the metal fence of the carnival, behind the bikes chained up on it, there's a row of trees that they used to climb on when they were kids. That's where she leads him to, not running; people would see them running, but walking together without talking, still feeling the ground unsteady below their feet. She gets there a pace ahead of him, leans against the tree facing away from the carnival and as soon as she's there he is there too, standing in front of her as she puts her arms around his waist, hooks a finger through the belt loop of his jeans; pulls him closer.

Liam forgets to look up, to see if anyone can see them. He's never cared what people might think, not when he feels the warmth of her hands through his shirt and is pressed so close he can feel her breath on his lips. But he pauses there, allows himself the time to enjoy the seconds before they kiss. For years now, everything has been different when they are alone.

They hear a noise; some of the local kids are unchaining their bikes and Liam and Róisín freeze, still holding each other, breath racing in unison. The seconds drag into minutes. Róisín hides her mouth in his shirt collar to stifle a laugh; he holds her tighter, smiling too, lets his lips graze the top of her ear, lets his body press closer towards her.

When the coast is clear she says, come on, we should get back.

His eyes meet hers, playful, daring.

Should we?

He doesn't want to let go, moves his face next to hers. But she places her hands on his hips.

My mum said she was coming down later, with Neil.

He takes a step backwards, swallows, then nods. He wonders if it would have made a difference to him, had his dad found someone new.

The sounds of the funfair return, and the lights come into focus again.

They stroll through the crowds like cousins, talking about the farm, about school, about nothing in particular, as Róisín nods and smiles at all the friends she sees. It's a warm night; the clouds are keeping the heat close to the ground, shielding them from the cold of the sky. Róisín sees her mum in the distance, raises her hand in a wave when she is noticed; asks Liam with a look if he wants to come and say hello. He replies with a smile.

Róisín's mum asks how his dad is getting on.

He replies about the year's crops and the newborn calves, about the second-hand turntable his dad tinkers with every evening and the roof needing repaired.

She suggests a roofer he already knows and he doesn't mention that he already knows about him, thanks her. She says that he is looking well.

The moon appears between the clouds and people from the village say hello as they are passing, and Liam, for a second, wants to put his arm around Róisín, to be able to stop feeling like he is hiding all the time except when he's with her, alone.

Dad says Róisín can come for dinner tomorrow, if she wants.

That would be grand, Róisín's mum answers, like she is encouraging her to be polite.

Yes, Róisín smiles, of course.

She knows what he is really suggesting.

We must all get together some time, her mum is saying, a proper family Sunday lunch...

I'll tell Dad, he says, though he won't – they haven't had a proper family Sunday lunch since his mum died. He shifts on his feet, faces Róisín, see you at school tomorrow I guess, he says; hands tucked into jean pockets, a shrug of his shoulders, and he is gone.

Róisín looks round the funfair. It is suddenly so small, already like a memory from her childhood.

You'll miss all this next year, her mum says, smiling like she expects to be contradicted.

Róisín struggles to find the words to reply.

She'd almost forgotten she was leaving.

SEVERINE HOLDS HER GRANNY'S ARM as they walk; she hopes her granny will interpret it as a show of affection rather than a physical support. Her granny never much wanted support, unless it was to counter an argument with her imaginary ghosts. Severine gets a cramp in her stomach thinking about them, about her granny and her visitors; about the way her hand flew around her head last night as if brushing away a pesky mosquito, not the memories of a lifetime ago. She hadn't seen her do that since she was a teenager.

Not far now, she says.

I've been making this walk for sixty years, I'm not going to forget the way now.

Severine loosens her grip.

That's right, her granny says. I'm the one who should be helping you.

I'm fine, Granny.

Her granny's face dissolves into a scowl, sweet rather than bitter on her old face, as Severine rubs her stomach.

You do help me, she says, and her granny takes her hand in a gesture that says she always will.

At the entrance, Severine pays the fee for one adult and one OAP as her granny sniffs at the price.

It should be free for you and me, she says. You should tell them who we are.

Who's that then?

The woman on the till smiles kindly at them as they pass the ticket office and head for the long, wide display room of the Bayeux Tapestry.

Severine can see how other people edge around them. She wants to explain that her granny's not dangerous; in fact, she wants to shout at them for being so bloody insensitive – this could be you, one day, you know? But she doesn't. She pretends not to notice their stares and whispers as her granny carries on conversations with memories, only gently taking her hand to try and bring her back to reality. She brushes away the thought that they might be staring at her too, so heavily pregnant.

Great-Grandpa Paul-François wants to see the green horse with red legs.

Great-Grandpa Paul-François died, Granny, a long time ago.

Now, where is that panel?

The horses are all dark blue and yellow, you see?

Her granny pulls away, begins pressing her face close to the glass as she sidesteps around the room.

There, see? Oh, do be quiet, old man. She's young; she'll learn. Won't you?

What's that, Granny?

Bright green horse, just like I said, see?

I told you there is no... Severine begins to say, until she sees the green horse with red legs, prancing in mid-air, dancing rather than running, oblivious to the spears and axes that surround it. The words catch in her mouth.

She's not convinced by her mother's memory-loss idea; her granny's memory seems to be sharper than the tip of an arrow. She feels that mild pain in her stomach again. No, pain is the wrong word, it is just a pressure, a reminder of what she's carrying.

Some tourists move behind them, abandoning their view of the green horse for someone altogether more important on the next panel; someone with a crown.

She should talk to her mama, persuade her against sending Granny away. Not that her mama is speaking to her much these days. This is not what she had planned for her daughter. Severine suspects she's always been a bit of a disappointment to her mama.

Do be quiet, you great fool! Nobody wants to hear you sing.

Severine turns. Her granny is poking at something in mid-air, and Severine can't help but smile.

No! her granny continues. Not even me! And she clasps her hands over her ears and begins to sing – I can't hear you, old man – *je dis que les bonbons, valent mieux que la raison...*

Let's have a sit-down over here, Severine says, conscious of her granny's stooped back as well as her singing; as well as the queue behind them.

Not yet, I'm not ready yet, her granny says, calming down. I haven't shown you what I brought you here to see. It's important.

You have to be more careful, Severine says. Try to concentrate on the people who are really here.

Do I embarrass you, just like I embarrass your mother?

I think we've both embarrassed my mother, Severine says.

Her granny chuckles.

Well, that's true, God knows.

What are you going to call him? her granny wants to know.

Severine sighs; she doesn't want to have this conversation yet.

It's not me that wants to know, you know.

She raises her eyebrows.

Your great-grandpa Paul-François has been asking.

Severine smiles.

I bet he has.

She tilts her head to one side, nods a few times, then holds her granny's stare. You know, Great-Grandpa Paul-François is very keen for you to have a sit-down.

Mais non. What he actually said was that I should hurry up and show you what I brought you here to see. And he's quite right, too.

Is it the Halley's comet border? Because I saw that when I was a girl.

No, no, not that old thing. There's something much more important for you to see. Now, let me think.

When, at last, the ghosts quieten down enough for her granny to find the panel she needs, she doesn't even look – she points from halfway across the room and says: There. Go. Look. See for yourself.

Severine does as she is asked, leaving her granny behind. She goes to look, and she looks carefully, and she looks for a long time.

Two red pillars are spiralled with gold. At their tops, two dragon heads breathe tongues of fire. Between the pillars a woman stands; she is wearing a long robe of gold with a red scarf covering her head and neck. A cleric stands to her side, beyond the pillars, and he is reaching out; touching her face, no, perhaps striking her. Below them is a naked man, a dagger, a winged monster fleeing to the right. Above them, the words: *Ubi unus clericus et Ælfgyva*. She doesn't know what it means.

Severine can see the texture of the cloth, stains that take it in patches from beige to brown, each thread of colour, the wonky lines of the pillar's spirals, the shading on the cleric's cloak. His fingers look long; his thumb is pointed where it reaches her face. The top of his head is bald.

What does it mean? Granny?

She turns around.

And then there is a rush of people trying to help – tourists, schoolchildren, the security guard who sits by the door and hands out the laminated information cards. So many people that Severine doesn't even move, she just watches while all these eager hands help her granny, check her pulse, feel for her breath, and finally go running to the phone for an ambulance.

HE WAITS FOR HER BY the closed brown gate, like he always does at lunchtime. They squeeze through the broken slats in the fence, her first, then him. The rain is floating instead of falling; Liam likes the way it lingers in the air; Róisín would prefer it to fall, like pumice instead of ash.

Shall we go to our island?

She nods.

Róisín knows it's going to be difficult to tell him the truth. She's been putting it off for a while now. Maybe another day won't hurt.

The stream is low. They could have waded across in bare feet, but instead they balance on the fallen tree trunk like tightrope walkers, unobserved.

They made the hut when they were still children; neither of them wants to mention how it's too small now. They crawl inside and sit on the old sleeping bags they zipped together to make a padded floor mat. They end up with their feet sticking out of the entrance – they never got round to making a door, so it's always been three-walled, with some rocks in the front. When all the wooden walls are gone, rotted away to more earth and soil and mud, the rocks will still be there, outlining a door-shaped gap on the ground – *Look, you can see the remnants of the front wall, and here: this must have been where the door was. Can you imagine what it would have looked like? Can you imagine the people who lived here, all those hundreds of years ago?*

Róisín feels sorry for the archaeologists of the future who will get their hut so very wrong. Sorry, and also glad. It's only fair.

He unbuttons her shirt slowly while she talks about Rome – she's studying ancient history as well as science; the teacher calls her a contradiction – he kisses the nape of her neck, touches her right dimple when she smiles. Her woollen tights are navy blue today, like her skirt, which unbuttons at her waist and then has to be unwrapped from side to side. She rolls over along the ground and he gently pulls the fabric until she reaches the end of the sleeping bag; still lying on part of the pleated skirt she rolls back over towards him. This is what they do – roll away and roll back again, meet in the middle of their secret childhood hut with their clothes half off and their hands damp from the stream's spray. His hand rests on her hip; hers on his shoulder.

You have stubble today, she says, her cheek brushing his chin.

He pulls her closer; the sleeping bag scrunches up underneath them until they are lying on an island within an island.

Theirs is not an urgent love; it is undoubted, whispered rather than shouted.

Stay there, she says. Stay inside me.

She kisses him, fleetingly, inhales the warm air next to his neck.

Liam rummages in his rucksack, his bare back white, patterned with criss-crossed lines from lying on the ground.

Look; no, wait. You'll never guess. He throws her a smile over his shoulder. OK, look.

He has brought binoculars with him; he's holding them out towards her, like a gift.

Do you know what day it is today?

She does know, but she doesn't want to spoil his moment – she feels guilty enough already.

Today is the day that Halley's comet will be at its brightest in the sky.

She smiles. However much he grows up, he will always be younger than her.

So I thought, you know, we could look for it.

We can try, she says, but it might be better to wait till later.

He looks disappointed, but it's too faint to be seen during the daytime; she knows it'll be masked by the sun. It is the dimmest appearance of Halley's comet for centuries. It's usually so bright – it's one of the Great Comets, one of the greatest – but this year it will be invisible to the naked eye. If you don't make a special effort to look for it though telescopes or binoculars, you would never even know it was there. It's keeping its distance; losing interest in the Earth.

Later then? Will you come to the farm?

OK.

There is a change now; a restlessness in the hut that he doesn't want. Róisín's getting dressed.

Where are you going?

I have to get back to school. We can't lie here all day.

Róisín gets back to the school gate on her own.

She slips through the broken slats of the fence and into the science block before the bell goes.

She stays after class to tell her science teacher about her acceptance to Imperial College, London. He was the one who recommended she apply there; without that push, she might have stayed in Ireland, continued orbiting her home on the same path. She's grateful.

You'll love London, he says. It's a bigger world, so it is.

His arms are wide, palms open, like even he can't grasp how big it is; bits of London leak out from between his splayed fingers and dance on the lab bench.

And he's right, that is exactly what she wants – the promise of a bigger world, a cosmos, an expanding universe. She's too tall to lie in an island hut forever. She knows it.

As she leaves the room, she blinks, brushes impatiently at her eyes.

Liam lies in the hut for the rest of the day.

The smell is of damp wood, the rush of fresh water over moss, cloud cover, familiarity, longing, loss.

⁖⁙⁙⁙⁙⁘

DID YOU SEE, SEVERINE?

Her granny is in a hospital bed; her words are slurred.

I've been with you all day, Granny.

But the tapestry?

They say you've had a stroke.

Well, I'm not surprised, with all these people fussing around me.

The room is empty.

But did you see Ælfgifu? She was very anxious that you see her.

Severine's mother arrives with sachets of fruit teas and flowers and slippers – her granny's slippers – and says: You're awake?

Well, of course I'm awake.

Severine puts her arm around her mama's shoulders. She knows that it is hard, not getting on well with your mother.

We're worried about her mind, the doctor says; she seems to be seeing things.

She's always done that, from time to time, Severine says.

Has she had a stroke in the past?

Her granny's voice rises in the room behind the closed door – I'm waiting to get her alone, you impatient old man, honestly…

Her mother follows the doctor down the corridor. Severine squeezes her hand before she leaves.

It's OK, her mama says, you go and talk with her. You're the one she wants to see.

Severine wants to tell her mother she loves her, but doesn't know how.

It smells in here.

Yes, Granny, it does.

Her granny is propped up with pillows now, and her eyes dart around the room.

Who's here? Severine asks, but she's ashamed of the question – she should be saying rest, your mind is broken, there are no ghosts here; if you pretend to be normal you might be able to come home.

She listens to the familiar roll call of ghosts like she did when she was a child; grandparents and great-grandparents and child-uncles and soldier boys, Brigitte who built their house and hangs around at the back, almost out of sight, so her granny says; and then there is Ælfgifu.

You think she's our ancestor?

Severine's not daft; she knows where this has been leading.

Her granny's eyes close over and she slips down her pillows. An alarm begins to sound.

She wakes again in the night. Severine's mama has gone home to get some sleep; they're alone in the room.

What will you call him? her granny says, struggling to touch the round bump of Severine's belly.

I don't know yet, Severine replies, there's a chance he might be a girl.

Her granny chuckles. You'll know soon enough now.

What do you want me to call him?

Severine is conscious of a tone in her voice that she doesn't usually use with her granny; she is talking gently.

François, her granny says. After your great-grandpa Paul-François, of course.

Her granny looks over to the door, shakes her head sadly, holds up her hand as if asking someone to be quiet.

But don't make him stay here, she says, pulling Severine closer. Tell him to travel the world. We have so many ghosts in this family already.

Severine looks around the hospital room; thinks about saying that there are no ghosts, that there never were any ghosts. That there is no such thing as ghosts.

But instead she takes her granny's hand and says, OK, he'll travel the world; we'll travel the world together. There are things that I want to see with my own eyes, you know, and I intend to see them all. I'm not going to work in our épicerie forever.

That's good, her granny says, hurriedly now. Perhaps you should go too. You should go now, though. Before—

I'm not leaving now, Granny! Why would you think...?

You don't have to stay with me.

Severine wants to hold her granny tight, but she's so frail she's afraid she'll hurt her and the expression on her face now – she looks paler, she looks like she's giving up.

It's OK, Granny, she says, tears filling her eyes. Stay with me. I'm not going anywhere. I'm not going to leave you. Please, I can't do any of this without you.

Her granny's eyes close, and Severine starts to panic.

I'm right here, she says, holding tight onto her granny's hand, everything's going to be OK.

Do you want to see me again?

It's such a faint whisper, Severine doubts she heard the words right.

What?

Her granny's eyes open, her expression now different to any she's seen before.

Do you want to see me again?

Of course I'll see you again, I'm staying here.

You don't understand. There's a price, to see ghosts.

You're going to be OK.

I dreamed of travelling once—

I'll call the doctor.

Don't you dare.

Her granny stifles a laugh, pretends to look stern but it's not her natural countenance; she can't keep it up for long.

You're not going to believe me, she says, but please listen anyway because you need to hear.

Her eyes close over again. Severine looks around for help, thinks of reaching for the alarm but something stops her.

You can see me again, she says, if you want to. It's a choice. You'll have to make a choice.

It's OK, Severine says uselessly. You'll be OK; I need you. Baby François needs you.

She feels alone, desperately alone.

Her granny smiles, opens her eyes.

It means staying here.

I've told you, I'm not leaving this room until you're better.

Her eyes close again.

Look for the comets, she says.

Granny?

Severine feels the pressure on her hand release.

Severine's granny doesn't wake up again after that. A series of strokes kill her in her sleep shortly before sunrise. But when Severine wakes up in the chair next to her granny's bed, it is not the nurses rushing into the room that she chooses to see. She doesn't even look at the dead body, her granny's expression still lingering on her lips. Standing in the corner, apologetically, Antoine looks the same as he did in the photos; he is still not quite a man.

Hello, she says.

I'm sorry about this, he smiles.

And there they all are, crowding into the room, too many for her to count; surrounding the bed where her granny has died and greeting her as they pass with a look of wonder, a hand to her shoulder, and a wry smile at the inevitable.

There are ghosts, she thinks to herself.

François? says Great-Grandpa Paul-François as he takes her hand and winks at her belly. It's a good name. I like it.

Severine opens her mouth to reply but has no idea what words to speak, and besides, she is trying not to cry.

Then Great-Grandpa Paul-François turns to the bed to stroke her granny's hair and gently kiss her forehead as if she were his daughter. Which, Severine realises, of course, she is.

- - - - - - -

LIAM'S DAD HAS MADE A steak and kidney pie with mashed potato; Liam pours water in pint glasses and sets the table ready for dinner.

His dad pauses by the sink after washing his hands, tired. The silence feels like it has lasted for hours. Liam takes a hand towel and pushes it along the counter so his dad can see it. It stays there, part folded and part crumpled, and his dad wipes his hands on his trousers.

Is Róisín still coming?

I think so.

They look at the pie; it will spoil if she doesn't get here soon.

It's more of a dinner than his dad usually serves – as if the promise of having a woman in the house encourages him to make it feel more like a home.

This summer, I'll get you properly trained, his dad says. About the farm.

Maybe we could look into a qualification, Liam says.

I can teach you. There's no need to go…

OK. Yes. That'd be grand.

Róisín is going to the farm for dinner, like she said she would; her mum is going out with Neil again, and it'll be a good idea to give them space. She doesn't mind about Neil. In fact she likes him, likes having him around, and that surprises her. She's not jealous that her mum has found someone new; it makes her feel free. Recently she's started calling her mum Adele to show how grown up she is – she wants to feel like they are equals.

When she walks across the field she opens her arms wide and imagines a world so big, so full of people, she would never tire of exploring it, her eyes fixed on the sky above until she slips on some sheep droppings, only just managing to catch her fall. Liam's always telling her the ground is just as important as the sky.

Liam looks up to see Róisín peering through the glass in the door. She is waving. She is smiling. When she walks into the kitchen it's as if the lights have been switched on – she kisses his dad on the cheek in a way that makes his father grin and pat her on the back; she turns on the radio and music, voices, stutter through the static then settle in the air, and she winks at Liam. His family comes alive again.

Thanks for coming, he says, and although it's delivered with a casual smile he means it more than he can say.

Róisín takes a sip of her drink. She's nervous, though trying not to show it – tonight, after dinner, she has to tell Liam that she is going away.

At dinner, Adele has gone quiet because she knows what it feels like to wait for a man to break bad news. When Róisín's father left he didn't sneak away in the night or drive off after a fight, he took her out for dinner to tell her he was going. And now a new man is avoiding her eyes and struggling with where to rest his hands, looking relieved when the waitress comes by because it gives him something to say.

Neil orders red wine and, when it arrives, he sips it in a way that barely reduces the volume in the glass. Then he tells Adele that his son has been diagnosed with autism. His ex-wife says she can't cope. She has found a boarding home that specialises; she wants to send him away; his heart is breaking.

This is not a man who is leaving; this is a man asking for help.

Move in with me, she says. Both of you.

She puts her hand over his hand. It creates a new family.

Over dinner they focus on talking to Liam's dad, don't say too much to each other; they both understand caution. It has been this way for several years now. They are scared to act like cousins, because then they would be acting like they were close, and they have to hide how close they really are.

Liam accidentally brushes Róisín's hand when he's passing her the mashed potatoes. He immediately apologises.

The want he feels makes his face burn.

Amo, amas, amat.

His dad doesn't notice.

When the dark starts to seep in through the window in the back door Liam stands, plates clatter into the sink, his dad wishes Róisín a good night, and then they are alone. She knows that it has to be now. She turns the radio off.

Something about this makes Liam's throat dry.

No, now. I can't wait, he says.

He speaks through breath that is fast and hard, like a man's, not shallow like a boy's.

We have to wait. Just till the light's off.

They always used to wait till Liam's dad's light was off; it seemed the right thing to do.

No.

Róisín knows that she has changed things, and she's not sure if they'll be able to go back. She never intended her leaving to be a betrayal. Is this what happens when something undoubted becomes doubted?

She lets him fuck her against the fence, her skirt hurriedly pulled up around her waist, his trousers around his ankles.

Afterwards he sits in the grass and puts his head on his knees. His sobs are the sobs of a boy. She doesn't know how to comfort him like this. She wishes she could.

I've found it, she says.

They haven't moved; they are both sitting on the trampled grass by the fence.

Do you want me to show you?

He takes the binoculars from her and follows her instructions. Nothing.

You have to keep looking. It's very faint – look away from any nearby stars, try to see just dark space, and then concentrate.

After a while, he makes out a smudge of light that could be anything; a bit of dirt on the lens, his thumbprint.

Why London? he says.

She doesn't answer. What answer can she give?

But you belong here, he says.

You could leave with me?

He doesn't reply.

I mean it. After school, you could come to London too. We'll find a whole new world, you'll see...

I can't!

She is shocked into silence by the force of his voice; he never shouts. He's never shouted at her.

I can't leave my dad, don't you see? he says, quieter now, trying to find words to explain. The farm, I need to help and . . . he's so sad. You could help, too? You do, by being here.

But Róisín knows she can't stay, not now, couldn't live on a farm with all this weight of silence, can't keep on keeping a secret like this; she doesn't want to live in the shadows, however much she wants to help.

It's only four years, she starts to say, meaning her degree, but somehow she knows it's going to be more than that.

This is a shite comet, he says. I can hardly see it at all, and the binoculars make a quiet thud on the grass. It's too far away.

Give it some time, she says, hoping there might be some truth in what she is about to imply. It's Halley's comet; it always comes back.

- - - - - - - -

AT FIRST, ALL SEVERINE CAN do is listen. She listens to their chatter and their affectionate bickering, listens as they discuss how grown up she is now: how very pregnant. She listens as they debate who the father is and smiles when they ask her, giving nothing away, telling them nothing of her life. She falls asleep to their words and wakes up surrounded by family and at last, in her pyjamas, two days after her granny has died, she begins to ask them questions.

Where is my granny?

Oh, she's a bit busy, pet. You'll see her next time.

With the next comet?

Yes.

How long will I have to wait?

Days. Or maybe years. Jusqu'à ce qu'ils décident d'arrêter.

Great-Grandpa Paul-François laughs, kindly. She had his hair wrong in her tapestry; he is not a white-haired old man, he's dark, handsome, with laughter lines around his eyes.

She promised.

You'll see her again, if you want to.

And who are all the others?

But Great-Grandpa Paul-François has opened the closet in the hall and is having too much fun trying on Severine's mother's hats to reply.

She watches the comet through binoculars from their attic window. It's faint this time, Halley's comet, not like the comet she saw as a child.

How many days do we have left?

One or two, I'd say.

Oh, it's you.

Hello.

Severine puts her binoculars down, turns to face Antoine.

Where have you been? she asks, sounding far more like a teacher than she intends.

Antoine smiles.

Playing hide-and-seek, he says.

With the other ghosts?

With the stars in Cassiopeia, and he turns his voice to a whisper. When we're not here, I like to think we're out there. Don't you?

She looks out of the window and tries to imagine what he means.

Never mind, he grins, your granny always said I had my head in the clouds.

She tries to remember all the things her granny ever told her. Look harder, she would say, look at the world, at the sky, and always at the ground beneath your feet.

Beneath Severine's feet there is just the same old carpet they've always had, but standing on it are twenty or more dead family members, watching her inquisitively. There are twin sisters in long dresses of lace, young men in the different uniforms of different wars. An old woman who appears to be wrapped in a towel; I want to take a bath, she announces.

Severine hears her mother calling and glances around the room. Pads barefoot down the stairs.

Mama?

Just thought you might like some coffee.

It is a peace offering for an argument that was never voiced, and Severine is glad, and grateful, and would very much like some coffee.

Severine and her mama sit side by side at the table, each holding their coffee with their palms wrapped round their cups, warming their fingers. They have the same skin, the same shape to their heads, the same way of blowing over their cups to cool their drink.

How are you? Severine's mother asks.

Ready to burst.

They both smile.

I remember when I had you.

I've seen the photo in the album.

Her mama looks tired, brushes her hair back from her face in a familiar gesture.

I'll be there with you, she says. I wasn't sure if you knew... I didn't mean to seem angry about it. I just wanted you to...

Go to college, have a career. Get married?

I just wanted you to be free.

Severine lets go of her anger. She hadn't realised it was still there until she felt it vanish.

Perhaps some things are better than freedom.

That's what your granny would have said.

Only sometimes.

That's true. She was a contradiction.

Just like us.

Even though her mama is crying now, there must be an unspoken memory of her own mother that makes her smile; makes her laugh despite her tears.

Severine wants to talk to her mama about the ghosts, but every time she tries something stops her. They would, surely, have appeared to her if she had wanted to see them.

But it's more than that. She has seen too often how people looked at her granny, the concern, the pity, the embarrassment of watching a woman lose her mind. She doesn't want that; she doesn't want to be looked at like that. She will try to keep the ghosts to herself.

What have you been doing upstairs? her mama asks, as if she could hear her thoughts.

Just resting, Severine says.

Her mama's eyes, red for two days, search her own. She reaches forward and tucks Severine's hair behind her ear.

You'll let me know if you need anything?

Severine nods.

All I need is to be here.

She looks up, to the window.

Or maybe outside for a minute?

They take the picnic chairs out to their back garden, even though the evening is drawing in and it is cold. Severine used to think that she could see all the stars there were to see in Bayeux, the sky was so full of them, until her granny told her that there were layers upon layers they couldn't see. Would every black space have a star in it, if we could only see well enough?

They wrap a blanket each around their shoulders.

What's in the old shed? Severine asks, as her eyes fall on it.

That was my grandpa's shed, her mama says; he built it himself.

So it's empty now?

Granny kept her gardening tools in there, and some other things she imagined she had to hide from me.

It seems funny, that a mother would need to hide things from a daughter, but perhaps all mothers are doing it and it's only the rarest daughter that realises and understands enough to leave well alone.

Do you think I could have a look tomorrow?

If you like, her mama says. I think she was keeping it all there for you anyway.

It feels good, to be outside talking with her mother, feels like something they should have been doing for years but haven't. She takes her hand and they sit in silence for a minute. Severine is glad that the ghosts have stayed upstairs.

Where's my father?

It's a question she hasn't asked since she felt afraid to keep asking as a child, but it feels right to ask it now, at last.

He wanted to travel, she says. You were a baby, but it was OK, somehow. He said he hadn't found his home, not here. She looks at Severine with a fresh worry in her eyes. Do you miss him?

Severine smiles, shakes her head. It is her granny that she misses.

You can't miss someone you never knew, she says.

Her mama thinks that, actually, you can; she has watched her own mother go mad with longing to speak to members of her family that she never knew.

Where did he go?

Across Europe first, she says, then... Africa, South America.

You didn't think about going with him?

Her mama smiles then, and shakes her head.

Because you needed to be with Granny, after Antoine...?

Because I had a home, and I had you, and I'd married a man who was too restless to ever stay in one place.

What was he like?

He was gentle, but distracted. And he was always whistling.

Her mama's expression changes, as if another forgotten memory has been rekindled, and it makes her face softer.

I always thought I wanted to travel, she says, it was part of why I loved him in the first place.

So what changed?

Life, she says, but Severine knows from the look in her eye that she means a new life; she is talking about what happens when you have a child. And what happens when you lose one.

It's colder now, she says. Time to head in?

Severine nods, allows herself to stop questioning.

There are fewer ghosts in Severine's room that night. The night before she was overwhelmed with how much family was around her; tonight she feels overwhelmed by the loss of them.

Some of you have left already? she asks anxiously. You'll come back, won't you?

With the next comet, says a ghost who hasn't spoken before.

Which one are you? asks Severine, but she regrets the question as a shiver of fear passes through her body. She knows who this must be.

If you stay here, in Bayeux, says Brigitte, holding out her hand.

Severine recoils. The skin on Brigitte's arm is weeping, red raw and peeling back in places to expose shrivelled muscle and blackened bone.

Brigitte stands where she is, stands taller, her arm still held out towards Severine, who finds her back is pressed hard against the wall. Brigitte's burns are spreading and her hair – a minute ago wild dark curls down to her waist – has caught alight and Brigitte's head, her face, is turning from a vicious red to the black of ash as her eyes still stare, open and pleading.

Severine clasps her arms around her belly, turns away – she can't help it, can't stand to watch this horror, and she has to protect her child.

Please, no, she says. Leave us alone…

But as she rushes for the doorway she sees the tall woman in the golden dress, a red shawl wrapped around her head and neck, a gentle smile on her face.

Hello, Severine. It's all right now.

Her accent is strange, foreign but not foreign; an inflection to her words that Severine has never heard before.

I am sorry, she says. I didn't realise what I was creating.

Severine looks around the room, but Brigitte has gone and everything is calm again.

I don't understand.

That's why I'm here, tonight.

Severine wishes she could kiss her cheek to welcome her, but instead she gestures towards the old chest by the window and with that Ælfgifu sits down and starts, softly, again, to tell her story.

Severine dreams that night of hundreds, no, thousands of ghosts clamouring to be heard, breaking from their disorderly queue and talking all at once. You're like children, she says, waving her hands around her head as she'd seen her granny do so many times, trying to swat the voices away like insects; you're just like children.

She wakes to silence in the night. Stands at her window for a moment, but it is not enough. She creeps down the stairs, avoiding the step that creaks, holds her breath as she passes her mother's room and pulls a coat over her nightdress. She turns the key in the back door as quietly as she is able to; she doesn't want anyone to follow her out here.

In the garden, she searches the sky for the comet. She couldn't see it out of her window, or from the back porch. Her binoculars show her layer upon layer of stars; more layers appear the longer she looks, every dark space fills with stars but Halley's comet is nowhere to be seen. At 4.30 a.m. the sky begins to lighten and the furthest layers of stars sink into the rising blue. Standing on the grass out by Great-Grandpa Paul-François's old shed she gives up the search; lets the binoculars fall to the ground with a quiet thud. The comet is gone, and besides, her waters have broken.

Halley's Comet

They walk into the village like it's carnival day, that's how it feels; like it's fun and wholesome and will never lead to arrows of fire and lungs pierced with splinters of wood. Ælfgifu stands with the others and cheers for the local boys who are going to fight, and she waves her flowers because that is what they do, at carnival time.

That evening she goes to collect water from the stream; their well is sending up mud and they say that the flying star means bad luck, that her family shouldn't trust anything when the stars come shooting through the clouds. What nonsense, she told Grandpa once, but still, she avoids the well and there – by the stream, she sees the boys from the procession, not off fighting yet, but playing in the water. They are like children, she thinks.

The night is warm but fresh and their clothes are piled by the stream's bank; one of them turns, raises a hand halfway then stops. Shaking her dark hair out over her shoulders she walks up to the stream, pretending not to watch him. He's emerged from under the water now, the one with black hair and a wave half formed, glancing at her when he thinks she's not looking. She kneels by the bank, and without meaning to she's slipping her feet into the stream and he's walking towards her. In the moonlight his skin shimmers. She slips off her dress. She invites him, and he accepts.

She can hear the sounds of the battle, her sisters and brothers hear it too; like a shared nightmare lingering after they've woken. No way to protect themselves so they sit outside on the grass and wait for whatever will follow. The screams – shapeless howls of pain that can't be comprehended. They threw flowers, she thinks, just yesterday, daffodils of hope that were more like the petals thrown into a grave. Even the young ones understand what is happening; no words yet to speak it but she can see the fear in their eyes.

The worst is when it gets quieter; wails of pain replaced by silence of death. From over the hill they appear, with their unfamiliar uniforms and flags; these are not their soldiers come to protect them. They are the other side, here to destroy. At the edge of the village a house is set on fire and the smell tells her it is not only wattle and daub that is burning; the animals, she thinks, and the thought turns to hope that it is only animals. The men shout in a language she doesn't know. Children scream. She gathers her brothers and sisters, tells them to stand behind her. Overhead the comet blazes.

She doesn't know why they do it. The arrows pass her outstretched arms and find their target in her brother's chest, in the face of her eldest sister who still has a flower in her hair. They set fire to their home. Her youngest sister runs to the next house, into the blade of a man who has blood streaming from his arm. He falls with her. Ælfgifu turns, looks them in the eye, holds her last sister behind her. They have killed everyone else. She's pushed to the ground. When her sister falls beside her, blood leaks from the gash in her neck. She doesn't know why they do it. They leave her alive.

At the sound of his voice Ælfgifu opens her eyes.

Please, he says, there is not much time.

She is holding her sister in her arms, blood dried now on her face and neck, her tunic dyed brown with it. She turns away from his eyes that had smiled at her through splashing water. She wants to die here.

He carries her to the stream, away from the village to where the smell is less thick. He follows the shooting star because there has to be some help and it is all that is left. He saw it, the bright flying star, on the battlefield, watched it from the ground where he lay, pierced, bleeding. And now here he is. He doesn't understand it. And there it is, the flying star, still in the sky.

They stumble through the night, following the flight of the shooting star; when he falls she takes over, supports him in her arms so they can keep going even though she doesn't know where they are going to. As the sun rises they see a building of stone high on the hill, an impossible shadow. They don't know if it's real or a death-dream but they start to climb. She trips, crawls up the steep hillside, feet bleeding against the stones. There are doors of thick wood; she beats on them with a fist and falls to her knees.

My child.

She looks up. A woman is standing above her; the doors are open.

She tries to stand, collapses into the woman's arms.

What is your name? she asks.

She doesn't know if her voice will work; she thinks she is dead.

Ælfgifu, she says, letting the shapes form on her lips and hoping the sound will follow. And—

She turns to the soldier boy but he is gone. Something in her changes. It is a loss too far and she will spend the next thirteen years trying to bring him back; trying to protect their child. She has lost too much family and she knows she cannot stand to lose any more and now – and now she allows herself to be carried by a stranger into the safety of ancient stone and shade.

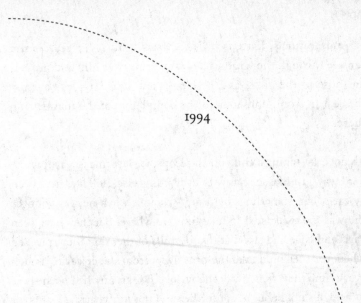

Comet Shoemaker–Levy 9

FRANÇOIS SQUIRMS ON HIS SEAT as he looks out of the aeroplane window, trying to turn far enough that he could press himself through the glass and into the clouds.

Look, Mama, he gasps, Mama, do you see?

They are over the sea; there is land rising up from the water.

Most of the Earth is water, his mama says, and below the water is magma. The land on top, it's just floating, like the croutons in your soup.

François laughs at the image – Mama is so silly – but he doesn't take his eyes from the view. As they descend through the clouds there is a moment when the world through his window is striped; golden sky, silver cloud, blue sea far below.

Look! he cries again. Mama, look!

And he turns, flattens his head back against his seat so she can see through the window, and she leans over him and presses her nose to the glass, and he laughs and kicks his legs against the seat in front, oblivious to the complaints of the man sitting there.

It's not easy, taking a child on an aeroplane. Severine is learning the hard way, just like she has with everything else. Holidays have been by car so far, sometimes by train – though when he was younger she was too exhausted to take him anywhere. But they have seen Paris and Nice and stood at the foothills of the Alps; they travelled whenever she could take the time away from the épicerie, though every time they went away she wished her granny had been there to help. It's not enough, not for her and not for what she wants for him, but she has tried to show him some of the world, at least the country beyond Bayeux. She has tried not to mention the ghosts that she saw in the days before he was born, because she wants him to have a normal childhood. Besides, she's not even sure they were real now, though she still dreams of their voices.

And so now, for her first plane journey in ten years, they are going to Scotland; to feel the cold and the rain and the beauty and the music, to climb the seven hills and to start seeing the rest of the world. Perhaps she will even have a moment or two to herself; to feel like herself.

Every time she thinks that she tries to unthink it, but cannot.

As they land, he squeals with joy rather than pain – if his ears hurt like the other children on the plane he certainly doesn't mention it. It's like he was born for this, Severine thinks to herself; they are part of the larger world. And she opens her hands wide, imagines whole universes contained between her palms.

She hasn't seen the ghosts for eight years – and for eight years now she has been the parent, the one in charge. It seems like a lifetime since she felt looked after; since she was allowed to be the child.

François is older now though, she thinks, more able to take care of himself. Besides, he is not afraid of travel – he seems to love it.

Maybe they can go and see all that world, after all.

He's never asked about his papa, and that's OK by her; she's had enough questions from her mother to last her a lifetime.

Actually, he's a nice enough man. He says he likes receiving the photos she sends, says to let him know if there's ever anything they need.

He works on a boat that travels the Atlantic.

They could have been good friends (the love thing was never going to work out; they soon realised it wasn't love that drew them together) and a part of her wanted to go with him, but another part of her chose to stay and now she doesn't really know why. Sometimes, though, she imagines a vast ocean, the brightness of so much water, the wide-open expanse of it.

Can I run on this bit?

François jumps with impatience; there is a moving strip of floor and he wants to fly along it, to race faster than he can on grass.

His mama checks behind her – they were the last to get off the plane; they are the last on the people carrier that will take them to the terminal.

OK, she says, run like the wind.

She is supposed to say be careful but that's not the kind of mother she wants to be.

His arms fly out as he runs. When he gets to the end he waits for his mama to do the same, come on! he shouts, but she doesn't run – she stands tall and waves at him as the flat escalator carries her forwards and something in him is disappointed.

*

On their first night, François wakes with a nightmare. He was on a dark beach, there were waves crashing against the rocks; there was cold and there was fear. The salt water filled his mouth when he tried to shout out, he gasped and choked, he had to save his mama... He opens his eyes; pulls the covers over his head and grips his toy tiger as if someone were trying to steal it from him.

In the bed next to his, Severine is awake too. This always happens when she leaves home: a knot in her belly, something between guilt and loneliness that haunts her in the night. She wishes the ghosts would appear now; even after all these years she misses her granny. She never really said goodbye. One day she thought she was surrounded by so much family, and then they were all gone, leaving just her and her child, a baby then, to wonder how the house could feel so empty when there was so much noise. She too pulls the covers over her head and tries not to wake her son, tells herself this is crazy, that it probably never happened at all, that she spent two days hallucinating after her granny died.

And then, of course, she knows that they have arrived.

Granny?

She pulls the covers away from her face to see the shadow of a woman standing by the door. This is not like it was the last time. Where is the rush of voices, the laughter, the playful bickering of people who have loved one another for decades, for centuries?

This is silence.

Severine tries to beckon Brigitte closer, but she won't come.

She thinks about getting out of bed herself, but something makes her stay.

They look at one another across the room, neither making a move.

There is a sound though.

What are you trying to say?

Please...

Severine stares. In the shadows Brigitte's face is obscured, her clothes are long and loose; her skin looks dark, but that might just be the lack of light. Severine looks down at her own skin, at her arms. She is visible in the moonlight coming in through the curtains. Brigitte must be hidden by more than shadow – she is fading into the air.

Come forward, she wants to say; are you here alone?

But François is sleeping and Severine does not say the words out loud and the ghost remains where she is, barely visible. Watching.

Severine rolls onto her side; from here she can see François's bed and she tells herself that he is what's real – the world is Severine and François and their holiday in Scotland, with wide oceans still to explore. It is her choice to make. She closes her eyes.

When she opens her eyes again Brigitte is gone, and she tries to deny the disappointment she feels.

François wakes early; he is in a new country that he has never seen before and he wants to go and explore.

Scottish breakfast? his mama asks with a smile.

He wrinkles up his nose to say no, pulls the curtains wide to look out at Edinburgh, where there are castles and bagpipes and looming hills of rock.

Half an hour later they are on the Royal Mile, standing before a stall of fresh fruit and flowers. François chooses the clementines for breakfast, holding each in his hand before making his selection, testing for their ripeness the way he's seen his mama do it, looking up to her with a grin. She buys herself a single tulip and threads it through the buttonhole of her coat; rests her hand on his head but he pulls away, already eager to see more.

Severine's not sure why she turned her back on Brigitte in the middle of the night. She never wanted to ignore the ghosts before – she spent most of her life willing them to appear. But before they had wanted to speak; they had been happy to see her. Now, their appearance seemed to say something else.

No, not their appearance. Brigitte's appearance.

Where is her granny?

As they walk up the cobbled streets, listen to the commentary about the castle – with François asking so many questions – take photos from between the cannons and eat ice cream despite the chill in the air, she catches herself glancing over her shoulder, looking into the darkened alleyways, behind closed blinds and along the shadows of the old town, wondering if Brigitte will appear again.

What are you looking for?

François pulls his mama away from a dark alleyway of steps that smells like a toilet.

Just wondering where we should go next, she says.

He doesn't believe her. She was hardly listening to the man talking about the castle and when he got ice cream on his face she didn't even notice. He had to wipe it off on his sleeve, and he doesn't like doing that.

Let's sit down in the gardens, she says; the gardens used to be a loch in the middle of the city. That used to be where they dunked witches, she says, and then she stops talking suddenly.

Is that a story you're not supposed to tell a child? he says, and his mama looks surprised and maybe a little bit like she's going to laugh.

I'm going to tell you a secret now, she says.

His eyes widen.

OK.

My granny told me when I was little, she says. And now I'm going to tell you.

*

François doesn't believe in Father Christmas any more. He doesn't believe in magic either; he is eight years old! So he scrunches up his nose at his mama's story of ghosts, and waits for her to tell him the real truth.

Well, you were named after your great-great-grandpa Paul-François, she says, do you believe that much?

Of course, he says, I've seen a photo of him, so I know that he was real. He's just dead now.

And of course that's when Great-Grandpa Paul-François decides to appear.

We need to talk, he says, fading in and out of vision.

Severine shakes her head.

I know, not now. Later. In the night. We can't stay long here. It's too far...

He's gone again.

Severine frowns.

The bagpipe player starts up again, and François clasps his hands over his ears and squeals. Shouting over the noise, he says, you know, Mama, there's no such thing as witches, and there's no such thing as ghosts.

- - - - - - - -

IN THE FIRST SECONDS AFTER Róisín wakes she doesn't know where she is, and she loves it. She looks over to the curtains – red and gold, thinner than expected – up to the ceiling with its ornate plaster-work and old-fashioned charm. Voices, traffic, laughter, unexpected sunshine. Her flatmate is making coffee. She knocks; passes it in.

Skies look clear, she says. You're going up to the observatory tonight?

Tammy sits cross-legged on the floor as they chat. She is study-ing French and Spanish; says it means she can live in pretty much any continent of the world.

But after she's left the flat and Róisín is on her own again Liam appears in her mind; every morning there is this moment, the flash of a different life, his face the last time she saw him, the shadow beneath his eyes, before he is brushed away. The sea is keeping them apart, the distance. It's for the best. She did the right thing; she's out in the world.

She rolls onto her side, decides not to get up just yet.

She doesn't have to work today. The party is planned for this evening.

The predictions are for the comet to explode in the atmosphere of Jupiter, in the early hours of the morning. A comet this size, colliding with a planet; it's the stuff of Armageddon.

That is what she wants to see, in her life. The power of something extraordinary.

Eventually she pulls on leggings and a jumper; changes the jumper for a T-shirt when she looks out of the window.

Below her flat there are people on the street, some waiting at the bus stop, others walking past the grocer's on the corner. A mother and son, hand in hand, are standing by the flowers and vegetables on display outside. She pushes open the window and French voices reach her on the air; she almost calls out to them before she catches herself – people in Edinburgh don't wave to strangers the way people in the country do. Still, the sun in Scotland can make people do unexpected things.

She checks the news on her computer for any preliminary observations. Nothing from NASA so far, just promises that the best is yet to come.

She closes the window; the people below have moved away. It makes her feel strangely alone.

Róisín decides to climb the hill a bit later than the others; she knows they're all going to be there together, at the observatory, and she feels like making her own separate entrance. She takes her time with the day, letting the anticipation build as she does some washing, as she listens to a radio play, as she thinks about phoning her mum but doesn't lift the receiver to make the call. Simple everyday things on a day that is not everyday, on a day that is once in a lifetime.

Patience.

Another hour slips by; the comet will know it cannot escape now, will be feeling the rush of the outer atmosphere as it edges closer to its fate.

She paces her flat, pulls on her shoes.

It is nearly time for sunset.

In orbit, telescopes orient themselves towards the stormy gas giant; in deserts, on mountains, terrestrial observatories prepare to record the collision in all wavelengths of the electromagnetic spectrum. There have been great comets before, but this is something special. Earth knows it, for once; the planet is at a safe distance, but it knows where to look, and it's learning how to wait.

Róisín is learning to wait, too; she's trying to stop cheating, to stop expecting something new to feel as powerful as something old. Things with Liam, they couldn't be the same; that couldn't continue, not as adults, not when they had lives to lead. A secret like that would fester.

And so she's gone home, twice a year, like she promised; has visited on Boxing Day and called in to the farm each summer, and they have gone back to being cousins, if not best friends – they are a long way from that. But cousins is something. Cousins is what it should be.

She shakes her head. Pulls on her coat, grabs a hat from by the door. It could be chilly, on the hill.

Tonight, Róisín will wait all night if she has to, for that perfect moment of destruction when the comet will split and burst, crash through the atmosphere and turn from ice to fire.

Some people say that comets seed life on lifeless planets. That will not happen today; nothing can survive on Jupiter, not even ice and dust and rock.

When she arrives, Sam is already there; he glances at her as she walks from the stairs to join the group, his eyes lingering a second longer than if there was nothing to say.

How's it looking? she asks.

Clear night, he says.

There are several other postdocs there, PhD students and one of the junior lecturers leaning over the computer's keyboard. We should get some good measurements from here, he says without looking up.

Róisín thinks about saying she is more interested in the view, then realises how unscientific she sounds.

Sam turns away.

Róisín thinks about Liam, then promises herself she will stop.

Comet Shoemaker–Levy 9 was trapped a long time ago, caught in orbit around Jupiter, never able to break free from the storms. Some planets collect comets, shielding the smaller fragile worlds from their impacts; that is what Jupiter does for Earth. It's a comet catcher. The solar system's best line of defence. You have to forgive its toxic atmosphere and raging hurricanes, when you know what it does. Jupiter is a self-sacrificing sort of a king.

Róisín's memories come to her uninvited; she is looking through the telescope, focused on Jupiter's southern hemisphere, and she is thinking about the touch of his stubble on her chin; the taste of his skin where she once licked fresh water from the crease inside his elbow; the way his thumb brushed her lips outside the school gate.

Sam has fuller lips, is capable of growing a far thicker beard, and wears glasses that accentuate his eyes. There is nothing unpleasant about him.

Sometimes Róisín feels the lack of love so acutely her eyes burn.

Someone has brought a bottle of wine, someone else some crisps and chocolate. Snacks fit for a children's party and drinks for an eighteenth birthday. They've planned to stay here for the night. They're going to watch the collision in the observatory and then go outside, drink and play music and spend a night on Blackford Hill.

Not just one bottle of wine: many. They've all brought at least one, some more. Someone has whisky. Someone, peach schnapps. They started with little plastic cups but soon they are taking swigs out of bottles.

The sky is black at first but after enough wine they can see it as purple, turquoise; a deep glowing blue that's filled with something more than darkness.

It's ready, someone says.

They cluster around the telescope, wanting to see with their own eyes; the computer display is inadequate for the mood they want to capture.

Sam looks at Róisín, steps back from the crowd.

They see a burst of golden-yellow red, a bright fireball igniting within the atmosphere of the gas giant. The comet has fractured into pieces, and this is the first of them, the bravest, letting go of its orbit and agreeing to burn. It lasts for a while; there is nothing immediate about this particular form of ending. It is not the miracle she was expecting.

Róisín looks through the eye of the telescope, imagines Liam doing the same. His binoculars made a quiet thud on the ground, the last time he saw a comet. He was angry. Perhaps he still is. That must be why he won't hold her gaze.

She feels a hand on her shoulder; someone takes her wrist.

Come outside, Sam says.

They step out into the dark, stumble along the muddy path and over the crest of the hill.

- - - - - - - -

SEVERINE IS WOKEN UP BY a terrible pain in her stomach. Something has happened, and she's no idea what it is, but it feels like something in her is breaking apart, something that should be whole is fracturing into pieces.

Didn't you realise? says Great-Grandpa Paul-François. He looks different, diminished. If you want to see us, there are conditions, he says. Your granny told you.

Severine clutches her stomach and her eyes close over.

She had lost consciousness, but she wakes again and a different ghost is there: Brigitte is standing at the foot of the bed. There are burns on her arms and legs; her skin is a raw mess of blackened wounds.

What are you doing here? Brigitte says.

Severine doesn't reply; she mustn't wake François, he must never see this, feel this horror.

Did we not make it clear that you have to stay in Bayeux? Otherwise we can't...

She remembers her granny's voice, her words from years ago.

But, surely, only when there's a comet in—

All the time.

Always? Severine thinks of all the places she wants to see, of the continents she has never visited, of the landscapes she wants to show François. She can't give that up.

She sits up higher in the bed, looks to the window and remembers; was there something on the news about a comet?

I'll go wherever I want, she starts to say, but when she looks back, the room is empty.

François is asleep, but Severine is wide awake now and her mind is racing.

To demand that she stay in Bayeux – it is ridiculous. They can't send burning strangers to threaten her into giving up her own life. She wanted to see her granny again but she never agreed to angry women appearing in her hotel room at night.

In the corner shadows Great-Grandpa Paul-François has come to check that she is OK. It is difficult for them to appear this far from Bayeux, it takes a force of will and uses up too much of their energy – they can't stay for long.

See that? Severine's granny says, shimmering in beside the bedside cabinet. She's missed the comet – she didn't even look through the binoculars.

She didn't miss anything, you daft old woman, he says. She felt it; I know she did.

We felt it. But not Severine, she's strayed too far. Her heart is...

She understood.

She'll be too late getting home now. We have to go.

It'll be different next time.

What if she stops wanting to see us?

Don't fret, he says, she won't stop. And besides, would that be the worst thing? You don't need to see something, to know that it's there.

LIAM LIGHTS CANDLES, SETS THE table before she arrives. He can hear Rachel's car approach. The farm is the only thing for miles, her car the only car.

And yet he waits for her to ring the bell, not wanting to seem too keen or too in need of company.

The bell doesn't ring.

A minute later he hears a knocking on the back door that leads into the kitchen.

He looks up, expects to see Róisín smiling at him through the dappled glass of the door. But it is not Róisín. Of course it is not Róisín. It hasn't been Róisín for years.

She has brought a bottle of expensive wine with her. The sight of it makes him feel more empty than he can say.

So instead he says, thank you.

She seems to find his formality endearing.

Lipsticked lips are pressed to his own; they miss slightly. He spends the evening with a smudge of maroon to the left of his mouth.

He fumbles with the buttons on Rachel's shirt, aware that he is being clumsy because he is self-conscious. He knows this is something he could stop; he's not even sure why he's still going.

Let's go outside, she says. He wonders if she's remembered his dad lives with him.

He nods OK; he prefers to be outside anyway. They go out through the back door from the kitchen, walk towards the old barn then turn left, towards the river instead.

Here's grand, she says.

He stops, surprised. It would be a nice view, he supposes, if there were light enough to see by.

She's brought a blanket he didn't even know he had. He guesses it would spoil the allure if he asked where she found it.

She's laying it out on the ground.

Her name is Rachel. So different from Róisín; so close that it makes him ache.

*

Rachel's lips explore his body; he feels like he's watching it happen even though his eyes are closed. He imagines himself as a younger man, a teenager, understanding for the first time what certain words mean; amo, amas, amat, he whispers.

What?

He doesn't reply. He thinks about asking her to stop.

When he opens his eyes he finds himself by the riverbank; he doesn't remember how he got here, only that he had walked through the dark in search of something that he couldn't find. And there beside him, Rachel's face is of concern, an earnest desire to help.

Liam, are you OK?

He almost laughs at the absurdity of the question: of course he is not OK. He stopped halfway through; mumbled that he couldn't focus, that he needed to go and see the river – the real question is what's she still doing here?

Maybe I could help, she says. If you tell me...

He just wants it to stop. Wants her sweet, genuine eyes to turn to frustration, her bare legs to walk away – he's not sure what happened to her tights, but her legs are now bare beneath her pleated skirt, which stirs a memory in his mind.

Your skirt, he says, and she smiles, not expecting a compliment but taking it as one anyway.

This is a man she would quite like to save from his demons. She's not sure what they are yet, but even at school, as teenagers, she could tell there was something. Why don't we sit down here, she says, by the river.

He does as he is told; feels a step closer to Róisín and feels an emotion he had forgotten.

I'm surprised you're still here, he says.

She reaches in for a kiss then gives him a smile.

Sure and we can take all the time you need, she says.

He feels ashamed; thinks of another time, another body. Undoes her skirt.

THE OTHERS FOLLOW RÓISÍN AND Sam outside; they are not alone, they are all on the hillside looking out at the sky, looking down at the city.

Sam whispers something in her ear. She doesn't catch the words.

There is laughter behind them, another bottle opened.

I want to be barefoot! someone cries, finding themselves hilarious. I want to feel the mud between my toes!

Over here, Sam whispers, leading her away. Beyond the crest of the hill there's a view down to the river, away from the lights of the city. She likes the fact that it's too dark to see his smile. Liam didn't smile all the time; there was something serious in his eyes. Something that made her need more.

Sam is sitting down, pulling her down too.

Come here, gorgeous.

She cringes; imagines a different man, a different moment. She's not even sure why she's doing it, but she doesn't really have the energy to stop.

He's laughing now; his eyes are aglow with a perceived danger, a sense that they are doing something forbidden. Róisín wonders if her heart should be racing, if she should be looking over her shoulder to check that they are alone, if her breaths should mirror the risk they are taking, but instead she closes her eyes and imagines herself in a childhood hut with no notion of danger, with no sense that they could be discovered. For her, exhilaration comes from something else; it's nothing to do with love being forbidden.

*

She finds she is crying, and is so embarrassed she has to pretend she's had an overwhelmingly good time.

I didn't hurt you, did I? he asks.

It's so ludicrous her tears are masked by laughter.

Of course not, she smiles, giggles. It was grand.

In a quieter moment, later, she'll remember the sound of that fake laughter and feel ashamed. But, for now, she doesn't have time to reflect on it because the others are shouting. Someone's realised what the hour is. Another fragment is about to collide.

It's time, now—

Come on—

What were you two—

Quick—

They all run back into the observatory, drunk enough to feel like they are about to witness something extraordinary, to believe that something extraordinary can be experienced together.

Comet Shoemaker–Levy 9 has a spectacular death as it splits and fractures and splits again and one by one the fragments catch fire in the atmosphere of the planet. They take turns watching through the eye of the telescope; there is no rush to see. It is spectacular but slow. The fragments burn for a long time – beneath them, they are causing a storm more violent than any on the planet.

Róisín is surprised at how slowly it happens, although she shouldn't be. A scientist should have known that the comet's broken pieces would take time to travel through the atmosphere; that they would disintegrate in a lonely death that would be less beautiful than the imagining of it. She was expecting fireworks, a series of bright explosions like timpani in light, but she should have realised that destruction takes time; that damage lingers on the surface before leaving a lasting impression.

She remembers a moment, in their childhood hut, by the river, a moment when she walked away and didn't realise.

SEVERINE GASPS; HER GRANNY'S VOICE, she's sure of it. She was here. It's a shiver of warmth that takes her back to a time when she felt protected, when she could allow herself to feel like a child pretending to be a grown-up.

Hello? she whispers.

Her voice will hardly make a sound. She imagines her granny's face, the crinkles around her lips, her laughter. Her eyes search every corner of the room, behind the door, between the cupboards at the end of the bed.

Granny?

She can't see her anywhere. And then it hits: this terrible thought she can't shake; what if they all leave now and don't come back? Is this her last chance?

She walks to the window, peeking out through closed curtains so as not to wake François; searches the sky for a comet, but sees only cloud cover and stars reaching through to edge them in silver, an orangey tint to the darkness from the city lights. They come with the comet and they leave with the comet, she thinks that's how it works. So there must be a comet somewhere up there, if she could only find it.

Open your eyes, mon petit, she whispers to François, who stirs in his sleep but doesn't wake up.

It's unfair, to do this to him, but she has to. What if her granny has gone and she's missed her chance to speak to her again? She couldn't stand it.

She touches his shoulder, lifts him out of his dream.

I'm sorry to wake you, François.

Mama?

We're going up to the hill; it'll be an adventure.

Why?

We have to see a comet tonight. I need to know if it's still here, I don't want to be too late.

She makes him put on layer after layer of clothes, like she is protecting him from a cold that he hasn't experienced yet. She wishes she had brought hats and scarves despite the mild weather and now her son is looking at her like she has gone crazy.

Even to an eight-year-old boy she seems like a madwoman.

But he does as he is told and soon they are creeping down the stairs of their old-fashioned B&B and closing the heavy door quietly behind them and walking hand in hand through the deserted streets of Morningside towards the unlit hill in the south of the city.

François doesn't really know what's going on but he's enjoying it. He's overheating in his layers but enjoying the fresh night air, the excitement as they clamber up a muddy path towards a big building with turrets and elaborate stone.

What is that?

I don't know, his mama says.

They have reached the observatory – the strange out-of-time tower with shadows down its walls, with brickwork at once crumbling and glorious, when the voices reach them on the wind.

He runs around behind it, his mama calling to him in shouted whispers, telling him to stay close beside her, but he doesn't listen; there's no danger here, just a new world to explore. It's dark, the ground gravelly and uneven, but there are lights twinkling in some of the windows and silvery moonlight catching the glass of others. And there are voices – over the other side of the tower, sitting on the grass, there are people laughing outside the observatory.

They are grown-ups, François sees that, but not really grown-ups; they're pointing at the sky and laughing and drinking and chattering, using words he doesn't know, long-sounding words that have the ring of something far away and mystical – interstellar space, galactic tide, hyperbolic trajectories.

He finds another path that leads from behind the observatory round to the summit of the hill.

Mama, he calls, not afraid of being heard.

They don't hear him though.

He runs up the path.

When François gets to the summit he looks back for his mama; he cannot see where she's gone. His fear doesn't come immediately, there is a moment of calm – she is on her way, of course. It is dark, that's all, hard to see; soon she'll appear. And then, after a minute, when she's still not there, a panic sets in but he stands quietly waiting, because his mama wouldn't leave him, not his mama.

And then something strange happens. He sees someone else. She is sitting on her own over the crest of the hill, hidden from the view of anyone except François standing at the very summit. She has her head resting on her knees; he can't see her face, she is more of a silhouette. Her loose hair blowing in the wind. It looks black, but that could just be the dark. And he has this strange feeling like she knows he's there but she's not going to turn around – like she's chosen to look the other way and nothing will change her mind now. He looks in the direction she is looking, and forgets to be scared. All there is that way is sky; night sky and stars. He's so intent on watching her that when he feels a hand on his shoulder he nearly cries out with the shock.

You got here first, smiles his mama – her voice is coming from behind him, so he thinks he can hear a smile.

He turns. She is not as calm as he thought, she looks different; he was wrong about the smile.

That's good, that you're quick, she says. Now there's something we have to find.

What do you mean?

There's something happening in the sky tonight. There's a comet that we need to see. It should be visible here, away from the street lights.

And Severine searches the sky without knowing that the comet has already fractured in the atmosphere of a red planet and burned, and disappeared into the storm.

François stares and stares at the sky. It is the first time he's stood looking up like this but somehow he knows it won't be the last. He's never looked at anything this closely before; he realises now his view of the world has been small. Layers of stars appear, each one on top of the other, stretching back further into the night.

There are lots of stars here, he says.

It sounds childish, but it is true.

His mama says he's right, but that somewhere among them there must be a comet. It's no use though; she can't see one. Why don't they help her? Look for the comets – that's what her granny said – so they should at least guide her gaze, help her to find the right direction. If François wasn't here she would shout out to them, demand they stop their comings and goings and tell her when she can see her granny again. She's always been quick with emotion – her worry turning to anger to regret. If François wasn't here she wouldn't shout, not really, she would call, she would wait for her granny all night. But François is here, so after a while she stops staring at the sky.

François, she says, it is not only the stars you can see. Look down on this city and think about how big the world must be.

Learn to love the heat and the cold, learn to get up in the middle of the night and see what no one else sees. And then learn to walk away.

She's talking to herself more than to him, thinking of the travels she never had and the life she can already see slipping out of reach.

What François wants to see is the woman with the black hair who was sitting over the crest of the hill. But, for some reason he doesn't understand, he keeps that to himself.

It's not fair, Severine decides, as she looks down at the lights of the city spread out below them, the shadows of the seven hills darker than the sky; when she turns she can see one of them, a reminder of the volcanic land they are standing on. It is not fair that the comet has left so soon. It's not fair that she has to stay in Bayeux. She deserves to live the life she wants, to explore the world and see jungles and rainforests and deserts of ice. When she was a girl she had so much energy, was so determined to see everything there was to see. And now?

And now she just wants to talk to her granny. She has so many questions. But it's not only that. Her granny, who everyone thought was crazy, who made the world come alive, whose smile made Severine feel special, and loved, and grown up when she was still a child – she misses her granny and Severine finds that she has to sit down on a rock at the crest of Blackford Hill and rest her head on her knees and hide her tears from the boy beside her, and she knows that in the morning she will return to Bayeux, and hope, and keep searching the skies, and that's where she will stay until a comet comes again.

- - - - - - - -

RÓISÍN DOESN'T MEAN TO PHONE; she can't help it. If she could see him instead she would.

Liam answers with Hello.

It's me.

Róisín.

It's almost a whisper, when he says her name. Why's he whispering?

Her breathing is too fast.

She wants to hold him. She wants to say that she was wrong.

She hears him swallow, he is breathing fast too.

There is another voice.

Someone's with you?

He doesn't reply.

She feels sick.

I didn't think.

Sam looks over at her. She's using the phone in the observatory.

Now Róisín is the one who whispers.

I'm sorry, she says, I'm sorry for calling so late.

And she hangs up the phone.

Liam cannot sleep, not for hours. The want he feels makes his cheeks burn; his skin is on fire. She phoned him. Why did she phone him?

When Rachel wakes he gets up, afraid she might think any of this is for her.

When she leaves, unhurriedly, with promises to see him soon – though he knows he will never see her again – with a warm hand on his arm, a look of kindness, and he is left alone, he reimagines the phone conversation. He rehears her voice, closes his eyes, knows her smell, her skin, her smile, her sounds.

Years of this, of stilted conversation, of glimpses of each other across rooms, of reserved Christmas cards, of having to listen to news of her life elsewhere. She's moved on again; she's in a new country, with a new man, has found a new life. This endless moving of hers, is that what she needs? Perhaps it is better than his version of life; staying, waiting, clinging onto a hurried glance and seeing meaning in her eyes as she turns them away, playing over and over in his mind the way it would be if they were together again, on the farm; the way her presence could recreate his home.

He reaches for a tissue.

He's not ashamed, not of this.

He wants more.

He wants Róisín.

The group camping out on Blackford Hill don't go home that night. They lie on the grass and talk about the things that drunk people talk about at four in the morning: past centuries and the vastness of the universe; what makes love true and whether or not the world is becoming a better place.

Róisín lies with them, but doesn't talk; she's too busy staring up at the sky and waiting for the faintest stars to appear in the voids between the bright constellations. She was disappointed in this comet, she thinks, in this night; perhaps that's why the pull of home feels so strong. She shouldn't have phoned him. Why did she phone him? But the longer she looks, the more stars she can see appearing, layer on layer, between constellations as familiar as her own dreams. It is not too late to make a new decision.

She leaves the group. The morning is early; there's no hint of light yet but the sky is changing, there's a shimmer to it that doesn't exist in the depths of night. She climbs the last peak of the hill and descends the other side, sits on the ground that is damp from dew and rests her head on her knees. There is a stream that runs behind the hill, beyond the trees and along through Morningside. She runs there, once or twice a week, in bright daylight; runs so fast her lungs ache and her breath burns in her throat.

Sometimes, it is as if she can feel him here. Liam. She tries saying his name without making a sound, feels her lips form around the m and part again, longing for more. She could hardly look at him, when she was home last, for some anniversary or other; both of them had gone to the party for each other and left without exchanging a word. She thought his expression was an accusation, at the time, but it was not; she knows that now, somehow, on Blackford Hill, with another man's taste still lingering, another man's touch still felt. It is as if he is standing behind her, watching her, waiting for her to turn and say it is OK. That their love is real. That she will come home. But he is not here; he is lying in bed with someone else.

Perhaps that is her own fault. Hers, and his.

She doesn't want to be haunted like this.

But she doesn't want the Sams of this world either, the confident men with their city accents and easy conversation. She wants the whole world, a life full of different people, the bright lights dancing between her outstretched palms like she'd imagined as a child. And though nothing so far has compared to what she left behind she knows what she's going to do. As the horizon blurs into a faded pink and she turns to see a child's silhouette on the top of the hill, she knows; she is going to keep searching, because there is something more for her to see.

Donati's Comet

One minute the house was bursting with life and then the men were gone and the women, safe but left behind, feel the weight of silence as they wait. Crimea – not a place they had even thought of until it was all they could think of. And then there was no word. The war ended, but there was no word. The men did not return. Instead, a comet has appeared in the sky.

Mama Bélanger has not taken to her bed – that they would understand – she has taken to her bath and is refusing to get out. The comet is not here to hurt you, they say, but she has convinced herself it is poison invading her mind that only water can destroy. She scrunches her eyes closed, clasps her hands over her ears.

No! she shouts. No, I will not listen!

The doctor shrugs and says she is getting old, which she is, though what he means is that she must be going mad. Her eldest daughter disagrees. But that evening Mama Bélanger is calm again, and they can hear her softly singing a lullaby from when they were children.

Her eldest daughter brings her fresh hot water for the bath – if she must lie in there for days, she reasons, better to do it in the warm than in the cold.

Will you not get out tonight, Mama?

She pauses, wondering if she should go on.

This comet will do no harm, she smiles, reaches forward to brush her mama's hair away from her face. I promise you that.

My sons are gone.

Yes, Mama, she says, glancing over, sadly, to the corner of the room. But your daughters are still here.

Mama Bélanger stands up and allows her daughter – who will one day be a mother and grandmother and great-grandmother – to help her out of the bath.

I want to show you something, Mama, she says.

Is there more I have to see?

Something more, yes, she replies, kissing her mama on the head.

She leads her out to the garden and they sit on the grass in the dark and gaze up at the stars overhead, and at the comet.

You see, Mama, she says. There's nothing to be afraid of any more.

And she looks over to the ghosts of her brothers who are sitting opposite them in the moonlight and smiles.

Our family is changed, but will survive.

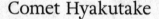

1996

Comet Hyakutake

FRANÇOIS'S MAMA IS FUSSING.

He takes the blackcurrant jam from the cupboard – they made it together at the weekend, fruit and sugar simmering in a pan for hours as they prepared the dough for the bread. He scoops out a teaspoonful, puts it upside down in his mouth as he watches her check there's milk in the fridge for chocolat chaud, the book for his bedtime story, a list of emergency numbers pinned to the wall by the phone.

It's OK, the sitter says. His mama told him she's a student from the university. We're going to have fun, she says to François, patting his blond hair as he pulls away and then, using a different voice to Severine: you too, enjoy your date.

His mama glances in the hallway mirror before she leaves. Her hair is loose, not tied up like it is when she's working, and her dress is red and gold, her arms decorated with bangles.

Be good, she says to François.

You know, I don't need a babysitter, he says, you could just trust me…

You're only ten years old. We'll talk about it later.

He scoops up another spoonful of jam and lets the rich flavours sink onto his tongue, waves goodbye.

In the restaurant, Severine starts telling lies and finds she cannot stop; the last ten years of her life have become a fiction for anyone who cares to listen. I spent a year in Vietnam, she says; the heat, the moisture, it fills your lungs, and the traffic – twelve lanes moving each way, criss-crossed, no separation between them, bikes, cars, buses, motorbikes, taxis, tuk-tuks, a mess of vehicles and if you want to cross the road, you just step out into it. It's a leap of faith.

And where will you travel to next? he asks.

The opposite, maybe Greenland. It's so empty, so big, you know? When you look on the globe it's a mass of frozen land. What would that be like?

He's leaning forward over the table, almost seems to be reaching for her hand.

I'd like to go to the desert, he says, to see sand dunes and hazy gold sky in every direction. I'd like to see a mirage.

Severine smiles.

A mirage of what?

Anything; an oasis, an iceberg, a civilisation.

I think I'd see the past.

But he shakes his head, not interested in that route; the past is done with, he says, I want the future. I'm only interested in what comes next.

François tells the babysitter he would like to read to himself in bed, and he selects the world atlas from the tall bookshelves in the study, climbing up on his child's plastic stepladder to reach it.

The sitter doesn't seem to know what to do, watches on to check that he's safe while he ignores her and carries his atlas down to the table, carries the stepladder back to the kitchen; politely wishes her a good night from the top of the stairs.

Goodnight, François, she says, turning back to the sitting room and marvelling at how a ten-year-old can make her feel too young to be a babysitter.

In bed, François opens up his atlas to the page he was up to: Indonesia, it says, and he traces his finger over the tiny dots of land that decorate a blue-and-white sea. Sangkapura, he says, rolling the consonants on his tongue, Belitung, Masalembo. The land here is drawn green and yellow and orange and he thinks that means there are mountains, rising up from the sea. Thirteen thousand, six hundred islands, it says, under Geography. He tries to think of something else with a number that big, but he can't.

Severine and her date go for drinks after dinner, rich red wine in a dark candlelit bar where they flirt over what the future will bring. Slim buildings of glass that stretch to the clouds, a colony on Mars where people will live in the orangey glow of starting over, cities built on the crisp water of melted ice caps. His hand on her knee. A glass nearly spilled, then saved. But this is not real life, and underneath the flirting Severine knows it.

On the walk home, it happens: a shiver of warmth, a rush of relief and Severine is not alone any more.

I'm sorry, she says to the man beside her whose name she's already starting to forget. You can't come any further. But thank you.

As he walks away, confused, she pulls her shawl over her head, around her neck; a smile already building somewhere in her chest.

The ghosts walk beside her, their steps turning to skips and bounds as their casual greetings become a flurry of words and questions and playful amusement.

By the time she reaches home, there are five of them; by the time she has paid the sitter and made her way upstairs to François's room, there are eleven. Henri from the 1750s is here, the sisters in lace dresses, and Great-Great-Grandma Bélanger with her wet hair in curlers. Behind them all a soldier boy shimmers out of view, and the laughter, the relief is bubbling inside her because they are here, and she is surrounded by family.

François is woken up by voices and at first he is afraid. He sits up in bed, listens hard and hears his mama – he thinks it is his mama – but she sounds different, and she's not making any sense.

You daft old man, she's saying. You think you can be funny now, do you?

And then she's laughing, and François is opening his bedroom door quietly so he can see who's there, see who it is that's making his mama sound so young and happy.

As he tiptoes to the banister he sees her, but he rubs his eyes, doesn't understand, because she is talking and laughing with no one at all.

Granny, she calls, arms wide.

François looks for his grand-mère but she's not here, and if she were then his mama would be talking in a different kind of voice, he's sure of that.

We'll watch it tonight, she is saying, quieter now, as if she's remembered he's sleeping upstairs and is trying not to disturb him. And I'll always be here, I'll stay in this house, I'll listen to your stories – but please leave François alone.

He sits on the top stair, hidden behind the banister, and shuffles down, a step at a time.

I don't want her scaring him, his mama says, and perhaps for the first time François does feel really scared, with the kind of worry that sits in your stomach and makes your throat go dry.

He pushes the door to the kitchen open and stands there in his pyjamas, looking at his mother, his toy tiger trailing from one hand.

Mama?

She smiles, a big open smile that looks like it shouldn't be hiding anything.

Do you want to go on an adventure? she says.

He stays by the door, unsure at first, not understanding, but his mama's eyes focus on him now and she kneels down beside him and says, let's go on a midnight adventure, just you and me.

OK, he says, his smile widening.

They open the cupboard, search inside for François's red tent, the one he got for his ninth birthday. It's more of a tepee really, light wooden poles holding up a triangle of red fabric with a door flap at the front that zips down; a red sleeping bag to match.

They make up flasks of coffee and hot lemon cordial – François's favourite. Bring the home-made pain au raisin left over from the shop (François was hoping there'd be some left for him) and a selection of fruit, clementines and pears.

François carries his rucksack on his back with supplies while Severine carries the tent and binoculars. He thinks perhaps this is going to be a good adventure after all. His mama was just being silly before.

Severine turns to check that her granny is still there, and she is; she is following them, she is smiling.

The night is clear, spring-fresh, clouds floating past the moon and carried on the wind. Even though it's a public garden, the gate's now locked – but it's not high. François wants to go first. He wants to be an explorer, like his mama said he would be when he was younger. He climbs easily, jumps down the other side.

Hurry up, Mama!

Severine gathers her dress up and ties the hem round her waist so it won't catch, climbs over and then they run through the gardens, searching for the perfect spot – over by the trees? Near the lake? François is excited now, his laughter carried on the night air.

And they find a space in the open, an oasis of grass bounded by trees for shelter and a clear view of the skies. They set up the tent and sit on the grass in front of it, flasks at the ready.

François likes it just the two of them, it's how it is at home most of the time anyway, except when his grand-mère comes by and brings him dried apricots and ginger. His grand-mère says that when he grows up he can be anything he wants to be, so he's thinking about that. He likes watching the chefs on television, and he likes drawing. But mostly he wants to discover new lands.

Severine likes that they're all here today, every one she's ever seen and heard of; it feels like at last the whole family is united. It hasn't been easy, waiting here in Bayeux – she is well aware of what she is giving up to have them here. They're sitting in a wide circle in front of François's small tent and she listens to their chatter without replying, not wanting to show how much she is enjoying herself; just wanting to protect François. She thinks her granny understands – in among their chatter she is quiet, watching Severine.

You don't have to worry about Brigitte scaring him, she says eventually, underneath the banter of the others, when only Severine can hear. François won't be able to see us. Not yet, anyway.

How can you be sure? Severine asks quietly.

He hasn't lost anyone yet, she says, and moves to put her arm around Severine's shoulders.

THE STREETS OF BAYEUX ARE golden in the evening light; the rivers reflecting the sunset, fading to black as they wind in and out of the petite arched bridges. It is so different to Scotland. A smaller city than Róisín usually wants to live in, but there's something about it that fits. Perhaps it was just a name she had always heard, wondered about, and it is charming, the way its history seems to blend with its present. Róisín stops on a bridge towards the edge of the main town, thinks of taking a photograph looking down to the bustling medieval high street, but doesn't. She's not a tourist here, she's going to make this place her home. For a while.

She positions her telescope to point out of her Velux window. There is no observatory at the Université de Caen Basse-Normandie, not like there was in Edinburgh or even on the rooftop at Imperial. But here she can study Planetary Sciences, the Earth as seen from the universe, not the other way round. It was time for a fresh perspective. That's what brought her here to Normandy.

Every few years Róisín moves, unlike her friends who are starting to settle down, from Ireland to London, London to Scotland, and now to France. She likes it here; she likes the pathways by the river, the old waterwheels that no longer spin, the spires in the distance that rise, modestly, above the homes and narrow streets. Ten years of looking away was enough, it was as if looking up for too long was starting to make her lose balance. But, as if to compensate, she has her telescope, enhanced over the years, as money allowed, shipped from city to city with her. It isn't ideal – it is too light here, she can't see anything too distant,

no faraway galaxies. But it is hers, and she has created it for a
night like this.

It matches, she thinks, it works, for this comet was discovered
by an amateur in Japan searching the sky through his binoculars.
She likes how that makes it personal, how one man, standing alone,
could find something so rare.

She's left a message on the crackling answerphone at the farm,
but Liam hasn't called her back. It has become what they do to each
other now. One phones, the other backs away. She wishes he had
returned her call tonight, just this once, but a part of her is glad he
hasn't; perhaps it's more honest this way. She thinks he never really
cared, that much, about the comets. Not when compared to the farm.

So she tells herself, but then she reaches for the phone again,
knowing it's going to be spectacular. She doesn't want him to miss
something so beautiful, and so surprising – two comets in the sky
tonight, one still distant, just approaching the inner solar system,
and one so bright; the unexpected eclipsing the anticipated. There's
a certain poetry to that.

The phone rings four times then clicks over to the answerphone.

This time she doesn't leave a message.

She puts the kettle on.

The kettle is whistling downstairs. Liam's never wanted an electric
one, until today. That whistling, calling him away when he doesn't
want to leave.

He dips the flannel in cool water again, twisting it before folding it into a neat strip. The windows are rain-dappled and dark. He
draws the curtains closed, as quietly as he is able.

Behind the house where Róisín grew up, Adele, Neil and Conall
wait outside in the garden. Róisín told them to look; said this time

was special. The adults have the binoculars that she gave them two Christmases ago. Conall has the pair he was given for his fifteenth birthday. He keeps turning them the wrong way round. He is cold, so he stamps his feet.

Róisín remembers a time when they lay outside on the grass, watching the sky; she remembers how much she wanted Liam to understand, to appreciate what she was showing him. It was unfair, to be so frustrated at his nature when he was so young, but it also made his indifference easy to forgive.

Not so when he told her, stroppy as a teenager, she'd best be getting back to wherever she was living these days, or when he hadn't read her first paper, or when he said manned space flight seemed like a waste of money.

It's harder to forgive a grown man, even when really they've done nothing wrong.

Clouds spill into her field of view and she tells herself that she must be patient. She knew that there would be clouds, but there is also wind. She heads downstairs to make a cup of tea, fills it with sugar. She doesn't want to sleep tonight.

She hears something happening in the street. A group of students, perhaps, coming back from a bar or on their way to a party – she doesn't know what. She hears voices shattering the night, a collage of tones and timbres, laughter, a shhh, the click of heels on pavement and a jangle of bracelets and then, something that sounds like a child. At first she thinks they're just passing but she hears them again, moments later; realises they are sitting in the garden over the road. They must have climbed the gates. Róisín wonders why they've done that. Then she forgets about them.

Liam's dad is sleeping now. Liam's propped the door open so he can hear if he's needed, and he's sitting in the kitchen on his own, accounts and letters covering the table. The farm is struggling. He thinks he'll have to sell some of their land, maybe some livestock too, downsize, focus on organic produce he can take to the farmers' market in town. His head is aching. The drone of the microwave seems like a constant in his life, even though it's only been on for three minutes. When it pings, after four, he pours tomato soup into a bowl and the warm smell of it fills the kitchen, soothing him for a moment.

But the longer the quiet lasts the more he is unable to move; Liam is anchored to the table just like he is anchored to the farm. His soup is finished and there is a red blotch of tomato on the tabletop that he's not ready to wipe away. He plays her message again. It is all comets and stars and galaxies; it is all Róisín. She doesn't even ask after his dad. His bowl clatters into the sink. He deletes her. He knows that upstairs his father has stopped sleeping; he will never wake up.

Róisín scans her telescope away from the clouds. There is only so long you can stare at what is in your way. Beyond them, and to the east, she can see Beta Andromedae huddled close to NGC 404. She says their other names aloud, rolling them on her tongue: Mirach and Mirach's Ghost. A giant star and a galaxy, so close they could almost be touching. Between them are 2.2 million light years of empty space. Her tea has gone cold; she thinks about making more while she sips it anyway.

She hears the people in the garden again, moves away from her telescope to look out of the window. They've put up a tent. She was right – there is a child with them, a boy, the only person she can see now. He's pointing at the sky.

She tries to hear their voices but not much reaches her, despite the open window; only snippets of conversation, a moment of laughter, the wind catching a loose flap of the tent's fabric.

It is red, their tent, only big enough for two. It reminds her of childhood, of something far away now and out of her reach.

She purses her lips, refocuses her telescope.

Liam climbs the stairs slowly. At the door, he waits. It is peaceful; there is that.

When he's sitting by the bed he starts to talk. He didn't know there were things he wanted to say, but it turns out there were, and now he's started saying them. He talks about the time he saw his dad arguing with his mum's ghost out by the stable after the last of the horses had been sold. He talks about why he was so upset when his dad gave his old red tent to the Kelly kids, who splashed it all over with leftover paint from the big For Sale sign on the wall of their barn. He talks about Róisín, how she'd left him behind to find a bigger world – bigger than the farm, so much bigger – and how she keeps on moving; always somewhere new. And someone new. He cannot ask her to come back. She never did what he asked her to do anyway.

He says he wishes he were a different kind of man, that he found it easier to speak, though now it's too late the words won't seem to stop coming. He talks about how the farm is his now, only his, and it is empty; how he knows it has become irrelevant to the world but at the same time knows it is all that is left of his home.

He wonders if this means he is being set free. Perhaps Róisín would see it that way. But freedom was never what he needed and besides he can feel the weight of his heart, just like his father's, that is tying him to a place and a past that was happy, once; that will not let him leave.

Do you want to see, Conall?

He is stamping his feet.

Here, I'll help you, if you want? Conall?

Adele holds the binoculars close to his face without touching, and he starts to shout. His arms knock into his sides, the flask of tea topples over. Neil bends to pick it up – no harm done. Everything's grand, you don't have to look.

The binoculars are removed. The shouts quieten down.

Conall stamps his feet.

Adele smiles. Not everyone has to watch the comet, she says. There's more to life, so there is.

Conall stops stamping his feet. He's seen a fox, at the end of the garden.

A moment later, it is gone.

Inside, the phone starts ringing.

Liam doesn't know who else to call.

SEVERINE TAKES OUT THE BINOCULARS and tries them out herself first, locating the comet, its tail and its nucleus, so she can help him find it; help him see.

You need to adjust them for your own eyes, she says, and he bends the eyepieces closer together, immediately getting the hang of it.

She watches his expression as he moves the binoculars to point all around the sky. He looks at the moon, at Orion, straight over-head like he's trying to see the top, the very top of the universe, until he loses balance, almost toppling backwards before catching his fall and letting the binoculars swing around his neck.

And that's what the strap is for, she says. Already he's holding them up to his eyes again.

To François, it is like looking at a new world, more foreign and magical than anything he has seen so far in his atlas. The moon has craters and mountain ranges, dry lakes that spread between skyscrapers of rock. And there are patterns in the stars, pictures that he can see how to make, like in the join-the-dots drawing book he had when he was still a little boy. He spins around, not afraid of falling again – why should he be afraid of falling on grass? – and then he sees the tops of buildings, magnified into the homes of giants, and then a window. And a woman.

Mama, look.

He points up to the open window.

What's she doing?

Looks like someone's got a telescope, Severine says, gently pulling the binoculars from his eyes. They'll get a beautiful view of the comet from there.

Can we get a telescope too?

Severine smiles, passes him a clementine.

You and I don't need one, she says. We've got special powers.

When his mama's not looking, François points the binoculars to the window with the telescope again. The woman is standing next to it, adjusting something, perhaps, and looking at the sky but never down to the park. He thinks at first that she's wearing a red dress just like his mama's, but then he sees that it's a scarf, wrapped around her shoulders. Her dress is black, like her hair that is tied back in a ponytail with wisps left loose and free around her face.

Guess what, his mama interrupts. He's not sure if it's because she thinks it's wrong of him to be spying on the lady with the telescope, but he puts the binoculars down just in case.

What is it, Mama?

She pauses – she hadn't meant to do this – but she feels a need to share their family, wants him to understand, now that she knows there's no risk of him being haunted by them. She never was much good at keeping secrets.

Your great-great-grandpa Paul-François is here, she says. Your namesake.

François looks around the empty park and forces a smile.

François isn't quite old enough to know that he thinks his mama is a bit embarrassing, but he will be soon. He has been resisting her stories of magic and ghosts for years, and now she is trying to pretend they are actually here.

He stares at the stars. He can't see anything very much without the binoculars; the sky has become smaller, somehow. There is no comet, and he can barely even make out Jupiter – it's just a star no brighter than some of the others. If he squints he can almost believe it's red, but even then, not really.

There's no one here, Mama, he says.

Oh, Severine, says Great-Grandpa Paul-François, he looks just like me – don't you think he looks just like me?

Your great-granny is here too, Severine says.

Where?

She's wearing a black dress, sitting next to Great-Grandpa Paul-François. She's very beautiful, with her dark hair, don't you think?

That's not Granny, that's the woman in the window.

What?

For a moment Severine is shaken, her faith questioned by a child.

She takes the binoculars and looks up to the window; there is a telescope but no woman, no one watching the stars.

There's no woman in the window, she says to François harshly, but then smiles at him because it is not his fault she is suddenly terrified that he might see things, but different things to her.

Well, maybe not now, he says, stubborn and sure of what he saw. But she'll come back. She's real, I saw her. Wait and see.

*

But soon he's forgotten about the woman in the window because the evening is getting cold and he wants to go into the tent; it was his birthday present and he wants to feel like he's really camping.

In the tent he says, you do know they're not real, don't you, Mama?

And it hurts, to see that look in his eye.

You're right, she says, I'm sorry. I was only playing.

Were you trying to be funny?

She smiles. It wasn't funny, was it?

He shakes his head.

There are no ghosts, she says. There's no such thing as ghosts.

She tucks him in and leaves the flask of hot lemon beside him, and goes outside to sit in front of the tent and watch the comet and talk to her ghosts knowing that he's safe, and asleep, and that nothing will scare him tonight.

We met on a night like this, says Great-Grandpa Paul-François.

No you did not, says her granny. Ma mère told me it was over-cast and damp, and you were in a bad mood.

There was a war on, what d'you expect?

I expect you to tell her the truth.

Severine pulls her shawl around her shoulders, hugs her knees to her chest; she's been looking forward to this for so long. Last time things were wrong, she'd left Bayeux and they were like shadows, and the first time Ælfgifu had told her a story so full of horror and love she could hardly believe it was happening. She'd wondered if it was the trauma affecting her brain, her granny's death and François's birth, too much life and death in quick succession for a mind to process.

But still – she'd stayed. She could have left, travelled the world like she always said she would; she chose not to. And now they have arrived again and she feels like her heart is full to bursting point. Perhaps it is worth staying for, if it will always be this way.

I was in the navy, he continues, we were on shore leave.

He was in the papers once, her granny chimes in, your hat at that jaunty angle, remember?

We were on shore leave, and we came to Bayeux for the Friday-night dance.

Enough of that, interrupts Brigitte. I built our home, my story's the start of it.

Severine glares at her, annoyed at the interruption from the only ghost who has tried to scare her, and Brigitte goes quiet again.

No, says her granny softly, Ælfgifu was the first, you are just the angriest.

But where is Ælfgifu? Severine says, suddenly feeling her loss.

Her granny puts her finger to her lips. Listen.

So Severine does, and she hears the voices of a girl and a soldier boy playing by the stream behind the trees – splashes of water and laughter.

Why didn't you come, she asks her granny, when we looked for the comet in Scotland? Was it because I couldn't find it in the sky?

No, sweetheart, she says, it's not something you find in the sky, it's about having the right patch of ground beneath your feet.

I'm home now.

And I'm here.

Severine closes her eyes, lets her head rest on her granny's knees.

Is there no one else here for you to visit? she asks.

But her granny just strokes her hair as if she were a child.

Severine tries to think – of all the distant cousins, great-aunts, new babies, relatives she only sees at funerals, at weddings – and she realises that hardly any of her family are left in Bayeux. It is just her mother, who won't see the ghosts, and herself. And François. Who doesn't believe in ghosts.

You said Ælfgifu was the first.

That's right.

How come?

Her daughter refused to leave. And then there was the comet, and the tapestry...

It's an embroidery, not a tapestry.

That's true, her granny chuckles.

Severine feels her body relax as the voices get quieter, one by one, until there are only three left.

Things are different now, her granny says. She will be the last.

Great-Grandpa Paul-François shakes his head. It's not a disaster, he thinks, more an inevitability. The proof that ghosts are no better or worse off than the rest of the population; they too need others to survive.

But she can't be the last, says Brigitte to Paul-François. My family needs more time to find their way home.

You could try being nicer to her?

She doesn't want to hear my story.

You haven't given her the chance.

I tried, but what's the point? She can't help—

Brigitte's dress catches fire but the flames shimmer into starlight.

Let's leave quietly, says Severine's granny. We don't want to wake her.

When Severine wakes up the ghosts are gone, and she is lying barefoot on the grass in the middle of the night, a golden shawl around her shoulders. There is a red glow coming from beyond the trees; it takes her a moment to realise that it's the beginning of a sunrise.

She wishes they were here to watch it with her, and she is stabbed through with loneliness. This is how it will always be, she knows, they will always have to leave, return and leave – and every time she will grieve for them all over again, but never be able to let go. She is trapped. She puts her head to her knees, misses the sound of the tent being zipped open.

Mama, look, François says, putting his hand on his mama's shoulder. Look at the sky. The sun is coming up!

He doesn't need the binoculars for this; he wants to see the whole sky with his own eyes as it turns into the richest, deepest, most golden red that he has ever seen.

He pulls his mama up from where she's sitting on the grass, leads her to the slope that rises from beyond the trees, drags her running – come on, Mama, faster – and laughing now, up to the top of the slope where they can stand, together, and stare at the glowing tapestry of colours in the sky.

- - - - - - - -

RÓISÍN'S FLIGHT LEAVES ON TIME at 9.50 a.m. and she lands in Ireland ninety minutes later with hand luggage only and a return flight booked for Sunday night. There are posters in the airport trying to advertise something through a pretty but airbrushed red-haired girl and a four-leafed clover. She doesn't know when the world became so cynical, when people became so airbrushed.

Today they're meeting at the farm. The funeral is tomorrow. She'll stay with her mum and Neil, unless Liam ... Unless Liam. She doesn't know how to finish that sentence.

She's filled with dread, softened by a desire to help, to hold him. This isn't her tragedy.

The hire car is cheap and tinny and an inappropriate bright yellow but she doesn't have the energy to argue. She parks it before the curve of the lane that leads to the farm and walks the last half-mile. She tries to quicken her pace, but each step takes longer than the last.

*

She finds her mum in the crowded front room with Neil and an array of cake and wine and black fabric.

I'm sorry I'm late.

You're not, people have been arriving all morning. Anyway, you're here now.

Her mum holds her in a hug for longer than usual, and then Róisín does the same for Neil.

Have you spoken to Liam? he asks.

Róisín shakes her head, brushes gently at her eyes.

She wants to see him, wants to help him more than she can say.

He sees her from the hallway, backs away from the door. He wants something that makes him feel ashamed. She left; he won't ask her to return.

A distant relative shakes his hand. It leaves a smudge of butter cream on his thumb.

She checks each room, one by one, scanning the faces for Liam's. Someone gives her a hug; someone shakes her hand. She's passed a glass of white wine, a plate. She stands by the back door, remembers being outside looking in. She remembers waving at Liam through the glass. She tries the door. It opens.

Liam is leaning against the back wall of the farmhouse. He is shaking. She reaches out her hand – an offering of more.

It's about to rain, she says.

I don't want to be in there.

There's the barn?

They don't run; this is nothing like childhood.

She waits for him to speak, trying to give time, space, not knowing how he feels but knowing his face, his eyes – he looks at her in a way that makes it difficult to breathe. He shakes his head as if there is nothing else to do, then he does the only thing he can; takes her face in his hands, kisses her as if the years in between had not existed, or had been a lifetime that he wants to erase.

It is fast and desperate, against the creaking walls of a barn no longer in use; the smell of the damp hay that lies in patches on an otherwise bare wooden floor. He holds her like his life depends on it, like she is the only thing left in the world. It is not gentle, not after all these years.

Afterwards they readjust their clothes. A shirt button is lost; neither of them mentions it. They don't smile, not today. Róisín knows that she has never felt what he is feeling. She is scared to interrupt his silence. So they stay standing where they are, both of them alone. Eventually, Liam clears his throat.

Did you get my message? she asks him, hoping that talk of something else might help.

Liam has to pause, rewind his mind to a time before these last two days, before everything seemed to exist in these stumbled moments. He's not sure if his voice even works any more.

About the comet, I mean?

Yes.

I'm sorry, do you… We can go for a walk or something?

He looks out over the field. It is grey and muddy. The fence to the left of the barn has blown over in the night, is hanging down in the mud. He has to tell himself to breathe.

Did you see it? he asks.

I did, yes, of course – her words come out as a jumble, she is so relieved he has spoken – I mean, I wouldn't have missed it. I watched it from my attic. It's fast, this one, she says, remembering their childhood, holding her breath. You could see it moving – really see it moving. Flying against the stars. It was one of the most beautiful things… You should have seen it. Maybe… Your dad would have…

He swallows, but doesn't reply; just lets himself stand next to her without speaking for a minute. He didn't want it to be like this, fast and rough. He didn't mean it to happen this way.

As they look out, a small flock of birds takes off from the trees at the edge of the field.

How do they know to do that? Róisín says. To fly at exactly the same time?

Liam wants to lie down, to close his eyes – he is so tired – but he can't. Someone is calling his name. She reaches for his hand. He pulls away.

I should go.

I'll come with you.

Liam shakes his head.

Don't push me away. I want to help.

You don't belong here, Róisín. It's OK.

Her hand drops to her side.

He turns his back; doesn't say goodbye.

Róisín stays where she is and watches him cross the field, his eyes fixed on the ground. He exchanges a few words with someone from the village by the front porch, wipes his shoes slowly on the front mat, and disappears back into the house. In a few minutes she'll pull herself together. Go and find her mum and Neil, give Conall the chocolate she bought him at the airport, his favourite kind, in the shape of a pyramid. But first she sits down on the floor of the barn and rests her head on her knees. Nothing she said helped him. She doesn't know how to help him.

In the corner she sees something glimmer, catching the light. She picks up Liam's shirt button, brushes off some hay and dust, holds it in her palm. She can feel it heat up from the warmth of her skin. She has an idea.

*

They open a bottle of wine that evening, Róisín, her mum and Neil; make a toast to her uncle, and then talk about her dad. It's funny how death can make some conversations possible that had seemed impossible before. Róisín can hardly remember her dad, if she's honest, just a sense of someone who was there and then someone who was gone.

Is he coming? she asks her mum.

He phoned, she replies; he couldn't get a flight in time from Sydney, so he's going to miss tomorrow.

How selfish, Róisín says, surprising herself by the words, and by her own anger. He's not even coming back for his own brother's funeral.

It can be difficult, Neil says, to face the fact that you can never see someone again.

What he means is that it can be difficult to face the fact that you've missed your chance, that there was a time when you could have made things different, but that moment is gone.

It's a terrible thing, he says, to realise that you're too late.

Yes, it is, Róisín says. And she means it, too.

She walks to the other side of the table and puts her arms around Neil's shoulders.

I'm glad you're here, Dad.

He puts his hand on her hand; knows they are a family.

Seventy thousand years. That's how long it will be until this comet returns. Its orbit is long; it gets to see a lot of the sky on its way. Even though it is small – smaller than Hale–Bopp, its competitor, the one everyone was talking about. Smaller than Halley's comet, the one everyone has heard of, the celebrity. But it is active; as it flies it spins, a curve ball of a comet, letting dust fly out, burn and soar, to create its own light on its lonely journey.

*

That night, Adele tries to find a way to tell Neil how much she loves him, but can't find the words.

Neil doesn't use words to tell her that it's OK, that he's here and he's staying. He kisses the top of her head, sets the alarm for the morning, wishes her goodnight.

I love you, she says, when the lights are out; I'm so lucky to love you.

That's my line, he says.

I think we should share it, she replies.

Róisín sits a few rows behind Liam in the church, watches the back of his head as he leans forwards and straightens up, stands and sits. She doesn't know the words for how she feels. There's love there, but also guilt for leaving, and a particular type of blame, too. He could have come away with her, where no one would have known them, where they could live however they wanted. She knows it would be difficult to do that, here.

He kneels again.

And her eyes can't move from the back of his neck, from the single shudder of his shoulder that tells her he is trying not to cry, and she wants to hold him; that is all there is, a need to hold him. Perhaps they can find a way.

He stands outside, shakes hands, tries to do small talk – never something he wanted to do at the best of times. She stays back, makes sure he can see her but doesn't get too close. They both re-member caution. They keep catching each other's eyes.

There's a hotel restaurant with crustless sandwiches and table-cloths of navy blue. There's a moment at the bar when their arms touch, accidentally, but not – a moment when they both catch their breath and the need for more makes them ache – and they take their drinks back to separate tables. There's Adele and Neil deciding it's time to leave, offering help that is politely refused, needing to collect Conall from his new school that is encouraging him to talk more, helping him interact. There's a car journey home and a kettle boiled, excuses made for an early night. And there's the kitchen door opening from inside once everyone is asleep, and Róisín creeping out.

You came.

Of course I came.

I don't know what to do.

I had to see you.

We have to stop.

Can you?

Please.

Me neither.

I missed you.

Voices muffled, murmured through a haze of need and warmth, a familiar taste, a longing for something out of reach, always, and the feel of his stubble against her chin, the urgency of his fingers. Something in him sounds like it is breaking, and he cries, not a single sob like in the church, gasp after gasp, tears hot and insistent, refusing to be held back any longer.

I can't leave, he says. I've thought about it. I know you think I should, but I can't. The farm would—

OK.

You don't understand. This farm. I have to save it. It's all that's left.

I said it's OK.

It is not OK, he says, thinking of tomorrow when she will leave again, thinking of a lifetime spent trying to resurrect something.

She touches his chin, draws his eyes back to hers.

I have an idea.

She leads him outside.

They lie on the grass, despite the cold, and look for a comet flying so fast they can see it move against the stars.

It's the brightest in two hundred years, she says.

There are a lot of clouds tonight.

He thinks that this was what she meant by an idea – searching for a comet again, as if all the answers can be found in the sky.

I'm coming home, she says.

Liam's not sure if he heard her right, if it can be true. He closes his eyes, holds his breath. Doesn't say anything. It's... what does it mean? What does she mean, really?

I promise, she says, leaning up, holding his face between her hands, planting a soft, swift kiss on his lips. I'm going to come home.

He opens his eyes. Smiles at her, puts his arm around her shoulders, feels the warmth of her head on his chest. Sees the comet. It is bright, she was right; it is moving so fast it can change the sky.

Róisín doesn't know how it's going to work but she thinks that just being here might, for a while, be enough.

When? he asks, his voice muffled in her hair.

She sits up, and he does the same. They look at each other and forget about the comet.

As soon as I can. There're a few things I need to finish, some of my work... But then I'll come home.

And you'll live here? With me?

With you.

All of a sudden something that seemed impossible has become possible.

Róisín thinks his expression is one of gratitude but Liam doesn't realise she's doing something he should be grateful for; his expression is one of hope, for a home rebuilt, for family.

There is no university here, Róisín thinks, she'll have to find some other job. Some other life.

Overhead, unobserved, the comet has gone again, slipped behind the violent chemical reactions of the sun; something so dangerous can appear so beautiful, when seen from a distance.

Róisín tells herself it will be good to come home.

She looks back up at the sky.

The Embroidered Comet

Ælfgifu watches her daughter work; lips pursed, eyes focused. The linen is stretched flat and taut across the frame. The parchment on top is covered in pinpricks – every line, every arrow – to create a colourless scene of holes. The cleric is watching. She dips a wad of fleece into the crushed charcoal and begins to dab it through the holes in the parchment.

They work side by side, Ælfgifu and her daughter, together in a room full of nuns and widows; everyone lost someone, some lost everyone, and now they will create the story. Footsteps approach. She feels her daughter's back straighten, looks up to see the cleric's hand brush against her daughter's cheek, her daughter's eyes downturned; you cannot disobey the cleric.

Come, he says.

Her daughter stands, follows him to the far table. Looks back.

Ælfgifu feels a panic that she hasn't felt for a long time. She's barely aware that she's embroidering the scene until it's finished, but then it is: a panel that will stand through time, be stared at by a child's eyes, an old woman, a man searching for answers he cannot reach. She adds lettering, includes her own name. She works through the dusk as the linen is cast in guttering shadows. The nuns are returning for compline but she has something she must do, and she doesn't know where else to get help.

She embroiders it larger than she ever saw it: a wild ten-pointed star with a core of glowing red and streams of yellow flying out behind. Below, five soldiers stand in amazement, pointing up at the sky; one has black hair and eyes she still remembers. Her daughter comes to help her finish, and when they step outside they see a star of thread and gold soaring through the sky.

There is a package by the door of their room. It is for her daughter. Opening it, the silk of red and gold sends shivers down Ælfgifu's skin. It's the most beautiful dress her daughter has ever seen, but she understands what it means; this is not the dress of a child, and gifts come with a price.

Come tonight, says the note.

Mother?

No, she says. No. You don't have to go.

Then he will take me anyway.

Ælfgifu didn't know her daughter knew about such things, but she is right. The nunnaminster is not safe any more and Beatrice, well, their abbess will not protect them from this. There's a limit to a woman's power, even an abbess with the confidence of Bishop Odo.

I will wear the dress, says Ælfgifu. He's expecting you, so I'll make him think you're coming. We don't have long.

But, Mother—

This time I will save my family, she says. I'll face him, and you must run.

Will I see you again? her daughter asks.

I promise, she says. Just follow the shooting star.

Neither of them understands that they are the only ones who can see the star, that there is no shooting star in the sky tonight.

Go quickly now, she says, gather your things.

I can't leave you.

But you must. Keep to the shadows, my love. And don't look back.

Ælfgifu slips off her habit in a gesture that makes her remember slipping off her dress, in another life, and lets the red silk fall over her shoulders.

You look beautiful, he says from behind her, but you do know where this will end?

She turns at the voice, so familiar, and she knows who she'll see.

I thought you were dead, she says to the soldier boy whose name she never knew, who helped her when she was ready to die. Who vanished.

I'm not here to interfere, he says, I just thought you could use the company. And of course I'm dead.

So be it, she replies with a smile.

As her daughter climbs the stone walls, Ælfgifu stands with her back to the door in a room she's never entered before, facing out over the cloisters. She can see the shooting star, though she knows now it is not there, just like the soldier boy standing beside her.

Do you like your panel, in the tapestry?

He shrugs, smiles. I think you got my eyes wrong.

Then your face with different eyes will last forever.

You have created a ghost, he says.

The comet that is not there speeds through clouds and does not dim. It races in front of the Horsehead Nebula, through the purples and greens and blues that make a whirl of dust alive with magic.

And what of you? he asks.

I have my own panel.

She holds out her hand for the first time and her fingers slip through his palm. There are footsteps. It has begun.

My child, the cleric says — he has a voice smooth as marble and just as hard. Turn now, I want to see your face.

It is working, so far: he believes she is her daughter; that he will get what he wants. She can hear his breath as his hand touches red silk. A man who believes he can have everything. When she turns, her eyes are defiant.

His voice rings out as he recoils and the shadows around the cloisters make the floor ripple like snakes. Where is she? he demands — but her daughter is free now, as the last rays catch the corners of the window and spark like flames from dragon heads. His hand rises, like she knew it would, and she laughs because she has saved the last of her family, and when the sun sinks below the hills the comet that isn't there glows brighter than gold.

When her daughter stops running she looks up to see that the shooting star has vanished. She does not keep running, unlike her family for millennia before her. Instead she does what her heart tells her to do; she begins to walk back to her home.

The next morning, she wakes to see her mother's ghost dancing in the stream with a soldier boy. Halley's comet glows on the borders of the Bayeux Tapestry, where an immortal soldier points in wonder at the sky and a woman with wild black hair is refusing to kneel.

The tapestry moves from England to France, and eventually to Bayeux, and her daughter, and her daughter's daughter, and daughters beyond that follow the shooting star in thread and gold. They refuse to leave it and they refuse to run from it and they wait for the shooting star to shine again in the sky – and as long as Ælfgifu's tapestry is close they know that, when it does, the ghosts of their family will appear.

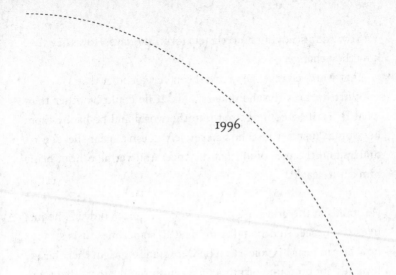

Comet Hale–Bopp

THE SUMMER PASSES SLOWLY FOR Liam, as he waits for Róisín to keep her promise. It seems too good to be true; something you say when you want to make someone feel better, but when it comes to it, when the months have passed and time is pressing up against you, a thing she will regret.

They talk on the phone, and he has to force himself not to ask her: is she coming home yet? He can't put this on her, she has to choose on her own. So instead they talk about their respective worlds – the earth and the sky, the ground under his feet and the planets over her head.

She has changed field, she tells him. She's not looking so far away any more.

He knows that she is trying to be kind.

Now she's studying how planets form, she says. How they live, how they change.

That word, change; he's never been very good at that.

What hurts is that he understands. If he could be other than what he is, if he could go out into the world and be happy there he would. Just because he's never left doesn't mean he doesn't understand the pull of all that distance. And yet he cannot bring himself to leave.

He stands at the grave. He doesn't kneel, or place flowers, he just likes the peace. And he talks to his dad, sometimes. It is strange how he can hear his voice, as if he were standing right there beside him. It's not profound or miraculous, nothing like that. Their conversations are remarkably mundane.

The fence has blown down, he says, this winter; like that winter a few years ago, when we mended it together.

At least I taught you how, his dad says – ever the farmer. It's your land, your fence. You can take care of it, sure.

And so he does.

The paperwork he despises, but it is necessary. He files papers for government subsidies, for European funding, for tax rebates; he signs cheques and letters and remortgage applications; he opens bills and demands. He uses his credit card to buy some new furniture; spends his Saturdays painting the living room, the hall, the bedroom, replacing the cracked glass in the kitchen-door window. But still he doesn't quite believe it.

When you have wanted something for so long, it is strange to think that you are about to get it. It does not feel how he thought it was going to feel. He is nervous. He doesn't know how things are going to work.

*

It is his father's birthday and he spends the day alone, although he has received cards; the family has made an effort. But he wants a day of being on the farm and not working the farm, of remembering the farm as it was. He plays Creedence Clearwater Revival, refusing to put on U2; it is a day like any other – he still has taste. He laughs when the record jumps, then comes to an abrupt end halfway through a track, the needle scratching as the arm clicks out of place. That turntable's always been broken. Some things don't change. Right, Dad?

Things don't change, not here, his dad says.

They're changing everywhere else, Dad.

Maybe so, maybe so.

I'm not ignoring it, not like you did. The farm has to change to survive.

He expects his dad to fight back, as he had when he was alive, but he doesn't. The house is quiet again, except for the grandfather clock in the hall. Its time is wrong.

He winds it up. Resets the hands. Turns towards the kitchen.

He is used to being on his own, but Róisín is going to change that.

He imagines her there. When she would arrive, for dinner, waving at him through the window with her hair pulled back into a ponytail, half of it flying loose.

And when they would pass in the corridor at school, each of them pretending to be too cool to talk to their cousin, pretending like it wasn't happening but all the time he would know, wait, count down the hours, the minutes until he could creep out of the school gate and run for the island, knowing she would do the same. And the way they were together, then; can it be like that when time has separated them and one has left, taken so long to return?

Even these thoughts leave him with a longing deep in him that is a part of him, now. It is who he is – if it were gone he would feel the loss of it just like he felt the loss of her.

But she is not lost.

She said she was coming home.

Two days. She has phoned to tell him when she will arrive, has given him the details of her flight, told him not to come to the airport.

I'll come to the farm, she said, and he didn't know why but didn't question her.

In the barn, he had needed her in a way that terrified him. It had been so different, so urgent, his arms, hands, even now, thinking of it, cannot remain still.

And he cleans the house – oh, he is surprised to find himself doing it; didn't expect to feel so anxious, so like he needs to impress – and he can't sleep, he gets up in the night to pace the fields, to remember how he was. Has he changed, after all?

Another day goes by, the last day, and he doesn't hear from her and forces himself not to call. He works, he spends all day and all evening working until he is exhausted, feels like he could sleep for two nights in a row, until he lies down and thinks of Róisín, arriving, tomorrow, Róisín coming home, and he cannot sleep. There is too much, too many things; things he can't name and doesn't even understand.

He turns on the radio.

They are talking about the latest comet.

The bar is busy. Such a French place, and she is glad of that – to have now something different from what she will have next. And they are kind, with their bottle after bottle of wine, their leaving cake dusted with chocolate, their understated goodbyes. But she knows that none of them can understand what she's doing, she saw the look of blank confusion on their faces when she told them. She'd had a fellowship opportunity; could have had three years' funding without the need to teach and then this – to turn down every job offer and move to a village in Ireland no one has ever heard of. Not even a village – beyond a village, to a farm miles past the nearest village. They would have understood her moving to the city – even in Bayeux she used to talk about going to a bigger city. But this?

You will come back, someone says in deep lilting French. It is her boss, a quiet, committed man.

She smiles her No.

You'll stay in touch, say the people she has worked with, searching for undiscovered planets beyond the known reaches of the solar system. We'll see you again.

She fields questions about what she will do, what postdoc she will find, what university she can travel to. She understands how they must feel. If someone else was doing this, she would feel as they do. Like it was a mistake.

The skies will be clear, she says, not wanting to admit that after being surrounded by all these people she's nervous about the isolation of the farm. She excuses herself from her farewell party at midnight, leaving the others to drink more Pinot Noir and wake up the next morning in one another's beds.

Her boss tells her she can always return; he will find a position for her, when she needs it. I'll let you know, she says, even though she knows that she won't, and as she steps outside she feels like she is running away, but that is OK.

Because how can she explain, to these people that don't really know her, that she is tied to a man so closely that she's realised she can't keep travelling the world without him. That she has fought the need to be with him, and she has lost, and now it is time to give in.

But the next day, arriving at the airport, she imagines seeing his face. She knows that he will be anxious, now, not quite believing she will be there. She remembers the way he used to see her and the way his expression changed into everything that mattered; the way he will see her again.

Is it real? he says.

She is standing by the back door, the one that opens into the kitchen. She has a suitcase with her, a bag thrown over her shoulder, another carried by its straps.

She steps inside.

Are you really here?

I told you I was coming, she says with a smile, but he cannot return it; he cannot laugh at this scene that he has wanted for so long.

He can't walk towards her either. He can't make that approach. It is as if he's rooted to the spot, unable to move, to speak until she steps closer and makes this true.

Perhaps he is afraid of something, he thinks, as he looks at her, as his eyes try to take in the woman standing before him. Perhaps he is afraid that it's a joke, that it is like someone who offers you a drink that tastes foul; when someone says they love you then leaves.

Are you not pleased to see me? she asks.

His face is burning. How can she be unsure, when he has been waiting for her all these years? It is like he's swimming in chlorine, can't see his way to the surface for breath.

And now she drops her bags to the floor, shuts the door carefully behind her and returns her gaze to him.

It's me, she says.

And she thinks that a hug is how it should start, even that has been so long. There was once one Christmas when they shook hands – so awkward, so far from what they had been.

It's good to see you, she says, as she steps forward, noticing that he doesn't step forward to meet her. She is worried about him. There is loss in his eyes.

How are you, today? she says.

They are not far apart now, but it still feels like a distance; the pull between them making the final step seem meaningful. She's unable to rush, so she takes it slow – stands in front of him, her jacket still on, a winter scarf in greens and gold hung loosely around her neck.

It's quiet here, she says.

You'll fix that.

She reaches one arm around his shoulder, one around his waist. Their bodies press together; his arms return her hug. They stand, for a moment, nothing pulling them apart, no pull at all, just this moment. And then a tipping point is reached; her hand brushes his neck, his fingers through her hair, his breath on her cheek, a word, her name, a sigh, her head turning away, so slightly, resting on his shoulder.

You are going to stay, aren't you? he wants to ask, but he doesn't. He forgets how to speak, forgets that he ever knew, and she whispers in his ear, like when they were children: It's OK, she says, everything's going to be OK now.

FRANÇOIS HAS HEARD HIS MAMA talking to herself every day this month, though before the weather turned cold she hadn't done that for ages. On the day it started she had been happy, giddy, dancing in the rain like the girls at school, but that's not true any more – something has changed, and now she is on edge.

He finds her in the study, looking at his atlas – well, it was hers once, but now he thinks of it as his – and he goes and stands by her, pointing out all the places he wants to visit.

She looks over her shoulder as they talk, even though there's no one there watching. She looks tired, more tired than he can remember, and he slips his hand into hers to bring her back.

This is Morocco, he says, pointing out place names on the page. Shall we cook something from Morocco tonight? And his mama smiles, her eyes back to his at last, as she begins listing the ingredients they need to make a tagine.

Pass me the coriander, she calls out as he climbs his plastic steps to reach the spice cupboard; and the cinnamon sticks.

François gives each stick a crack before throwing them into the pot, smelling the spice on his fingertips and then reaching for a handful of sultanas. The spiced sweet smell of lamb and apricots mingles with music from the radio as they cook together; it is a smell he will remember, as an adult, try to replicate but never be able to capture.

Watching them from the doorway, Brigitte stands unnoticed. She doesn't want to see them like this but somehow she can't bring herself to turn away. Severine is getting restless in Bayeux, Brigitte knows that much, even though she's trying to hide it from the ghosts. But they're dead, they're not stupid – does she really imagine she's fooling anyone?

François's certainly not fooled, and he's only ten. He can see something's changed. But the thing is – and this is what really scares Brigitte – she thinks he's on Severine's side. He's encouraging her to dream of going away; he wants the angry bit of her to win. The bit that will take them away from Bayeux, away from France, across the continent and beyond reach.

It is not fair. None of this is fair. Brigitte will not allow it.

Severine thinks they have no idea that she longs to leave, that she dreams of a wilderness to explore. She smiles, when they reappear day after day, when she finds Great-Great-Grandma Bélanger in the bath every morning.

They cluster around her as she works, pleading with her to play hide-and-seek when she needs to be laying out that day's display in the shop window. Antoine and Henri have taken to checking the latest deliveries of sweet oranges and avocado, but as she's trying to get them to stop throwing fruit to each other her mother arrives, points out that the light in one of the fridges has gone. Severine replies with a thank-you, biting back the comment that obviously she already knew, that she will deal with it when she can. And the worst of it – waking up every night with nightmares of fire, with the sound of a woman screaming and a child's cries. Severine never signed up for that. She never agreed to be haunted, not like that, and the angrier she gets herself the worse it seems to become.

Brigitte comes during the day sometimes, stands quietly in her long gown, her hair twisted into a plait, her eyes full of a terrible knowledge she doesn't convey.

When are you from? Severine asks, one evening, her voice hardened at the edges.

Fourteen fifty-six, she says, not elaborating on whether that was the day she was born or the day she died. You don't know what it's like, to burn.

Severine wishes she hadn't started the conversation, but at least Brigitte is calm now – perhaps she can be reasoned with.

What happened to you? she begins, but then François comes into the room – it's as if he knows when they're here – and Severine pulls her son into a hug and turns away from Brigitte, and when she turns back she is gone.

When the ghosts leave this time, they don't really leave. They return, day after day. Severine is surprised by this, at first, but soon comes to accept it – this comet will be visible for months, they say on the news, well into next year. Still, she was a fool not to appreciate the peace she had before, when the ghosts came for just a few days, every few years.

What is wrong with Brigitte? she demands of her granny, who is sitting in the old study, pretending to read the copy of *Thérèse Philosophe* her husband once gave her.

Her granny puts down the book and smiles at her.

What is it she needs?

Her granny's expression is full of sadness and so Severine sits in her mother's old chair and says, you didn't tell me the whole truth, did you?

You chose to see us.

No, I chose to see you. I didn't know that meant getting the others into the bargain. Brigitte...

Brigitte's scared that you are the last, and that her time is running out.

What will happen if I am the last?

We will go, ma petite.

Where?

Her granny shrugs. It doesn't matter, we will be gone.

But the rest of you don't give me nightmares.

Brigitte's story is different.

How so?

There's someone she can't let go of. And she can't control the flames; she had a terrible death. It still haunts her.

Severine softens.

Then I need to help her.

Her granny looks up at her, shakes her head. We all tried, at one point or another – we don't have the answers she seeks. And there's a risk. François...

What do you mean?

Please, Severine, she says, please. Don't push it.

Her tone is different now, far away, and something in it makes Severine want to hold her close, to tell her she is going to be OK.

If you let someone else's loss take over your life you can lose something of your own, her granny says softly.

Don't you think I might know something of compromise already?

Her granny laughs, returns to herself as she returns her eyes to the book. You know, you can make us all leave, if you want to, she says without looking up again. Or if that's too hard, you can just leave yourself.

In her épicerie, the next morning, Severine tries something out.

She turns her back to the room, stacking shelves, and tells herself that there are no ghosts. She has been ridiculous, imagining she had to stay here, in this place, in this town, for all of her life; there is nothing holding her here. When she turns round to face the room, the ghosts are gone.

A customer comes in, orders some of her tomato and lentil soup with a baguette. Picks up some biscuits from the counter. Pays. Leaves again.

Severine is alone. She made them disappear.

All of a sudden she is scared of what she's done – where have they gone? She wants their voices back, their playful jokes. She didn't even say goodbye to her granny. She didn't want to hurt them, to banish them forever...

She wishes they would come back.

And then she is not alone any more, and Antoine is sitting on the floor in the corner reading a comic book with Henri, and her granny is peering at the broken light in the fridge as if nothing has happened. And she is relieved, and grateful.

Antoine looks up.

I dare you, he says with a grin.

What?

You can do it – he turns a page – you can go and see the world. That's what I'd do, if I could. Don't worry about us. He looks back down at his book, smiles at something on the page. After all, he says, we're already dead.

In school, François is learning about the Hundred Years War, which was not a war that went on for a hundred years, but three of them – war after war after war. It is not like the history lessons they had at his old school. It seems more serious; he feels like they wouldn't be teaching this stuff to children. It didn't really end with the last war, just like it didn't really start with the first – it started a long time before that, in 1066, but he thinks it probably didn't start then either. Everyone is the product of something else.

The first war of the Hundred Years War went on for twenty-three years. And the next lasted only twenty. The last was the longest one of all and that started in 1415 and had Jeanne d'Arc in it, when she was the same age as François, with her visions and her strange faith, and her conviction that the voices she heard were real.

François thinks it's probably a good thing his mama doesn't know too much about Jeanne d'Arc. It might encourage her. There is something going on at the moment, and he's wondered if he should talk to his grand-mère about it, but has decided not to tell tales. It's not just that his mama is talking to herself in the house; she's started acting weird as well, weirder than usual. The other day she asked him where he'd like to go, if he could go anywhere in the world. It's like she's plotting. He's not sure yet, but he thinks there's a chance she's going to take him on a real adventure. Now that *would* be a good thing.

That night Severine is woken by Brigitte screaming. She tries not to listen, but it doesn't work. Something too horrific for words happened centuries before she was born, and she has to feel it, every night.

What is this about? she tries.

She thinks she can smell burning skin.

Stop this, please.

The room goes quiet; the fire flickers out.

What is it that you want from me?

I know you're planning to leave, Brigitte says.

And how do you know that?

You are planning to leave, and you're going to take François away with you.

Leave my son out of this.

Your son—

The flames threaten to engulf the curtains.

Stop it, Brigitte!

Severine tries to be calm, despite the intensifying smell, the smoke that makes her eyes burn.

Stop it and talk to me.

But Brigitte can't stop these flames any more than she could stop the fire that killed her. Her voice comes out as a growl, skin curls off her arms and she is gone.

As the sun rises, Severine remembers what Antoine said, and goes looking for him. She doesn't want to be told what she can't do any more, she wants to talk about all the places she wants to see, to take François – the promise of all that world they have yet to explore. And one of the ghosts, at least, will understand why she wants to leave.

IT FEELS DIFFERENT, TO LIAM, to make breakfast when he knows he is going to share it with Róisín. The coffee smells stronger, fresher, looks a deeper colour of black in the mugs once it is poured. He makes up a tray, feeling like a character in a film: coffee and juice, toast with marmalade and strawberry jam. Carries it up the stairs so they can have breakfast in bed.

Of course, it feels different. They are different. But it also feels different from anything else. When Róisín wakes up she has this strange feeling of knowing that she has nowhere to go – nowhere that she has to be; no work that she has to do. And it can't go on. She is going to have to find something to do. This is too like a holiday.

But then he slips back into bed beside her, and his bare legs lie against hers, and she remembers the first time, when he had kissed her, quickly, like if he didn't kiss her fast he was going to back out, pretend it was only a joke, and she had been so shocked. Not that she hadn't thought about it, she had, many times, but still, she'd never thought he would actually do it; never thought they would kiss like this, in his bedroom – the same bedroom they are in now – while his dad was out at that farmers' union meeting and there was condensation clinging to the windows that separated them from the insistent rain. He had pulled away, been ready to apologise she thought, but she hadn't let him. She had pulled him back, while his eyes looked at her in disbelief. They had kissed and not known what to do next so they had kept kissing, had spent the afternoon kissing. They were young, at first. But now, he is a man, and some combination of his rough stubble and his sure hands, his eyes that are so like those of a boy, his voice that is deeper than she remembered, the lines already forming on his forehead, his skin, the skin of a man who works outdoors, who understands what it is to manage acres… All of it makes her put the breakfast tray on the floor and reach for him again, still half amazed that she can, that she has made this happen.

Liam smiles now, a half-sigh, half-laugh, as her hands push him back onto the pillow, as her hair falls over his face. He, too, remembers how she had been older than him (it doesn't feel that way now), less afraid, or so it seemed, when she had taken her shirt off and told him to do the same. I want to see, she had said, I want to see you, and that had changed everything that he was. How he had stood still for her, allowed her hands to touch his chest, the flicker of a smile on her lips as her hands moved up over his shoulders, down over his stomach, making him hunch over from a tickle he couldn't laugh about, that did something else to him entirely. His breaths had come in stop-starts, he remembers, as she took so long, so long to unbutton his jeans. Now his breathing is less desperate but still fast; his thoughts more conscious but still not controlled; his exhale comes with a deeper voice as she guides him inside her again and his memories dissolve into some continuous present version of the past.

Róisín thinks, in the shower, that she must go out today. She will go to the village, see if she can find some temporary work.

Liam doesn't knock on the door, does not come and join her.

As he leaves the house he sidesteps around the large box that was delivered a week ago. It is Róisín's telescope that, for some reason he doesn't understand, she has left unopened in the hall.

She walks from the post office to the pub at the end of the high street, feeling like she is too big for her surroundings. When she was a child this street had seemed long, with the green opposite, and the old wooden benches named for people that no one can remember but with surnames they all recognise: families that have lived in the village for longer than anyone knows, having arrived no one knows when.

She looks up to see that the butcher's has closed but the baker's is still open. She goes inside and orders a sticky bun, for old times' sake.

Are you back for a visit? Keira asks. Keira, who has worked here since she was old enough to reach the till, who wears the same apron her mum used to wear when she worked here – and look, she still does. Róisín smiles as Keira's mum appears from the door to the back room, curious to know who has come in, not quite recognising the voice.

Róisín, it's you. Staying with your mum?

Róisín smiles, considers her words.

Actually I'm staying on the farm for a bit, with Liam.

Mother and daughter smile and nod. Keira twists the corners of the paper bag, sticky bun inside, and spins it over once, before handing it to Róisín.

In the pub, she asks: Any part-time work? I can waitress.

They have started serving food. She wonders if they get tourists here now – she has noticed a couple of B&Bs that weren't there before. The isolation of this village makes her long for them to arrive.

Let me think on it, sure, the owner says. Haven't seen you round here for a while. Staying with your mum?

Mmmm. Róisín smiles – well, let me know – and leaves.

They have a family dinner on Friday – Róisín, her mum, Neil and Conall. She suggests to Liam that he stays home, this time, just until she's had a chance to see, to test the water.

So, you're staying on the farm? her mum says.

For a while, says Róisín, fake casual, taking a sip of wine.

That'll be grand, says Neil, give Liam a hand. It must be hard, running that place alone.

Her mum smiles, Róisín smiles. This is going to be tricky.

It's nice to have you home, her mum says, taking a sip herself. Don't get me wrong, it's wonderful.

Róisín nods, spikes some peas with her fork.

It's just, what happened with your job?

It's just a sabbatical, Róisín finds herself saying. I can go back.

And will you?

I'm not sure yet.

You seemed to like it in Bayeux.

Róisín doesn't reply, though she did like it – thoughts like that aren't helpful at the moment.

The sun has set but the blinds are still open, letting in the dark of the garden, letting in the cool of the night.

A silence sits around the table with them, the silence of what everyone knows but no one will say.

We're just two people, Róisín thinks. Two cousins, living together, it's not so bad as all that. But she knows that to other people, to her mother, it might be that bad. And even so, her mum hasn't said anything. No one has told her to leave. There have been no arguments. There is just this silence.

She goes to slice a potato, sees that her hand is shaking.

Neil glances at her.

Her mother gets up and closes the blinds.

Róisín sits next to Conall on the sofa as he loads up his favourite computer game.

Two player, he says, selecting 'Astrogirl' for Róisín – it's been her avatar since they started playing together, that summer she came home from Imperial.

Well, this isn't going to be fair, she jokes, you've had a chance to practise and I—

But he's already beaten her in level one with a swift move she can't even begin to replicate.

Have you forgotten how to play? he asks.

No, she says, leaning forwards, just needed a kick up the—

Conall laughs loud and hard as he bumps into her on-screen and nudges her joyfully on the sofa.

As they play, Róisín forgets to worry about what people think and remembers how nice it is to be at home, with her family. Her mum gently touches her shoulder.

Liam remembers a time from before he lay out in the field with Róisín to watch the comet, when the house always had music playing. His mum would run from room to room, searching for old boxes they could use to build child-sized cities with sheets for tunnels and torches for street lights. He doesn't remember her being sad, she never seemed sad, though she must have been – he was so young when she did it he didn't know the right questions to ask. But the music was replaced by the sound of his dad taking apart the old turntable and trying, again and again, to put it back together while water dripped in from the roof and the fences blew down and the only time he could have fun was when Róisín came round and filled the house with her dreams of the sky. And now she is here. Though she is late coming home.

It is dark outside and he finds himself pacing from room to room, trying to push back the emptiness that threatens to infringe on the farm even now. It won't do, not now Róisín lives here. So he sits on the floor and starts to unmake his dad's turntable, laying out the components around him so that each one can be cleaned and checked and refastened, in an attempt to remake what has been broken.

Róisín approaches the farm's kitchen door slowly, unable to shake the look in her mum's eyes over dinner now that she has left the warmth of her home. Perhaps, when she was younger, knowing that her home was there made it easier for her to leave, she thinks; her solar system has always had her family at the centre.

She wonders if she needs to have a conversation with Liam, but she doesn't know what that would be. For the first time she consciously questions herself: would everything really be OK, if they weren't cousins? It was more than their being cousins that made her leave before, that made her reluctant to return. She wasn't running away from a secret, she was running towards a world full of mystery and freedom, and she's not sure if she's ready to stop exploring it.

She stops a few feet from the door, steps round to the side and leans against the wall of the farmhouse, out of view. She has tried to forget about the stars and the world that calls out for her to travel, to see the things she's never seen. But it's not working so far. So instead she decides she will set up her telescope on the farm, after all – avoiding something doesn't mean you're longing for it any less, so why pretend? The light from the window shines out into the dark and she can see the first snowflakes of the year glittering in the air, not ready to settle on the ground.

She doesn't want to go inside yet.

She doesn't want to have these doubts.

Liam has opened a bottle of wine, tall candles in the centre of the table, with a Beatles record playing on the turntable that had always been broken, that he has fixed. His dad left it unfinished, but he is not going to do that – not to the turntable and not to the farm. It is warm in the kitchen, the windows hazy with heat from the stove. Now all he needs is Róisín, and time to fix everything else.

He sees her through the window in the kitchen door, looking in; a smile spreads across his face, his arm rises in a wave. She looks serious for a minute, but he runs up to her, lifts her inside and spins her in his arms with a laugh.

You'll not guess what I've done, he says.

She raises her eyebrows, follows him to the turntable sitting proudly on the kitchen table.

He points to the record, holds his arms round her waist as they both listen to it playing smoothly.

I fixed it, he whispers in her ear, before kissing her neck.

She turns to face him.

Was it broken? she says.

If she had known, she would have bought him a new one for Christmas.

1997

Comet Hale–Bopp

FRANÇOIS CROUCHES OUTSIDE THE DOOR, some instinct making him feel more hidden if he is low down. Inside the room, his mama is talking to herself again, and he has decided that he needs to know what it is that she keeps saying.

Why did you make the shed? she says.

Does she mean the shed in their garden, the one that is his den?

You knew, didn't you?

François backs away from the door, crouches in the corner.

You wanted to escape, too.

He hears footsteps, thinks about running for the stairs, but then her walking stops and her voice softens.

I do understand, she says. That's the trouble. I understand just fine.

He creeps downstairs, keeping to the far side by the wall; he doesn't want the steps to creak the way they do, sometimes, in the night, when his mama heads down to the garden, imagining him to be asleep.

In the shed, François pushes his toys to one corner – toys he hasn't played with since he was little, model figures and storybooks and even a child's bicycle that he has outgrown. He hasn't come in here to play for a long time, a long time in his world, not since he was at l'école primaire, at least; not since he grew up, as he has done this year. There are boxes stacked around the walls, some made of cardboard, others plastic; some covered under blankets so he could sit on them, pretend he had his own sofa in his own den, when really there was no actual furniture in there.

But there is some furniture. One piece of furniture. There is the old cupboard at the back that looks so dusty and boring that he's never bothered looking inside. Only now he reaches for the handle.

The door opens easily. There's no lock. No secrets. And inside there are mostly books. The top half is lined with shelves, the shelves crowded with old-looking books in dim colours with thick spines. The bottom half has no shelves and contains a suitcase that he vaguely recognises. It is their suitcase, the one they used to take on holidays when they still went on holidays, when he was a child.

He pulls it out from the cupboard and lays it on the floor.

The flimsy padlock comes off the zip easily – it's not a real lock, it is like a child's toy intended only to stop the zip from winding free in the baggage hold, not to stop the contents from being disclosed.

Upstairs, Severine and her granny sit side by side on the bed. They do not want to fight. Her granny looks older now, which is odd – most of the ghosts appear like younger versions of themselves.

It's not a good thing, Severine says, that we are all tied to our ancestors like this.

It's not so simple, her granny says.

Then tell me.

Her granny looks past her, as if looking beyond the camera's lens to something outside of the scene they're in.

It was wonderful, she says, to see him again, you see. He was still young, when he died.

Great-Grandpa Paul-François?

He said it was up to me, if I wanted to see him, and I didn't even have to think about it. I said yes, yes, yes. I didn't want to be alone, in this house.

You had Mama.

She was a child. You know what company children make?

She does; Severine knows that well enough.

I didn't even realise that I was staying in Bayeux for him, her granny says. I stayed here because it was my home. At first, anyway.

What happened later?

I didn't want to let him go. It was… she shrugs. It was too much fun. And I was too lonely without him.

There was a moment in the hospital, as her granny was dying, when Severine had felt the loss more than at any other time; a moment before the ghosts had appeared and offered her hope. It still returns, that feeling, bites into her like cold reality after a dream.

In the case, there are clothes. New clothes that he hasn't seen before – clothes for his mama and for himself. He pulls them out, lets them scatter on the floor around him as he searches deeper, and finds passports, birth certificates, money – why is there money hidden in this cupboard in his shed? – maps, maps of France, driving maps, timetables of trains and boats, maps of

Europe, money in currencies that he doesn't recognise, that looks like fake money, but somehow he knows this is not pretend. Everything they would need to start a new life, away from Bayeux, is in this case.

It is strange, her granny says, to realise that you have another chance, but that it is slipping away.

I don't understand.

It can't last; I know that now. We have a generation left, perhaps, that's all.

And then what?

She shrugs her shoulders then looks up to the sky, waves her hand as if inviting Severine to look from one edge of the universe to another.

Don't worry, she says, anger can't last forever.

You're talking about Brigitte now?

It controls her, that's the trouble. She's not ready to leave yet; she finds it too difficult to let go.

François repacks the case, and does the zip back up, although the padlock is broken now and won't secure properly. He puts the toys back to where they were, scattered about the den, and tries to make it look as if he hasn't been here. Then he reconsiders.

He had a toy, a tiger, that he loved when he was younger. He used to carry it everywhere, stopped when he became embarrassed, when the teasing of other kids made him ashamed. He finds it in one of the other boxes, stacked in with a multicoloured xylophone for a two-year-old and a wooden yo-yo – he has no need of them – and carefully pulls it out, trying to tuck in the loose thread that is coming undone from the seams.

He unzips the suitcase and places the tiger inside, along with the clothes and maps and money, and puts the suitcase neatly by the door of the shed so it will be ready, when his mama is. Ready for when they will leave.

While they cook dinner, François keeps grinning at Severine, as if he has a secret, and he looks so pleased about it that she's going along with it. She lets him crush the garlic – one of his favourite jobs in the kitchen – laughs as he climbs up onto a chair so he can lean down on the garlic press with all his weight.

She's accidentally laid three places at the table – one for her granny – but she pretends the serving mat is for the hot casserole dish, and she thinks she gets away with it. François doesn't tell her she's made a mistake. He just smiles.

Is it good? she asks.

You have outdone yourself, Mama, he says. How grown up he sounds sometimes! And he continues: You know Luc, from school? He says he calls his mama and papa Julie and Pierre. Do you think that's funny?

I think it's OK, she says, parents are people too.

Can I call you Severine then?

Yes, she smiles, I suppose you can.

François thinks this is something of a turning point now. He is a grown-up, not a child any more, and he and Severine are going to go somewhere far away. He's just got to wait till she tells him where.

I want to go to South America, he says.

Why South America?

We're doing South America in Geography. The rainforest is the last untouched wilderness.

Severine thinks about that for a minute.

What about Antarctica? she says. That's untouched, and it's certainly wild.

His eyebrows furrow. He hadn't thought of that. They've never done Antarctica in Geography.

Can we look it up in the atlas?

After dinner, she smiles.

He stands beside his mama, beside Severine, and they both stare at the page. It is different from every other page in the atlas: a pure white land of ice in the blue sea – a world of two colours – and miles of empty space.

Who lives there? he asks.

Penguins, she says, and after a minute, maybe sea lions as well. And some birds, I think.

What people?

I don't think there are any people, she says. I told you it was untouched.

No people at all?

François likes the idea of a snowy wilderness even more than all those trees in South America. Though he can't imagine a whole continent with no people – he didn't know there was such a thing.

Will you come with me, if I go as an explorer? he asks his mama.

A smile warms her face.

You're not too old, are you? he says.

She laughs. I'm only thirty-five, François. Then she pulls her son into a hug. And of course I will.

Brigitte is different that night. She perches on the end of Severine's bed, quiet and soft.

Severine is tired like she's never been before. She's had nightmares every night since the comet arrived last year. Every day she takes François to school and runs the shop and cooks dinner and listens to all the other ghosts, but tonight she is going to try to stay calm despite her exhaustion and listen to Brigitte.

Do you want to tell me your story? she asks.

Brigitte is staring out of the window at the black of the night.

Maybe I can help?

Someone was taken from me, Brigitte begins, and stops again abruptly.

We've all lost someone, says Severine. Perhaps it's time to let it go. We all have to let go eventually.

And Brigitte can't help it. She thinks about the fire and it catches light around her, thinks about the screams and the room is filled with noise that she can't stop, even though Severine is covering her eyes and burying her head in the pillow and stifling a scream of her own and it feels like the whole room is alight, the house collapsing into rubble, and then it stops.

Brigitte is gone.

Severine sits up. Enough. It has to be today. There is nothing she can do to help Brigitte, nothing she can do to change the past, but she can make a new future for herself – and for François. A future with new places to explore and no ghosts to haunt them.

François hears a knock on his door. He thinks, as he wakes, that it wasn't real – just a house sound, like the noises that always appear in the night. But there it is again, three knocks, and the door handle to his room turning.

François, his mama whispers.

Mama? he says, and then sits up. I mean, Severine?

You should get dressed, she says.

What time is it?

Dawn.

Why are we getting up now?

We have to get to Paris.

This is it. The time has come, sooner even than he thought it was going to.

What are we going to do in Paris? he says, eyes wider. She is smiling now, peeking out of his curtains.

We're going to get a flight.

To South America? Or Antarctica?

London first, she smiles, lets the curtains fall back but puts the bedside light on. Then, anywhere you want to go.

When François gets downstairs his mama is waiting in the hall with the suitcase from the shed. She doesn't mention his tiger, maybe she hasn't even opened it yet. It feels like an adventure, this night-time leaving. Although, it's not really night any more – the outside is brightening, it looks fresh and clean, and colour-tinted from the stained glass in their front door.

They take the train to Paris, watching the sun rise higher through a hopeful sky, François gazing out of the window as they race by fields of cattle and orchards of apple trees, his eyes flicking back and forth as he follows the scenes.

What is this village called? he asks, with each station they pass through, and Severine smiles at how much she doesn't know, even this close to home.

Then there is a long bus to the airport, François climbing up the last few steps to sit on the high seats at the back, by the window again – looking out until the early morning catches up with him, and he closes his eyes, drifts back to sleep, his head nodding against his mama's shoulder for a moment before waking with a jolt, straightening up to stare outside some more.

A plane!

It is low in the sky, only just taking off. They are close.

*

And then they are inside the terminal building, queuing to check in their luggage, François watching as it wobbles along the conveyor belt then disappears from view.

His mama is holding their passports now, and their boarding cards. They are queuing again to get through security. François is impatient, wanting to run through the empty doorway of the X-ray machine, wanting to see if he makes it beep.

Severine stands beside him in the queue. She's not excited by the X-ray machine. She wishes the queue were longer, finds to her surprise that she is dragging her feet, looking over her shoulder.

They both pass through. Their bags are not searched.

Someone offers perfume to her in the duty-free boutique; she shakes her head, repelled by the scent.

Come on, Mama! François calls, his energy sending him running between the aisles of bottles and chocolates, just bold colours to him. The lights are so bright he wants to jump and shout.

Severine has stopped. He runs back, takes her hand.

But now, she is looking for them. Her granny would come, surely, wave her off to show her that it's OK, that she understands and that she is happy for her. But her granny is not here. And Great-Grandpa Paul-François, he'll arrive at the last minute, she thinks, he has to. He'll be there by the gate, lounging against the end of the row of neat seats with pale blue cushions, laughing at the way François runs between them, scrambles through the rows in his excitement. But they arrive at the gate and Great-Grandpa Paul-François is not there. She sees a man with dark hair, a walk she recognises, a way of swinging his arm, and she rushes towards him until a woman appears carrying two coffees and passes one to him. This is not Antoine, this is just some man, some stranger to her. She even looks for Brigitte, angry Brigitte, with her blackened skin and her seeping blood, even that, even the horror of that, would mean that they care.

And she thinks that Brigitte needs her help.

But this is what Severine wants – she wants to see the world, to experience it, not spend her life waiting for the ghosts of people who no longer live in it.

Her granny had said she hadn't had to think about her choice. You are offered the chance to see someone you love again. Is that even a choice?

Yes, yes, yes.

Are they not going to stop her?

And all of a sudden Severine finds herself standing in front of a man in the airline's uniform who is asking to see her boarding pass and she can't, she just can't, there is something inside her that is breaking and she steps back, calls her son to her, leans on a seat for support and understands, finally, that she can't leave them. She can't be responsible for them disappearing and never being able to return. Even though there is a part of her longing to escape, there is that other part that is longing to stay, to be surrounded by generations of family that make her feel loved and accepted, that make her feel young, and more – that make her feel that she is a part of something bigger than her world. Who is she to break that connection? She can't do it and so she gives in, she accepts, she shakes her head and doesn't board the plane. She holds François in a hug that he's squirming to escape from, just like he's squirming to get on the plane, pulling her by the hand, desperate not to be left behind until he looks at her face and understands. They are not going to travel the world. They are going home to Bayeux. He should have known his mother would never leave.

He stops trying to pull her towards the plane, and lets her hand drop. He doesn't cry, and he doesn't shout, but he knows that the next time she makes a promise to him he's not going to believe her.

Is it the ghosts again, Severine? He speaks with a hint of accusation, of frustration in his voice. It is like he has become the grown-up, she the child.

No, she says, pulling him closer than he wants to be again. It's me, it's my – but she can't find the words to explain to her son, so set on adventure, so aware of how big the world is and how much he wants to see, that, after all, her heart won't let her leave.

LIAM IS TALKING ABOUT SUSTAINABLE agriculture. There is some new code that's been brought in – she's only half listening, picking up words here and there while she thinks about what she's going to do, how she's going to live – something to do with nitrates, protecting water from pollution, soil P levels, nutrient management planning. The state of the world's water is something she's never considered, and something that he seems to think about on a daily basis. She wonders about how long it will be until we can launch manned space flight to other planets, if we'll find water on Mars, on Titan, how a planet develops water in the first place. She doesn't notice that his tone has changed, that he's playing, that he doesn't expect her to care about nitrates; obviously he doesn't. But he keeps on going, allowing his voice to spill words about creating a sustainable balance between soil input and output, about stocking densities and waste management (he's quite enjoying himself now) as he moves behind her chair and reaches down to kiss the back of her neck.

They're in the forest, walking through the afternoon's low light, filtered through spring leaves and lost in the still-damp covering of moss and mud on the path.

Where are we going? Róisín wants to know.

Just walking, he says. Might find a deer, maybe a badger.

But what they find is a squirrel.

This is not a wilderness, Róisín says, resisting the temptation to stroke its bushy tail.

Liam's kneeling on the ground, trying to coax it closer with some of her fruit-and-nut bar.

What shall we call her? he says.

Be careful, they bite, you know.

She's not going to bite me, sure. Are you, Susie Squirrel?

The squirrel gets closer, goes for a peanut, takes a chunk out of his thumb.

Five minutes later, and the blood has nearly stopped gushing from his thumb into the undergrowth. They have coloured the leaf mould red.

How did this happen? she says, and he laughs. Some creatures bite, he says, it's not deep, it doesn't hurt.

But she takes his hand, inspects the bite, has no idea how to fix it, scrambles around in the rucksack for some kind of first-aid box.

When she looks up again, he's wrapped a handkerchief around his thumb.

Problem solved, he says.

Róisín's not so sure.

At home, she notices the white handkerchief lying by the sink, stained in red, and a shiver runs down her spine.

Liam throws it in the machine, whistles his way upstairs.

He gets up early, because he has to. When the night is still creeping about the farm and the cold is biting its way through the single glazing and she no longer feels the need to get up with him, she rolls over, pretends to be sleeping as he creeps out of the bedroom, down the stairs, to turn the key in the back door and close it as quietly as he can when he leaves.

Once he is gone she rolls over again, onto her back, lies in the middle of the bed and stares at the ceiling, imagining there were no ceiling, imagining she could see all the way to the stars.

She doesn't get up till late. She enjoys this time of being on her own, of not always being one of two.

But then she runs out to where he is working, tells him to be careful of his thumb. She had a sudden premonition that he could hurt himself – hurt himself badly – when she's not there to help.

Liam looks at her like she is insane, then grins. He's not going to hurt himself. Still, it is good to know how much she cares.

They go out of town for dinner, drive over to Galway and ask for a corner table, the one hidden beyond the bar. The first bottle of wine goes down fast; they order another to have with the main course.

She's talking about being away, describing the flats where she's lived, the people she has known. We saw Shoemaker–Levy 9, she says, from the observatory on Blackford Hill – did you see it? she asks, but doesn't wait for a reply – that was the one that collided with Jupiter, there's still a storm raging because of it, churning up the surface of the planet.

She thinks she is talking too much, but perhaps that's how it always was with them; a conversation filled with her dreams. Until he reaches over and takes her hand: Maybe the planet is more interesting for the storm?

She lets a moment of understanding undo the past hour of not getting each other, doesn't mention the great storm on Jupiter, the thousands of storms that make the planet what it is.

In Bayeux, she continues, I set my telescope up in the attic – I had this top-floor apartment – and I watched . . . Her voice trails off as she remembers his dad's funeral, struggles for words until there is a voice:

Róisín?

Keira, from the baker's, is walking over to them.

Róisín pulls her hand away quickly. Prepares herself for a conversation that must be filled with lies.

He worries – of course he does – as he begins work, as he works through the morning, as he doesn't go home for lunch.

By dinner time he thinks he has a solution.

We have to just tell people, he says.

She looks at him like he is insane. She doesn't even smile.

That won't change a thing, she says. They already know.

In the evening, the phone rings and neither of them makes a move to answer. Her mum's voice leaves a stilted message on the answerphone. It would be good to talk, she says.

In the night, waking him on purpose but trying to make it seem like a natural thing, a thing that just happens. He is blurry, moving to get up as if it is time for work, until she pulls him back.

I want to travel, she says. We haven't left Ireland in almost a year. I want to see—

I've got work to do.

So did I, she says; spoken for the first time, this mention of what she has given up. I don't even have any friends here—

It's the middle of the night, he says, as if that's any kind of answer.

Yes, it is.

They spend the rest of the night both believing that the other has gone back to sleep.

But you don't have to keep doing this, she says. She is angry now. This farm is too lonely. There are things in the world we can't change, but a job– it's just a job – that can be changed. So change it.

If Liam had been there to hear her, it would have been a good speech. He might even have been persuaded by it.

She thinks that, if she insisted, she could probably get him to leave the farm. She allows the thought to stay with her, as she serves lunch to the three tourists in the pub, as she stares out of the window, uses her break to search the skies with her binoculars for a comet that is almost too faint now to be seen. But something about that knowledge makes her feel so cruel she pushes the thought away, promises herself she won't start another fight. Liam belongs on the farm. And Róisín, perhaps, is searching for something other than belonging.

He is cleaning out the stalls when he hears someone arrive, the grate of an engine finding its way over the noise of the cattle. He's not expecting a visitor.

His hands are dirty; he wipes them on his trousers but Adele doesn't move any closer.

She's not here, he says. She's working in the pub today. Sunday lunch. He smiles apologetically at her wasted trip, and at something else entirely.

People are talking, she says.

He is sweating beneath his shirt, aware that he smells of livestock. He thinks briefly about the new calf that was born last night.

Adele turns and walks away without saying anything else.

Róisín and her mum can be very alike sometimes.

The calf is with its mother, for now, but Liam knows it can't stay that way. They will be separated, so that the mother's milk can be bottled and sold, so that the calf, which was a male, can be sold. So that he can keep this going. He knows that the sooner they are separated, the easier it will be on them both. He doesn't know of any other way to make a profit on a farm. Every time, though, even now, he feels a sadness about it. He knows what it is like to be separated from your mother.

Your mum came by today, he says over dinner.

Róisín shakes her head. She's still not ready to do this.

She goes to the fridge, looks for a corkscrew in drawer after drawer before she realises the bottle has a screw top.

Do you know what everyone's saying about us, in the village? he says.

I don't care.

Wine spills over the side of her glass.

Shall we go out later? he says, his voice different, softer.

Where is there to go?

I was thinking we could visit our hut.

That's not still there, is it?

She had almost forgotten; she can't believe that she'd almost forgotten.

He smiles. Sure it is. I'll show you.

It is twilight when they arrive by the stream, by the log that still bridges the bank and the island, although it is not the same log, of course. That one was swept away in the storm five years back or more. This one is a replacement.

Liam lets Róisín cross first.

Halfway over the log, Róisín stops, turns back. I can't believe this is still here, she laughs, arms out for balance; it seems smaller than it did when we were kids, you know?

As the water rushes over the pebbles and stones it bubbles up, reaching her feet, her toes through her trainers, but she doesn't care.

It is so quiet out here with nothing but the sound of water and the smell of leaves, of a late-summer evening, just before the leaves turn. She's almost sorry when she reaches the end, steps onto dry land – not that it is dry, really; it's damp from the stream and muddy. She turns, holds out her hand. It's your go, she says.

Liam makes his steps smaller than they would naturally be, almost heel to toe as he crosses the log, like he would if he was a little boy trying to show off. He stops in the middle, sways side to side for effect.

On the opposite bank, Róisín has turned to shadow in the falling light, but he can see her eyes; she is watching.

Are you clowning around? she says, hands on hips, and she is the image of who she used to be; strong-willed, in charge, pretend grown-up.

She takes his hand once he is across, leads him the few paces to the entrance of the hut. They have to crawl to get inside.

They lie down on their backs, two pairs of feet sticking out of the doorway, an old sleeping bag undone on the ground beneath them. They fill the space, barely room left between bodies and walls. It feels warmer in here, although it can't be really, it is open to the elements through the door, through gaps between stones and branches once populated with leaves and moss.

Róisín turns to the wall, tries to make out the shape of it in the darkness. It is not completely dark, in here, the moonlight, starlight is enough, now her eyes are used to it. She reaches out a palm, touches the rough handmade wall that is only a few inches from her face.

Liam reaches out a palm, touches her shoulder.

They imagine, of course, there is no one walking by the riverbank. To them it is as secluded as it ever was; invisible, existing only for them. They don't think about where they throw their clothes, ending up in a tangle around their feet in the doorway. It's not a night for thinking about what people will say or how they're going to explain or how they are going to shape their future when their love is all about the past.

Instead, they let themselves become who they were, side by side in their childhood hut that was always a bit too small, even before they grew too big. She lets her cheek brush against his, feeling his stubble like she used to; he lets his lips brush against her shoulder, her stomach, as cautiously as if he were a boy, and they return to a moment when this was all that mattered.

They wake shivering, the cold a more thorough cover than the warmth of the sleeping bag they share. Liam puts his arms around her, holds her close as she buries her head in his chest. She is shaking.

Here, I'll warm you up, he says, but she's shaking her head as well.

Let's go, she says, getting up. It's time.

Liam feels a stab of loss, mixed in with longing, and can't explain why it seems so familiar.

WHEN SEVERINE AND FRANÇOIS GET home the ghosts are not there. François stands quietly by the door as his mama rushes from room to room, calling out to no one. I'm back, she shouts, I'm here. He sits down cross-legged on the floor in the hallway and pulls over the suitcase – abandoned by Severine as soon as she stepped inside – and sets it down in front of him.

The zip makes a slow, grating sound, and he doesn't rush; he feels like something in him is changing although he couldn't say what it is. He opens the top, holds it in his hands for a moment, then throws it backwards to make a quiet thud on the carpet behind, and he looks down into the muddle of clothes and maps and shoes and his old tiger and feels like he is looking into his childhood from beyond it. He pulls out the tiger, leaving a trail of clothes tumbling out of the case, and stands up.

Severine rushes up the stairs – she had thought they would be here, waiting for her return, ready to congratulate her on making the right decision, but perhaps that is a scene that would only happen in her imagination. She slows, checks a bedroom, stands outside Great-Grandpa Paul-François's study. Surprising herself, she knocks on the door.

Inside, Antoine is curled up under Great-Grandpa Paul-François's old desk, but when he sees her he crawls out – younger now, a boy, François's age – and looks at her with his head tilted to one side.

You wanted me to leave? she asks.

He brushes down his T-shirt, stands straight.

No, I wanted me to leave.

Severine thinks she can see Brigitte shimmering into view, but she vanishes again, and instead of searching for more ghosts she kneels down beside Antoine, remembering what this room looked like from the viewpoint of a girl.

Well, how's this: I set you free, she says.

Oh, that's sweet, he smiles, but not how it works. If you get one of us, you get us all. Besides, there's someone else I'm waiting for.

She looks up to see Great-Grandpa Paul-François sitting behind the desk, a book raised in front of his face, a chuckle already resounding around the room. Henri from the 1750s is looking through the shelves, pointing out the books he likes to the sisters in lace dresses, and others appear, their clothes reflecting different centuries, and her granny – her granny calls her name so she stands and turns and sees her granny as a young woman, with dark curls and a knowing smile: Welcome home.

When François gets to the top of the stairs, his tiger trailing from his right hand, he sees all the doors have been thrown open except for one, and he knows that is where Severine will be. He walks towards it, raises his left hand to the handle, but stops; finds himself again on the outside listening in. He can hear his mama's voice, chattering away to no one, describing the journey, the airport, the return, then skipping on to conversations that make no sense to him: something about U-boats and oceans – he turns the handle and steps inside – something about tabby cats, and Severine's laughter rings out and she doesn't turn, doesn't see him there.

He remains where he is for long enough to see that she is happy, and that the conversations she is having with herself are more captivating than the ones he wants to have with her. Then he turns, leaves the room, walks quietly down the stairs into the kitchen, opens the bin with the foot pedal, drops the tiger inside, and thinks about making some soup for dinner.

You all look different, Severine says; you are younger.

Her granny smiles.

We knew you were thinking about leaving, she says, and Severine's eyebrows rise and fall again.

I thought I'd hidden it well.

You didn't need to hide it—

Apparently I couldn't.

That chuckle, those laughter lines.

I tried to tell you it was a choice.

And now?

You have made up your mind.

Yes.

Severine thinks it is strange, how much comfort can come from a decision once it has been made. She looks around the room, wanting to sit down, but the only chair is occupied by Great-Grandpa Paul-François, so she sits down on the floor, cross-legged, and the ghosts sit down with her.

So, who is going first? Severine says. I want to hear everything. I want to know where I have come from.

It started long before us, says Great-Grandpa Paul-François, finally looking up from his book to join the conversation.

Before Ælfgifu our family lived in England.

Before that maybe Rome.

How do you know?

Just guessing.

There's a good chance we're Romans.

But why start there? Severine teases. Before we were Romans we must have been something else.

And they talk about the movement of great continents, about volcanoes and earthquakes and the start of humankind, the first boats, the first fire, what it must have been like to journey through an ice age, and by the time they have stopped talking it is dark outside and it is late, and Brigitte is there again – she is calmer now she knows that Severine is staying in Bayeux. She might have time, she thinks, after all, even though the world is changing.

You'll be back tomorrow? Severine asks as some of the others start to disappear. I'll make dinner – family dinner – and that's when she remembers that François must be downstairs on his own. She stands up, knowing that she has to go just as Brigitte has appeared, but she can't help that.

I'm just going to check on my son, she says.

Brigitte doesn't reply, but Severine thinks she sees a hint of jealousy in the way Brigitte looks at her, before she blends back into the air.

Walking downstairs, Severine thinks she will suggest chocolat chaud for tonight, but when she reaches the kitchen François is not there. He's not in the front room either. She checks the clock – it is later than she thought. She has lost track of time. But she will make it up to him tomorrow.

She finds François upstairs in bed. He's sleeping, so she backs quietly out of the room and turns off his light.

*

Brigitte is waiting for Severine in her bedroom.

Are you ready now? she says.

And Severine sits herself up in bed, pulling the covers around her shoulders because there is a cold draught coming from the window and, for once, Brigitte does not burn.

I'm ready, she says, I want to hear everyone's story. Are you ready to tell me yours?

Mine's not a happy one.

Pas possible.

Severine smiles, kindly, she hopes, though Brigitte is not one to laugh at quiet jokes.

Travelling is not the only way to see the world, Severine says, and this is something that has been slow in appearing to her, but it is no less powerful for that. She doesn't say any more, she just waits as Brigitte settles herself down on the edge of the bed and begins, at last, to tell her story.

In the afternoon François sits in the front room with Severine and his grand-mère, who is sipping her brandy.

I'm going to go to Antarctica, he says, and his grand-mère raises her eyebrows as if she thinks that is a bit too ambitious.

South America? he tries. To the rainforest!

And she laughs. Maybe we'll try somewhere in Europe first, she says, for a holiday?

She starts talking about Italy, describing ancient monuments and vineyards and how she's always wanted to go, and François thinks that it would make a good start to his adventures.

Can we go, Severine? he asks. Please, can we go?

But Severine's head is centuries away, in a France as foreign as any country, filled with battles and angels and crackling with fire. If she could just close her eyes she would be able to see it, Brigitte's world. To breathe it all in.

Well, what do you say? her mother insists, and she is dragged back to – not reality, that would be the wrong word.

Sorry, Mama?

Shall we go, the three of us?

To Italy?

Well?

I can't go away, she says, I don't want to leave Bayeux. But you could take François?

He doesn't understand why she won't come, even for a holiday, and for a moment he wants to cry but he won't. What would be the point when she's already made up her mind?

Well, then, says François's grand-mère. You and I are going to see the Colosseum – Yes, he says, refusing to be sad and clambering up on the sofa – and the Circus Maximus – Yes! – and perhaps we will travel south, she says, to the Sibyl of Cumae. François's eyes widen and he jumps as he says Yes! and tumbles down onto the cushions and grabs his grand-mère in a hug that nearly, but not quite, spills her brandy.

Later, while Severine and her mother are standing together preparing the dinner, she says: Be careful what you listen to, Severine. I don't want to lose my child to this nonsense as well.

Severine sighs. I fixed the lights in the shop, Mama, she says. I'm running a good business, I look after this house, what more do you want?

Perhaps you should make some friends, go out...

I don't have time for friends, she snaps.

And what about François?

But before Severine has the chance to reply François has arrived and is saying – Mama, why have you laid too many places at the table?

As she looks up, she can see the ghosts have quietly appeared and are sitting around the large dining table, each at the place she had subconsciously laid for them. She thinks, briefly, about laughing off her son's query and taking their mats away but she can't do it. It would seem dishonest. She doesn't like hiding things, and she's certainly no good at it; besides, keeping secrets is no way to protect a child even if you are scared of losing him. So instead three living members and five of the dead members of her family sit down together for dinner, and she knows that when the ghosts start to fade again, one by one, she'll tell them that she no longer longs to see the world and promise that she'll be here in Bayeux for their next visit – and her granny will smile, and softly say, I know you will.

~--------~

RÓISÍN STANDS OUTSIDE THE BAKER'S, trying to work up the courage to go in. A man passes her on the street, someone from the village. She doesn't recognise him, although he nods at her as he passes. She avoids eye contact.

Her fingers crush into her palms. She tells herself it is ridiculous. It is almost autumn, that is all. This chill is nothing more than the autumn air, the anticipation of damp leaves decaying underfoot.

The bell makes a ding-dong sound as she enters. There is no one else in the shop, and for a moment she thinks the sign should have read closed, but then Keira appears from the back. Her eyes don't know where to settle.

Just a baguette, Róisín says. And, perhaps, the coffee-and-walnut cake.

She doesn't move forwards to the counter, keeps her distance as if she were talking to an animal in the wild.

Keira smiles, puts her baguette in a paper bag.

Just the one slice of cake?

No, two.

The slices are boxed and paid for. Róisín finds herself standing out on the street again, lost for breath, a fine trickle of sweat gathering at the rim of her hat. It is too soon for winter accessories, she thinks, leaving the hat in place, turning from the village again.

She hears a shout – her name – and looks round to see Keira waving to her from the corner. The urge to run takes her by surprise; she's not a child, she shouldn't have to flee from her choice or be scared of what this woman might think. Keira doesn't matter. The people in this village don't matter. Róisín turns and walks towards her, head held high.

Did I forget something? she asks.

Keira looks confused, then smiles. Would you like to get a cup of coffee?

Coffee?

Yeah, you know… She tilts her hand to her mouth as if drinking from a cup, and laughs at Róisín's expression.

And Róisín laughs too.

Sure, sorry, coffee. Yes. Thanks. That sounds grand.

Tell me about your work, Keira says, her eyes lighting up. Róisín had forgotten that about her – she was always asking questions at school, always seemed like she wanted to be there, to know more.

At first, I was studying binary stars.

Keira nods, encouraging her to continue.

Our sun is on its own, but a lot of stars come in pairs, and orbit each other.

Do they ever crash together?

Not exactly, though there can be a transfer of… Sometimes material from one of the stars gets sucked into its partner, so one gets bigger and bigger and one smaller and smaller. And it's useful – it tells us things about them. What I was looking for were systems where one of the stars – the one that had been growing – got so big it collapsed into itself and became a black hole.

So you can see them, black holes?

Indirectly. The orbiting star – the one that was shrinking – gives off a particular type of radiation.

Keira's grinning. Sure I'd love to see a black hole, she says. Imagine it! And her hands are wide open as if trying to hold empty space between her palms. I wish...

Róisín likes her; she had forgotten that she'd always liked her. It feels good to talk about things without feeling like there's hidden meaning attached.

Tell me about the bakery. The cakes are grand...

We're doing well, she says. Business is good in the summer – you've seen the new B&B?

Funny to think of tourists coming here.

Keira nods. Funny to think of you coming back. I'm not sure I would, if I could be on a mountain top looking through a telescope at a black hole.

And although Róisín never looked through a telescope on a mountain top, or saw a black hole – not in the way Keira describes it – the image of herself living that life is so comforting that for a moment she can't find the words to reply.

Liam refixes the fence that always blows down, shares out the cattle feed, drives to the market and back again, and can't shake the worry from his mind that perhaps Róisín doesn't belong here after all. He could have lain in their hut all night; he doesn't care about the cold or the rain, or what people might be saying. He had wanted to stay but Róisín – he recognised that impatience in her, and knows, too, that look she gets in her eyes when she's describing her work, her old work, the sky she still looks to when she thinks he's not watching her.

When his dad died there was a moment, sitting by his bedside, when he thought about leaving. But as he reached forward and closed over his dad's eyes he promised himself he would stay, because that's what his father would have wanted – yes, he would stay and recreate their home. And he is trying, has been trying, to fix everything, to rebuild what was lost. With Róisín it had seemed possible, though what is possible and what is impossible seem blurred to him, sometimes: perceptions rather than facts. Besides, this was never Róisín's farm to save.

Can a home be recreated from a distance?

He doesn't know the answer, but he has started considering the question.

He leans against the shed and asks himself what he is doing here.

You're running my farm, his dad says.

My farm now, he replies.

Your farm, so it is.

And Liam turns and half expects to see his dad beside him, that weary look in his eyes; stubborn, too. But there is no one beside him. There is no one left who needs him to stay.

Halfway back to the farm Róisín stops in the middle of the field and knows she has to turn round again.

She doesn't care, she realises, what people might think about her, because the truth of it is that people probably don't think about her that much at all. She doesn't care if there's gossip in the village; she has been worrying about the wrong thing, when there was something far more important to worry about.

She'd forgotten, too, what it was like to have a sense of purpose, but she has one now. She strides back through the village and beyond the green towards her mum's house. It is time to face this, while the leaves are still golden and before the snow sets in.

Her mum's home is so warm; that is the first thing she notices. It is comfortable too. Welcoming, full of family. As soon as she steps in the door she wishes she had done so sooner.

Neil lets her in, holds her in a hug while Adele rushes down the stairs.

How good to see you, she says. Her voice sounds as though Róisín has been living on the other side of the world, not the other side of the village.

You too, Mum.

And all of a sudden she is choked up, almost ready to cry. How absurd, she thinks, as she blinks the tears away.

We've been watching the comet, smiles Neil, with the binoculars you got us. Conall's enjoying it, I think. Aren't you, Conall?

They are outside in the garden, the whole family together, sitting on her mum's new patio chairs, surrounded by late-flowering plants and late-evening sunshine.

It's quite something, to see it there every night, he continues. It's strange to think it will be gone soon.

Róisín nods. Might be a decade before the next one, she says. It's been a busy few years, for comets.

Why is that?

She shrugs. Sometimes these things just happen, she says.

Her mum brings out tea and cake, sits beside Róisín and chooses her words carefully.

Do you miss studying the sky? she asks.

And Róisín is stunned by how simply the question can be put, and by how obvious – how undeniable – her answer is.

*

Two hours later, and Adele is glad she didn't say anything more – there was no need. She holds her daughter tight, through her sobs; she tells her that it is OK, that it will be OK. She tells her to study the sky, and to travel the world, and to live her life the way she wants to. She tells her not to feel guilty, because it is no one's fault, and that she tried. She tells her that she loves her.

Róisín spends the night looking through her telescope, searching for the comet that is now obscured behind layers of cloud and mist.

Liam comes in to see her once, twice, but he doesn't stay and he doesn't return after that. He knows that he is not what she's looking for tonight. He falls asleep while the sky is still dark, hopes he will wake with her beside him in the morning.

But as the dawn breaks, Róisín knows she has made her decision, and now it is tears rather than the mist outside that obscures her view of the last of the stars. She packs up her telescope, carefully dismantling each component and wrapping them safely before placing them back in the box.

OK, Liam says. This is not like when they were children.

And she looks at him in surprise. Was he expecting her to leave? Does he want this, too?

OK, he says. You have to do what you have to do. I understand. So I'll come with you.

Róisín lets his words sink in. His expression is soft but not excited, and she knows that he doesn't want to travel or to explore, not the way she does. She doesn't want to have pushed him to make this offer that won't make either of them happy. It feels wrong. She shakes her head.

I can't sell the farm, he says, still talking, I can't lose it altogether. But maybe someone will rent it. Or I can bring in management.

And she is ashamed of how little she has told him of herself, how much she has hidden of her present while they tried to relive the past.

You don't understand, she tries.

I know you came back here to help, he says. After Dad... And it was so kind, he says.

No—

But now it's my turn, to do what you need.

Liam—

You're not happy here.

As he says the words out loud, for the first time, their full meaning hits him and he feels his hand begin to shake. If he hadn't said it, she would have had to.

You just need distance from where you grew up, he says.

No, she says, her eyes already stinging at the cruelty of what she's going to have to say. It's more than that. I need distance... to be on my own.

He doesn't understand; that is the opposite of what he needs.

I want to travel and to change, she says, and to know different people and become a different version of myself.

But you are still Róisín.

I'm so sorry, Liam, she says. I don't think you should come with me.

He stares at her in disbelief.

You won't enjoy it...

And she can't bring herself to say what she knows; it is something that she will never say out loud: that she wants to spend her life with people who are driven to explore the world, not those who are willing to follow.

He says that he doesn't understand, that he's sorry he didn't offer to leave sooner; he lies and tells her that he wants to see the world too – they can see the world together. He shakes his head as she describes all the ways that they are different, revisits conversations they had that were one-sided, different views of the world that didn't match up, until eventually he stops because her mind is made up and he knows her well enough to know that it can't be changed.

Where will you go? he says.

But she doesn't know the answer yet. Not back to Bayeux, although she would like to – she was only halfway through her post, there was so much more to learn there, to see – but she's too embarrassed to go back. She's going to her mum's for a while, to apply for jobs and see what opportunities come her way. So instead she tells him some of the cities she's always wanted to go to – Tokyo, maybe, she says. Or New York, I've always wanted to go to New York. I want to be surrounded by people, lights – her hands wide as if trying to hold all that life between her palms, before she realises how thoughtless it is to be talking like this, when he has such loss in his eyes. She looks down to the ground.

He wants to tell her that she knows nothing of isolation, has no idea what it's like to have no family left, but he doesn't say that out loud. He wants to tell her about all the things he has been trying to fix, all the things she hasn't even noticed, how he was the one who rebuilt their hut year after year, like a promise – but this time she is making no promise to return.

You'll be OK, she says later, standing by the door with her bags packed. She means it as a question but Liam doesn't reply, he doesn't say a word. She wants to say that she's sorry, but she doesn't really think those words would help, not now. So she turns and walks away, and doesn't look back.

Halley's Comet

They thought Brigitte was mad, when she built her house brick by brick with her own hands. When she refused to marry, denied all the men in the town, was once seen chasing a soldier out of her door with the point of a blade. She would stand on the roof, they said, like a witch, arms raised to the sky and her wild hair – like she was possessed, they said, just like her mother. But that was not until later. First they shut their doors to her and kept their menfolk away from her and watched, and envied, and waited to see what wild Brigitte would do with the stones as she laid the foundations for a home that would be hers and only hers.

Brigitte told the story to her son on the first night he was born, rocking him back and forth in her arms by the window overlooking the spire of the cathedral. Her home, the home she had built, stood on the edge of Bayeux. From the front of the house you could see the town, the waterways glistening in the summer light, her mother's house, but in the other directions – nothing. No more houses or streets or marketplaces, just the wild roll of the countryside out towards the sea. Do you see what I built? she whispers to her son, turning from the front window and carrying him to the back of the house. I can be a part of the town or a part of the world – and as she looks out towards the steeper hills and prickle of bracken, the clouds rolling in on a restless breeze, she knows which direction she feels pulled in today.

When the baby is sleeping she lays him down in the bed, covers him with her blanket, and closes the door so she can make her way to the roof. Before the baby was born she did this every night, watching the sky, watching the people stare and point, then laughing from over their heads to see them scatter in fright. She can't cower at home, she can't stop being Brigitte. She climbs the stairs to the flat roof and walks, unafraid, to the edge, looking out over the town that is shaded in the purple silk of sunset. A strange peace, she thinks to herself, after most of her life has been spent during war, when the sight of soldiers in the streets, newly arrived or blood-soaked and carrying the dead, was more common than children playing. But she has her home.

She hasn't taken the baby to the church yet. She thinks perhaps she never will; why should she follow their rules and agree to her son's name being written in their book, like a forced confession of how this child came about? No, she doesn't need to tell them anything; doesn't need to give a father's name or pledge a baby's allegiance to a religion she doesn't believe in. She will name her son tonight. That is all that matters.

There is a strange star in the sky. It reminds her of something she saw a long time ago, when she was still a child, when she

began to notice how people crossed the street when they saw her
mother walking towards them. Even as a young girl she knew
the whispers were directed at her family. She didn't cower then
either, she stood taller and stared at them over the street, giving
her mother all the time she wanted to talk to the dead. Not like
her aunt, with her pretty twins, who told her mother to hide, to
keep it a secret. Brigitte would not hide, nor ask her mother to do
so. It was something to be proud of, not feared; that's how she saw
it, even pretending, sometimes, when she was young, to hear them
too – especially when the other children refused to talk to her.

The flash of red catches her by surprise and she turns, ready to
curse whomever it is that's dared follow her up onto the roof. The
woman's face makes her breath catch, though, and her words are
spoken in a tongue she barely understands.

There is no time, she is saying, or seems to be saying.

Who are you?

I am sorry.

And she looks down to the streets that are no longer empty,
that are lit with torches carried by the family of a man she knows,
though she wishes she didn't remember his face. She looks over to
see the flames on the roof of her mother's house, screams out in
fright, turns to run, to help, but she is too late. They are here, he
is here, downstairs, and suddenly she realises: she has to protect
her son.

There is not time, the woman is saying, her red dress whipping
around her slight body in the breeze, and Brigitte understands,
runs to the stairs, hears the creak of wood as the door is broken
and the stamp of men's feet up the stairs even as she is running,
barefoot, down.

She stands in the doorway, panic gripping her throat at the sight
of the man holding her son, still wrapped in her blanket, sleeping
but starting to stir.

No, she says, trying to block his exit. She is taller than this man, but his boots crack on her bones and she falls to the ground. She clutches at his clothes, tries to scratch at his skin, whatever it takes, but she is outnumbered now, the flames are taking hold and the baby, her baby. She doesn't realise that her dress is catching fire, that her skin is about to burn; all she knows is that they are taking her son.

She stands in a circle of flame that is spreading, destroying her home. Walls fall. The roof craters in. Her black hair – once falling in wild curls to her waist – burns faster than lightning. The sky is alight, too, and full of thunder without rain. Her scream catches in her throat, comes out as a growl. Words are lost in the sparks but caught again, in her eyes, in her glare that defies the burns eating away at her skin and confronts the man where he stands on the grass, in front of the house she built, that blanket held in his arms. The torch that lit the flame held high like a victory.

To the north there is a falling star, a silver light moving across the sky faster than any star she has watched before. But now her skin is black and shrivelled, curling off her bones, and this is what she sees: the man, the flames of red and gold, and her lost child – the baby she hasn't named yet, whom she should never have left sleeping while she climbed to the roof of her home to stare at the sky.

2007

Comet McNaught

THEY TALK ABOUT NOTHING, WORDS thrown across the kitchen as onions sizzle, fish glaze, courgettes roast.

What d'you do last night?

Did you hear?

Was it good?

François is happy to talk about nothing, listen to the chatter as he fries and whisks. Every movement is precise despite his speed, every word calm despite the raging heat. The excitement, the bustle of the kitchen; he loves it, just as much as he loves it when it stops. It is funny, he thinks, how he used to dream of a frozen world, and he has ended up working in this sweltering one. The speed and smell and sizzle of the night, the sense they each have of where everyone else is, what everyone is doing; plates, knives, fish, tomatoes, herbs lined up and ready to go, everything is ready, every movement fast. Scallops perfectly golden-browned, thirty seconds in butter, salt, and parsnips – a new addition – roasted and slim, with a red-wine jus and chocolat.

The head chef returns, the conversation quietens, there is focus throughout the kitchen: there's a clarity, too. When it goes quiet, it's as if François doesn't need to breathe; the world becomes the dish he's creating and there's beauty to that. François knows he is good at this.

The head chef nods, walks on.

People come from all over the world to work here, to learn to cook in this kitchen. François has learnt technique here, but he learnt how to cook by heart when he was still a child; that is what makes it instinct.

Getting back to his flat at 2 a.m., windows and shutters flung open; at last he has time to breathe. His shirt is thrown over the back of the chair as he welcomes in the cold night's air. A pint of water followed by a bottle of beer, a Jacqueline Taïeb record on the turntable. A message from his mama on his answerphone: Look at the sky. And come for dinner tomorrow, yes?

He smiles, drinks more water, falls asleep in his jeans. Then wakes two hours later and walks to the window.

He is not the only one on the street. That is the first amazing thing. The next is the quiet – a buzz of silence, a ripple of something extraordinary in Paris. Then there is the comet: the brightest thing in the night sky. It is beyond visible; it is unmissable.

He doesn't understand how he didn't notice it before. He'd always thought of himself as somebody who noticed things.

He wants to pass it on, so he sends a text message to Hélène; she'll be asleep, probably, she has lectures in the morning, but just in case – it is so beautiful.

*

Hélène is woken by her phone beeping in the night. She doesn't mind. She smiles at the message – six months together and he can still surprise her. He was the only chef in the restaurant who didn't ask her out while she was working there, though every time she went to the kitchen to collect the orders she was willing him to look up at her.

On her last night they went to Le Sans Soucis, and he was quiet at first; she thought he would stay for one drink and then disappear from her life. It made her braver. Enough to claim the seat next to his as soon as it became available and to finally forget to be shy in front of him. When everyone else had left, they stood outside and said their serious goodbyes like they'd never see each other again, before racing along the streets as if they were competing in the Olympics and running up the stairs to his apartment, exhausted and laughing, hand in hand.

And now he says there's something beautiful in the sky. She thinks about getting out of bed but it's too cold and it's 4 a.m. so instead she huddles under the duvet and falls asleep again, waking happily in the morning to a low sun and a layer of frost that makes the grass crunch under her feet and the roads sparkle.

But François stays outside, staring up, long after the crowds have dispersed. For some people there is only so long you can admire the sky before your neck starts to ache. Not for him; he feels like he could search the skies all night for patterns in the stars, for mountains on the moon, for a comet that moves – yes, he thinks it has moved – between the constellations while he holds his breath and refuses to blink.

When he gets home, he writes a recipe for his mama. He wants to thank her for something, though he is not sure exactly what.

He doesn't hear back from Hélène. She must be sleeping.

A few hours later he goes for a run, despite having been up all night. He has the feeling that something is happening; that something is about to change.

RÓISÍN ARRIVES IN HAWAII, NATURALLY taking to the routine of staying awake all night and sleeping as the sun blazes down. She names the galaxies she sees, though they have catalogue numbers already; she names them after people she has known in research groups across the world. The group in Hawaii laugh over midnight breakfast, trying to guess which colleagues she liked and which dwarf galaxies she's named after professors who had become too fond of their own voices. Her results are good; she'll get another paper from this trip. She has moved across the world, sending postcards of new cities to her mum and sticky chocolate to Conall.

Guess where I am? she texts Keira one night from the observation room, the sky too beautiful to keep to herself. On a mountain top, looking through a telescope at a supermassive black hole in the centre of the Andromeda galaxy. We've discovered they might help galaxies form – isn't that amazing?

Well, I invented a new kind of pistachio cheesecake today, texts back Keira. Beat that!

She laughs – it is true; even though Róisín has invented a new program to analyse the radiation detected from some of the most distant galaxies in the universe, she has never quite mastered the art of baking.

She is exhausted after her shift but she still finds it hard to sleep; she closes her eyes and sees the stars, wants her day to begin all over again. She walks through the mid-morning sun to the canteen, where some of the others are already drinking.

A nightcap? Gerhardt suggests, pouring her a glass of ouzo – none of them know why there is ouzo in the Mauna Kea observatories, but it comes in handy – and they slip easily into talking about their observations, their spectra, the questions they each have about the universe that drives them to search the skies.

Róisín tells them half of her story; the half that involved watching comets race through the clouds as a child, the half that loves to feel free in a universe that is so big, the half that feels the beauty of the sky like an ache in her chest.

The other half of her story she doesn't share. Liam is still there, a part of who she is, and that is as it should be – everyone has a first love, she thinks, and it is personal, and it is precious, and it is in the past.

The storm lasted for two days, and it seemed endless. Even now the rain has stopped, the sky is so dark and low it feels like an effort to walk through the fields, as if the clouds are resisting the movement below.

Liam trudges through the mud of the field, but just as he gets to where he was going the skies open again and a shatter of lightning tells him it is futile. It is only lightning, he tells himself, but he also knows it is the last time – in this moment, he gives up on trying to fix the fence that he has mended every year, after every storm, since his father first built it.

As a young man, his father believed that hammering wood into ground would make a strong enough root to last. It was an act of faith.

As a young man, he wanted to be just like his father.

It is heartbreaking, he thinks, the things people believe they want when they are young.

In Toronto, Róisín starts a relationship with one of the engineers she's been working with. Jie is part of the team designing a component of the *Rosetta* spacecraft that will be woken up from three years of deep sleep to land on Comet Churyumov–Gerasimenko.

We are looking for prebiotic molecules, he says, in his unfamiliar Canadian twang.

You mean you're searching for life? she asks.

The precursors to life. And other things.

She smiles; she loves that idea.

To the *Philae* lander, she says, holding up her orange juice in a salute. Long may she travel with the comets.

He has fine black hair that tickles her chin, and trendy glasses that she likes to push to the top of his head, despite his protests. He is very easy to be around, perhaps because he is a happy man, by nature; when he wakes up in the morning something in the world always makes him smile.

Where were you before Toronto? she wants to know.

I spent three years at the Université de Montréal.

And before that?

PhD at McGill.

She nods, makes sense; perhaps he doesn't like to be too far from home.

I had a year in Antarctica though, Jie says, as if he can read her mind and doesn't want to be seen as homely. That's impressive, hey?

Her eyes widen.

Tell me more.

He laughs, undoes the top button of her shirt. They are together for three and a half months before parting amicably, and she enjoys every day of it.

But she thinks of Liam. Remembers that intensity in his eyes and feels the weight of it. Her mum says he goes for Sunday lunch sometimes, and she is glad of that. She hopes that he has learnt to see the fun in life, the beauty; hopes it is not cruel of her to think that.

Liam arrives at Adele and Neil's house at midday on Sunday; he is invited every week, and about once a month he makes the effort to go. He finds their kindness strangely hard to take, finds he returns to his home feeling more alone than if he had never left it.

Over lunch Adele mentions Róisín again – she is proud, of course, and he understands that. But he struggles for words to reply, even now, even after ten years, can't quite bring himself to ask questions about her life.

She has been to Hawaii.

She has made new friends in Canada.

She is improving her French.

There has been no one else, for Liam. He doesn't want the dishonesty of pretending he can love someone else, or the superficiality of pretending he doesn't need to.

But the next week, when the phone rings on Saturday to invite him for Sunday lunch, he doesn't answer it. He will not be spending Sunday lunch with her family again.

·⸺⸺·

FRANÇOIS AND HÉLÈNE STAND OPPOSITE his mama's house, on the other side of the road. She is nervous, and he doesn't really understand why – he's been looking forward to this.

She's not like other parents, he says – trying to make her feel better. Hélène is the first girl he's introduced to his mama; he thinks they will like each other.

No?

No, really. She's fun and young and we cook together, make up new recipes and . . . oh, she was the one who told me about the comet.

I forgot to look! Oh merde, I'm sorry.

Hélène glances over her shoulder, as if she's thinking of running, but he puts his arms around her waist.

Do you need to go for a drink first?

She hits him gently on the chest.

Hélène is so keen to make a good impression she's promised herself she's not going to drink at all – something she reminds him of now.

Yes, but that may not work with Mama ... He leans in closer and is pushed away.

Stop trying to kiss me and let's go, she says, marching across the road ahead of him, her scarf blowing out behind her in the wind.

François greets his mama with two kisses, bending down to reach her cheek. He's not an especially tall man but she's a small woman, petite in every way. She's had her hair cropped short and dyed rich brown, and she's wearing elegant trousers and a shirt, a slim gold chain with a twist running through it.

She spreads her arms wide. See, she says, I made an effort – special occasion.

Mama, this is Hélène, François says, a smile playing about his lips. Hélène – Severine.

We meet at last, Severine says, kissing her cheeks.

François turns to his girlfriend, takes her hand; I knew it would be OK, he thinks.

I've made Sunday lunch, Severine says. But first, try this new red. It is divine.

She turns away, looks over her shoulder and laughs at something they can't see.

There's a second's pause that feels longer than that, to François.

That's a white, he says quietly, all the nerves he hadn't felt before hitting him.

Yes, like I said, a new white, laughs Severine, her hand waving quickly around her head. Here, Hélène, come in. Let me take your coat.

They sit in the front room and François relaxes again as Severine talks about cooking; how she had learnt to bake from her granny when she was just a child, sharing recipes for pain au chocolat and madeleines. How she stocks the widest range of spices in Bayeux – boasting about her shop now – spices from all over the world, she says. What are your favourite countries, Hélène?

Hélène is studying Spanish and Portuguese at university, she tells Severine, accepting a second glass of wine.

You want to travel? asks Severine, eyes alight.

Hélène smiles. Actually I want to be a teacher, she says, but Severine doesn't seem to hear.

You should take François to the rainforest, she says. He always wanted to see an untouched wilderness – remember? She laughs. Remember, when you were little? I was very proud of you.

François feels himself going red.

And then you decided to explore Antarctica, she continues, because it is so remote, I think – but you were only ten so you said it was because there were no people there, only penguins.

But François loves being around people! Don't you? says Hélène, suddenly sounding nervous again, looking at his hand as though she wants to take it but isn't quite sure if that's allowed.

I'll get the next bottle, he says, stepping through to the kitchen to avoid more stories. But then he looks at the dining table and something twists uncomfortably in his stomach. Hélène has followed him through. She slips her hand into his.

François quickly re-lays the table while Severine is still in the other room; it sounds like she's talking on the phone now. There were six places set, inexplicably, so he packs up three. He hasn't seen her do that since he was a child. Hélène looks like she's going to ask a question but he shakes his head; he doesn't have the answers anyway. What could he say to her – that occasionally, when he was a child, his mama could hear voices? No, he cannot share that. She has been better for years now. It would embarrass her.

And anyway, the lunch is perfect.

You're the real chef, he says, as they move on to the second course, not me.

Tell your fancy restaurant they should hire a woman, instead of all you men.

Hélène laughs.

François is proud that his mama's still so feisty.

I'll tell them, he says. Believe me.

I just don't understand why they're so late.

The restaurant?

No, the others. My granny said they'd be right through.

François feels another prick of worry, before Severine laughs at herself – what am I talking about? she says, looking around the table at the empty seats – and he smiles and drops the issue even though he is struck by a memory that he can't shake off for the rest of the day.

Hélène takes a sip of the wine, gently steers the conversation round to her own granny's seventieth birthday while François seems lost in his thoughts.

And Severine – she knows that look she saw on his face, remembers it too well from the day she found his tiger in the bin and watched him from across a table full of ghosts that he couldn't see while he politely, perhaps kindly, ate his dinner and didn't make her feel ashamed.

*

Later François and Hélène walk home from the station along the Seine. They are quiet now, talked out from the day with Severine; François likes to be quiet, sometimes, and he likes that Hélène seems to understand, for now at least.

But his mind is not quiet, it is filling with memories that had almost been lost; a holiday to Italy with his grand-mère that his mama refused to join, an argument he didn't understand about relatives he had never met. And then, as he gets older, the memories solidify; Severine laughing at a parents' evening when the teacher told her he was dreaming in class instead of concentrating, taking out his report card when they got home and writing over his C with a big red A+; climbing up to the roof together when he turned fifteen to look out over Bayeux with a bottle of red wine for his second birthday celebration that year (the first being with his friends – Severine had the grace to stay well away from that one); teaching him the recipes she had learnt from her granny, and how to adapt them, how to create. It was as if, when he was a child, there was a moment when she seemed to be slipping away and then she returned, became his mama again and, as he grew up, his friend. But now…

François?

He looks up to realise that the rain has started, and Hélène has pulled her coat over her head.

Your place is closer, she says with a suggestion in her eyes. Come on—

He takes her hand and they run the rest of the way to François's apartment.

But as the door closes behind them, and Hélène slips her arms around his waist, she says: That was a bit weird, with the table…

She laughs. He can't.

I mean, how many girlfriends does she think you have?

And François finds himself pulling away, walking through the kitchen to the window where he looks out through rain-patterned glass.

François?

He doesn't reply.

I'm sorry, she says, I didn't mean to make fun. Here, look at me.

He turns, sees that she is wearing his red bobble hat that he hasn't worn in years – it looks ridiculous. He can't help but smile.

Where did you…?

Severine gave it to me.

She takes it off, pulls it over his head instead.

Looks good.

He raises his eyebrows.

I liked her, she says. Really.

And François returns to the playful man she knows as he carries her to the bedroom, bobble hat still on his head.

RÓISÍN REWRITES HER CV, AND then writes it again; planets to binary star systems to galaxies at the furthest reaches of the universe – she wants to see it all. She fills out the job application form, requests references from her old jobs and her current one: Toronto, Amsterdam, a recommendation from Bayeux. She has always longed to see New York, and the fellowship there would be perfect.

She watches the universe from a laptop screen showing real-time satellite images. Her fellowship, if she gets it, will be looking further away still; further away than she's ever looked before. The oldest galaxies in the universe, now, and she'll be studying them when they were young, when they were children – when they were still forming into what they would become.

We can see what's happening at the very edges of the universe, she thinks. What an incredible thing to do. By looking far away we can look back in time; we can see the birth of galaxies.

She adds some finishing touches to her covering letter, prints it out, signs it, reads it over again. She hopes that she has captured her experience, her commitment, her patience and meticulous research.

And also, she hopes that she has conveyed how much she loves what she does; the universe is pretty miraculous, she thinks, and that is not something that she wants to get lost among the detail.

Liam takes a stall at the farmers' market in town. Everyone else seems to be going to it these days, so he figures he should give it a try. He hopes it might bring in some money, although with the cost of reserving the place he's not convinced it's going to work. He has beef for sale, different cuts of meat, sausages and burgers, and he stands there, from 8 a.m. until 1 p.m. watching the crowds arrive and mingle and eventually leave again.

He covers his costs, just about, he thinks, counting up what he has sold as the nearby stalls start to pack up and the winter sun finally breaks through the clouds. He isn't expecting any more customers, and the child's voice takes him by surprise:

Sausages and chips, Mum, please...?

He looks up to see a little boy, maybe three, maybe four years old – he's not sure, he has never really been around kids since he was one and he can never tell their ages. The boy has a mess of blond curls and hazel eyes, and is clutching onto his mother's hand to pull her back to the stall that she had been walking away from.

She turns, the recognition crossing her face a second before her smile catches up.

Hello Liam, she says.

Rachel.

He had heard that she'd got married, though he didn't know she had a son.

She laughs, a little nervously, says, well, I think we'd like to buy some sausages for lunch.

Her son picks up packet after packet, looking for what Liam isn't quite sure.

How are you? she says.

Grand, yes, thanks. And yourself?

Oh, she sighs, you know, exhausted, busy, sure – and a laugh again – good, she says. Very well, things are…

You look well, he says, smiling, then turning to the boy. Found some you like the look of?

He shakes his head at the offer of money; a gift, he says.

He has this strange urge to speak to the child, to run with him through the last of the stalls, chasing patches of sun through the shade.

But then mother and child are leaving. Good to see you, Rachel says, as she turns. Take care, Liam.

And they are gone, and the market is over, and Liam packs up the last of his produce and makes his way to the car.

There is a heaviness in him that he can't really explain as he drives home, out of the town, past the villages, back down the single-lane track that leads through frosty fields to his farm. He hasn't made enough money to make it worthwhile. He won't go back.

He never discussed having children with Róisín, it never seemed to be what she wanted and besides, perhaps it would have been wrong. But now, as he walks up to the back door, lets himself in to a silent house, imagines how different it would be if he could have had that life, he realises that he would have loved to have had children with Róisín. The picture of it, the imagining of it, is so strong that he sits down at the kitchen table, rests his head in his hands, and allows himself to feel the emptiness.

Róisín recognises the university postmark and rips open the neat white envelope – a letter from Dr Joshi at NYU.

We are pleased to say…

Impressed…

New satellite data…

She contains her excitement – only allowing herself a smile before setting off to the shops. Conall will get Reese's Pieces today; his new favourite.

Later she phones her mum with the news. There are congratulations and shouts to the rest of the family, Neil calls out – knew you'd get it! – and there's the sound of music and a bottle of wine being opened.

So you'll be moving to New York?

The phone line crackles; she can almost hear the distance between them.

For three years, she says.

And you're happy, pet?

Oh, Mum, Róisín says, already imagining the new city she will get to explore.

We'll have to come for a visit, her mum says, you'll show us round the university?

VIP tour, she laughs.

She knows that her mum is proud of her.

Have you seen the comet? Neil calls.

Neil wants to know if you've seen the comet, her mum repeats.

Róisín pauses, tries to remember the name.

Erm, I haven't had the time…

Conall thinks this one's the best, Neil shouts from the kitchen. Don't you, Conall?

McNaught, she says – she's just looked it up online – Comet McNaught. And she promises herself to look for it tonight, to have an evening closer to home, to search the skies for a comet that can be seen with her own eyes. To allow herself to remember before she moves on again.

⁻⁻⁻⁻⁻⁻⁻⁻⁻

BRIGITTE IS BY FAR THE most beautiful of the ghosts. There's an elegance to the way she holds her head high but she's not pretty; she has a long face that is almost angular in the way it reflects the light, and a stubbornness in the way she will never apologise. And when she is calm – as she is now – Severine can see a sadness in her that is missing in the others. They have accepted what happened to them; they have moved on. Brigitte is not able to.

I want to help, Severine says, I just don't know how.

Brigitte sits, poised, on the end of the bed, her eyes looking out of the window.

I'm trying, Severine carries on, I'm not leaving, and I'll still be here when you return. But none of us know what happened to your son. We don't even know his name.

She thinks, for a quiet moment, that Brigitte is going to let the tears in her eyes fall. Instead she looks at Severine.

It's easier to burn, she says. I'm not angry at you.

I understand.

I'm just angry.

And Brigitte catches light, flames devour her hair as she fades and the ghosts leave again with the last glimpse of the comet.

François wants to comfort his mama, but it is hard to do when he has no idea what has made her so upset. He arrived for lunch, thinking he could surprise her with a new version of his crêpe Suzette, but he doesn't want to cook that now; Severine is curled up on the sofa in the front room saying that her family is gone.

I spoke to grand-mère yesterday, he says, thinking she is worried about her mother. She's doing well, all things considered.

It seems to make things worse.

She'll leave too, Severine says, and she won't come back.

Mama, no one has left. Grand-mère and I, we're right here. I'm just up the road in Paris.

Severine looks up at him, as if recognising something new in his face. François, she says, Hélène is nice. A sweet girl.

I like her, he says, feeling suddenly defensive. He's given her a set of keys to his apartment; she said she was going to come round later.

I like her too, Severine says, seeming to sit higher now, as she brushes the hair away from her face.

Come on, let's make lunch, says François. We can have anything you want.

Well then. Something from when I was a girl...

She lets her mind fall back to when she was a child, standing beside her granny in the kitchen.

I'd like roasted tomatoes with rosemary, please. With fresh brioche.

He laughs at her choice. And red wine to go with it?

Of course.

At home that night, François can't sleep. He doesn't want to wake Hélène, so he steps quietly out of the bedroom and goes to sit in the lounge. The skies are cloudy tonight; although the curtains have been left open he doesn't look out, instead he stares into the air in the middle of the room and breathes. He's not sure how long he is sitting there, but it is long enough that the night gets less dark; there is a purple tint to the blackness outside when Hélène comes to sit with him, curling her legs underneath her, resting her head on his shoulder.

I recorded something for you earlier, she says. While I was waiting for you to get back.

On TV?

Yes, there was a programme about South America. Your mama said you'd wanted to go, so I thought—

I was young.

I think you'd still like to go, really, she says. Wouldn't you?

He can tell that she's thought about it, though he can't picture Hélène wanting to go to any kind of wilderness.

Maybe I would, he smiles. One day.

She springs up, grabs the remote.

Here, she says. Let's watch a programme about an untouched wilderness from the warmth of your living room.

And he reaches to tickle her, gently, but she is too fast and they end up in a tangle of limbs on the floor by the sofa.

The programme, though, is not about an untouched wilderness; it is about the opposite. It is about generations, millennia, of change. They are both leaning forwards, towards the images of the rainforest, forgetting to watch the sun rise outside.

Geometric human-formed earthworks found beneath existing areas of rainforest; he can't believe it, though it is wonderful, he thinks, how the landscape can evolve like that. Different scientists argue over the details, some convinced that people cleared the forest in order to farm, others believing the climate itself meant the rainforest had to retreat. But all of them are excited, it seems to François; they are like explorers, he thinks, and he remembers how he had imagined visiting new lands, how he had dreamt of adventure in the wilderness.

I always thought the rainforest was untouched, he says to Hélène after the programme has finished. But it's not.

Is anywhere, really?

Antarctica, I guess, he says, smiling at how he'd once stared at a map of the ice. Though who knows what they'll find under all that ice, some day.

That thought fills him with a longing to discover something for himself; for the first time since starting his job he feels like a restaurant kitchen in Paris might be too small for him.

Would you like to go? he asks.

To Antarctica? Too cold.

To anywhere, he smiles. The rainforest?

She shudders. Too many insects.

He looks away.

Have I spoilt it for you? she asks, and he looks back at her in surprise.

Because you don't want to go?

No, because it was inhabited, she says. You wanted it to be a wilderness...

Not at all, he says, and you're very sweet. Actually I think it's wonderful. It was inhabited, farmed, lost and—

Reborn? says Hélène. Resurrected?

She giggles at her choice of words.

It recovered, says François, more serious than Hélène. It keeps growing and changing – he looks at her, her laugh fading now – somehow it survives.

He wants to tell Severine about it, leave a message on her answerphone to match the message she left him about the comet, but he doesn't. It is not conscious, but somehow the gratitude he felt then is retreating now, and being replaced with something else.

Comet Skjellerup–Maristany

The sound of the war wakes Paul-François at night again, the blasts of battle and worse, the groans of men whose skin is rotting; slow deaths, as vivid as if he were lying among them. They gave him a medal when he returned – still, he doesn't know what to make of that – a medal for killing men, or for not being killed. Perhaps it is just a medal for surviving.

His wife wakes beside him – she seems young to him, though they are the same age – eyes of concern, as though she is looking at a stranger in her bed. They did not really know each other when they married; they met as teenagers when he was on shore leave. And war changes people, that he is certain of now.

Paul-François, she says, will you come back to me?

But he doesn't know how to answer that. He leaves the bedroom and creeps down the stairs that creak so that he can stand outside. The cold helps. The sky. There is a stack of wood at the end of the garden; he's been collecting it though he doesn't know why, but tonight he starts to build – he needs to create something after all the destruction he has seen. He has forgotten about his wife upstairs but she has followed him down and now she helps, as they saw and hammer wood through the night.

They finish what they are building as the dawn begins to break, and the comet overhead fades into the orange sweep of the horizon. Paul-François stands back, looks at the structure he has built.

It is a nice shed, says his wife, trying to make him smile.

But Paul-François still feels the weight of what he has seen; he doesn't know if he can ever be the man that his wife married.

I remember your laughter, she says, placing his hand on her belly. I still believe it will return.

His unborn daughter gives his hand a little kick.

I remember it too, he says, and she smiles.

That is how it begins.

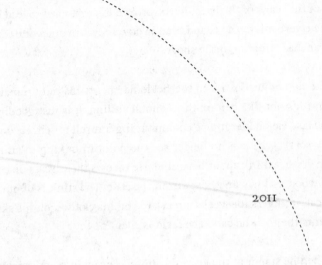

Comet Lovejoy

LIAM KNEW IT WAS COMING but still he is unprepared for its insistence, for the way it makes his chest tighten – there hasn't been a comet this bright in years. He doesn't look up, it hurts too much, but he can feel it watching him. Perhaps that makes it worse; to be visible but unable to see.

He shakes his head. To be haunted by a lump of rock thousands of miles away. There are things closer to earth he should be worrying about.

He no longer allows himself to think about Róisín.

That's a lie, obviously.

The colours of the world are earthy, here; browns and greens and the murky froth of a churning river. Frost comes overnight then melts during the day, causing wood to splinter and crack – he sees it in the walls of the barn, in the broken log that used to lead from the riverbank to the island, that is now only a mangle of bark and branches clinging to the shore.

One day he walks out to the field and shoots his only remaining cow. It's not like before; this is not a culling, it is just goodbye to the last, sick heiferette he couldn't bring himself to sell. He doesn't say sorry – he can no longer see the point in talking to animals. He doesn't think about her name. He throws the carcass on a pyre of wood and hay and boxes from the attic. The stink is of burning meat, it lingers for weeks afterwards on his clothes, on his skin. It taints the food he eats. The farm is silent now.

When he stands at the graveside his eyes wander from the dedication of his dad's headstone, rest briefly on his mother's matching one, then stray behind to members of his family that he never knew. They have lived on the farm for generations, and been buried in this patch of land beneath his feet; it is strange, to feel the weight of this history but get no comfort from it.

One by one he reads their names, for the last time – he has decided that he won't be visiting again – like a roll call, a school register: Gone, he says, instead of here. Gone, gone, gone.

He stops opening his post; bills and bank statements, legal letters and birthday cards all go straight onto the fire. His denial does not discriminate. The lacy cream paper of a wedding invitation crackles and twists away to embers beneath a threatening demand for a loan repayment.

He sits out by the broken section of fence and allows himself to watch the sky. He makes a map of the night, marking on constellations, galaxies, stars that he can't name, a swirl of cloud and the position of Comet Lovejoy. Without meaning to, he draws it on the top half of the page, leaving space for the farm below it. He leaves it blank for a while and he thinks about ripping it up or burying it in the mud, but stops short of acting each time he is about to let his anger surface.

Then, at around 2 a.m., he draws a herd of cattle, horses galloping down by the stream, sheep herded into the west field and four people sitting out by the barn. He draws it like a child's picture, stick men and women with round smiling faces, the barn a four-walled box with square windows, the grass like little spikes rising up prettily from the ground.

Mum.

Dad.

Liam.

Róisín.

He skewers the page onto the broken wooden pole of the fence and heads back indoors.

Róisín has bought new furniture for her apartment, a bookcase and matching coffee table; she unpacks the boxes that have been delivered, half builds the shelves before getting bored with the job and heading outside.

It's like a fairy tale, New York, one sprinkled with a harsh reality but full of more surprises than she'd imagined when she dreamed of living there. She walks past the university, a group of Japanese women stopping her to ask for directions; she's pleased, she must look like she belongs here now, and this is a city that takes years to get to know.

Where should we go? they say.

Sure that depends on what you want to see, she smiles.

They laugh loudly, as if rising to the challenge of the twenty-four-hour buzz of New York.

*

She calls her mum from the North Woods in Central Park, finding a stone where she can sit and watch the stream away from the crowds that gather even in December.

We've chosen a dress you'll like, I hope, for the wedding, her mum says. We're thinking dark blue for you, like the night sky.

It sounds beautiful, she says. I'll try it on as soon as I land.

We'll be there, her mum says – she sounds excited – we'll come to the airport. Can't wait to see you!

Me too, Róisín smiles. Put Conall on, I want to tell him about this new flavour of ice cream I've found.

It's the middle of winter—

Yes, but it's avocado and prawn – it's non-season specific.

To her surprise, after saying her goodbyes, Róisín lifts her phone again, looks up a number in her address book that she hasn't used for a while. Her old boss in Bayeux answers – Róisín, you're coming back to us? – No, she laughs, but maybe I could call into the department for a visit while I'm in Europe?

They've worked together on a few projects over the years, searching for clues that planets might exist further away than can be seen. It's funny; when she lived there she imagined herself to be so far away from Ireland, but now, they're like neighbouring villages when compared to a flight over the Atlantic. She can't shake a feeling that she left something behind in Bayeux. Perhaps, she thinks, she was in too much of a hurry to leave.

SEVERINE TAKES FLOWERS TO HER mama's grave every weekend, the colours changing with the seasons. Sometimes she leaves cakes or pastries too, and occasionally a bottle of Calvados brandy or amaretto. She hasn't seen her since she died, but she is waiting patiently and she thinks today's the day – this comet is special, she knows it: this one is a sungrazer.

You do know this is very cruel, her mama says, appearing at last and standing beside her. I can't even drink that.

But you remember the taste?

Her face lights up. Maybe some biscuits next week?

I'll see what I can do.

Her granny's shaking her head, her arm linked through her mama's – they seem closer now than they ever did when they were alive – and Severine joins them, linking her arm through her mama's and kissing her cheek before resting her head on her shoulder. Welcome home, she says.

Severine?

She turns, surprised by the voice; she had forgotten François was going to be coming today.

She tries to brush away the voices as if she were swatting flies away from her face. Then she stops.

I was wrong, you know, her mama says, that time in the kitchen. I understand now. You don't lose people by listening. And you don't lose people by speaking, either.

So, standing at her mama's graveside with her mama's arm linked in her own, Severine tells François, adult to adult, that there are two ghosts standing beside her.

Back in his own flat, François opens bottles of beer for himself and Hélène. She's looking out of the window, watching the snow.

It's the coldest December on record, she says.

He looks out at the snow as well; sees its beauty, and thinks of ice. It makes him long for something he can't describe.

He hasn't told her about that conversation with his mama yet – he doesn't know what to make of it, the voices returning again after years of silence. He doesn't want to think about what it might mean.

He misses his grand-mère; perhaps he could have spoken to her about this. Although she wasn't one to put up with any nonsense.

Hélène's hand on his shoulder is startling, the warmth of her leg next to his helps bring him back to earth. Her lips do the rest.

He wakes again, startlingly early. It is getting to be a habit. He gets up without waking Hélène, creeps to the kitchen to stand at the window. The snow has settled during the night; the world has turned to a perfect untouched white. He breathes out.

Hélène wakes and knows that François is up again, looking out of the window, probably, but she doesn't follow him there. She's tried that before, and it doesn't make him any more likely to sleep through the night.

The NASA website says this comet will be difficult to see; it is bright, very bright, but it is too close to the sun. It is going to fly through the blazing heat of the sun's corona and it may not survive. Even if it does survive it may never come back, they say, and Severine guesses that the damage sustained would make it unpredictable.

Ten... nine... eight... shouts Antoine to Severine's mother – they are both acting like children today, playing hide-and-seek – and there's Great-Grandpa Paul-François crawling into the cupboard under the stairs.

Her granny presses her fingers to her lips.

Severine shakes her head, looks at her calendar with a smile that fades. She may not have very long, if this comet is heading towards death.

The view on her calendar is an iceberg floating in a clear sea.

She hasn't heard from François since she told him about the ghosts.

*

In the restaurant, François's hand slips. He curses; he is a fool – his mind was elsewhere.

He wraps a blue plaster around the cut. So unlike him, to let a knife slip.

It was the heat, he says to himself. He is no longer enjoying the heat.

For a second, a fraction of a second, he thinks about walking out. He could leave this job, travel the world, see temples and oceans, cook fishcakes and snake curry in places he has only seen on TV. But there are customers waiting and there are people in his life he cannot leave.

He needs to be more careful with his knife, that's all.

He carries on cooking.

At home, Hélène says she will kiss him better.

Then we could go out? she says. Sophie and Marc are in Le Baromètre. A few drinks?

Yes, he says, you're right. Let's go out.

Into the snow, she smiles.

He reaches for her hat on the side table, pulls it down over her eyes as she giggles.

Tall white candles twinkle in old-fashioned iron holders. The lights are low and warm, the voices around them animated. A dog stands by the fire, shakes his coat dry as snowflakes melt to water and scatter into drops of rain. It is busy, so François and Hélène share a chair, their arms around one another as they chat to their friends, telling stories of the restaurant and the troublesome customers, the manager whose face is redder by the day, the waitress having an affair with the head chef and how they are all pretending they have no idea it's going on.

You can't hide *passion*, laughs Hélène, her voice dipping play-fully at the end of her sentence, squeezing François's arm. And for the evening he forgets to worry about his mama and he forgets the claustrophobia of the kitchen. There are just his friends and Hélène and the heat of the bistro and the frosted glass and the falling snow outside. How perfect, he thinks, to live in a frozen white world.

On the way home he starts saying something he hadn't meant to say; he's not sure that he's ready to share it but the drinks have relaxed him and he feels so close to Hélène tonight.

Do you believe in ghosts? he says.

It is just the beginning of a conversation, for him, a way to start, but her reaction makes it the end of the conversation as well.

Don't be silly, she laughs – and she has a nice laugh, a young laugh, and it echoes between the tall buildings either side of the street. Are you feeling OK, chouchou? she says, still giggling, as she puts her hand on his forehead and he knows that he's not going to tell her about his mama.

Severine is trying not to sleep. Brigitte doesn't come in the day very often but she'll come in the night, Severine knows that.

You're looking for a way to help her? her granny says.

I'm trying…

You're a kind girl, you always were, says her granny. But how do you find someone when you don't even know their name?

The father?

Her granny shakes her head. There is no record of him having a son, even though he remarried.

What?

His first wife died, he remarried. We found her name in the parish records, your great-grandpa Paul-François and I. She had a strange-sounding name.

Yes?

I wrote it down, I think. I kept all my notes in the shed – they might still be there.

Why didn't you just tell me?

The answer's not there, Severine. I'm so sorry, I know what it's like – and I know she can't let it go – but you should. Brigitte's son is gone. And I think perhaps you should be thinking about François instead.

In the night the worry creeps up on Severine, not about the ghosts but about the living: that look on François's face. Was she wrong to tell him? Perhaps there are still some things that a mother should hide from her child. But she doesn't want to hide. She is a daughter, and a granddaughter, and many generations beyond that too; why should she have to choose, between her ghosts and her son? Just because the women in her family have a history of losing their children, doesn't mean it will happen to her.

She tries phoning him, of course, but she gets no answer and she doesn't leave a message. He will come for Sunday lunch, she thinks, like he always has. She will give him time, and gradually he will come to understand about the ghosts.

- - - - - - - -

THE WEDDING IS ON THE Sunday afternoon. They have sun, a glittering frost, a slight breeze, bouquets of bluebells and a photo that each of them will frame to remember: Adele and Neil, Conall and Róisín, in silver and dark blue. A second wedding for them both, there are no white dresses or confetti here; it is stars and comets, it is calm, and it is family.

Only an overheard phrase can obscure the beautiful night sky: He never even leaves the farm.

Did Liam reply to the invitation? Róisín asks her mum in a quiet moment, her arm slipping comfortably around her shoulder.

She shakes her head, just slightly, sadly. These days he stays away. We haven't seen him since last year. Should I have insisted?

Of course not. Róisín kisses her mum's head – she is a few inches taller than her mum now, she doesn't remember when that became the case.

I could phone?

No, don't worry. It was his choice to make.

I suppose so.

He was always stubborn, Róisín thinks. The last time she saw him he was leaving the village shop a few days before Christmas, three years ago. She was out with her mum – she started walking towards him to say hello but he turned away. It's been much longer than three years since she heard his voice.

She catches up with Keira; they wander over to the village green and sit on the bench, hands wrapped around their takeaway coffees for warmth. Keira has brought her some walnut cake. Róisín has a gift too, a small print, which she hands over with an embarrassed laugh.

Sorry it's not a full poster, she says. It was all I could fit in my case...

Keira unwraps it, claps her hands and grins, wide-eyed.

It's just a photo of the Horsehead Nebula, smiles Róisín.

It's beautiful!

I'm glad you like it.

And although Róisín doesn't ask, Keira mentions, in among the village gossip and news of the new cinema that might open in the next town, that no one has seen Liam for quite a while. After a moment of understanding, the conversation moves on to other things, and Róisín is grateful for that.

At dusk they stroll back through the village, arm in arm.

*

Driving out to the mountains, she spends a day walking with her mum, telling her about the people she knows in New York, the way the sun turns the windows of skyscrapers golden, the energy of the crowds that fill the streets with character. They pick early wild flowers to take home, arranging them in delicate glass vases along the windowsill when they return in the evening.

She helps Neil outside in the garden – they sand and varnish an old wooden bench and picnic table, ready for the spring – and she plays computer games like when she and Conall were young, not minding when she loses every level; winning and losing was never really the point.

She lies in bed, windows open to let in the cold, a hint of dew in the air, and thinks that perhaps she should go to the farm, but she doesn't think she would be welcome there. She reaches for her phone instead, dials the number that she still has, and waits as it rings out and clicks over to an answerphone without a message. She would have liked to hear his voice, she realises as she hangs up the phone, but he has made it clear that he doesn't want to see her. She tries to get to sleep; tomorrow she is going to Bayeux.

Liam counts seven days on his calendar, seven days since he last drove to the supermarket that has opened outside the town and exchanged some words with the teenager working the till. Hello. Thank you. That's OK, I can manage on my own.

He can still see something in the way people look at him, as if they've heard the stories and want to know if they are true. Sometimes he wants to tell them that he did nothing wrong. Most of the time he just doesn't want to be reminded at all.

He counts the tins in his cupboard, the plates in his sink. He washes them carefully and puts them away.

The world is busy, he thinks. That is all.

It has been a long time since anyone else was in his home.

He hears a crash, and looks outside at the latest broken tile that has fallen from the roof. Another thing he must try to fix.

The comet is still there, in the sky. It hurts his eyes to look at it. But it will be destroyed in the sun, this one – he heard that on the radio. This is its one chance, its only chance to see what it came to see. Perhaps it's up there waiting for it to happen.

He remembers something Róisín once told him about Comet West. It had an orbital period of two hundred thousand years – when they saw it, the prediction was that its next visit to earth would be two hundred thousand years in the future – but no one knew that as it approached the sun it would break. It split into two pieces, so they thought at first, but looking closer they could see it was many, too many to count. This one comet, one amazing comet that he saw in the daytime sky when he was a child, had got too close; had fractured into pieces that would never be whole again.

He goes outside at sunrise, picks up the pieces of the broken tiles that have fallen from the roof – more seem to be coming down every day. He doesn't rush, and he doesn't hesitate. There are birds awake already; the comet seems stationary overhead. It's been such a long time since he saw the sky change, he's given up believing that it can.

He looks at the roof, knows that he needs to go up to see what is causing all the damage, besides the ice and the rain and the time. Perhaps it has just been there too long, he thinks. He walks round to the ladder propped up against the back of the house, raises the extension as high as the steps will go. When he reaches the top of the ladder, he can stretch to the attic window, pull himself up by the frame, make it to the roof. The patches where tiles are missing look bare and vulnerable. He can see a pool of water by the chimney, where one of the leaks must be coming in. So much to fix. So much he has never been able to fix.

From the roof he can see the whole of the farm – the cowsheds, now empty, the barn with its door hanging off, fields that are turning to mud, old fence posts leaning over in the wind like old men. Not a single person in sight. He's not afraid of falling, he realises as he looks around the farm that he was unable to save, lifting another loose tile from the roof and balancing it neatly beside him. And as he watches the scene that doesn't change, that seems frozen in its decay, he thinks that, perhaps, it would be good to fall.

EVERY SUNDAY FRANÇOIS GOES FOR lunch, without reminding Severine that he is coming; every Sunday she has lunch prepared, with a wine chilled or given space to breathe in advance. Every Sunday he checks the table and since that day, after he noticed the comet, there have been two places laid, as there should be, not six, as if she is losing her mind.

He thinks perhaps she was just missing her mother, or was being metaphorical, or needed some time away.

We could go on a holiday somewhere?

She scoffs, lifts a tray of roast potatoes but it slips from her hand and clatters to the floor.

The next day he buys tickets for them both to go to Iceland. It will be the first holiday outside of France they've had since he was a boy.

What makes you imagine I would go away now, she says, when I've never done it before?

Everyone needs a holiday, he says quietly, gently. He was trying to be kind.

If you want to go away then you go, she says, you don't need my permission.

Come on, Severine, don't be like that.

I can't leave the ghosts.

There's no such thing as ghosts!

She looks angry for a second, angry at his words or the volume with which he spoke them. He didn't mean to shout but this *is* ridiculous.

Severine sees her son's expression and the guilt hits her. All his life, she has been putting the ghosts first.

Are we having a fight? she says, trying to soothe him with a smile, and François sees his mama's face return to what he knows. I'm sorry.

I only got the tickets for us to go together. Both of us. It will be so different – a different world.

He holds his hands wide, to try and show her how much more there is for her to see, but to Severine his palms moving further apart seem like mother and son, with increasing distance in between. She shakes away the thought.

Try this wine, she says. I think it will be perfect with our boeuf bourguignon.

He wants to put his arm around her, but doesn't know how.

Moving to the window, he looks out through the frosty glass to see a woman standing in the street, looking straight at him. It is a strange feeling, a jolt of recognition stronger than scent. But then she is turning, holding a mobile phone to her ear, and the spell is broken and she moves away.

Later, Severine is pensive, rocking on her armchair of hand-carved wood.

Maybe you are right, she says. You should go travelling; go anywhere you want. Go see the world. I've always thought you should see the world.

I like it here.

That's what he says, but what he's thinking is that he couldn't leave, not when he doesn't understand what's wrong with her.

I always used to want to travel, she says, wistful now. That was my plan, you know, to travel around the world. So, if you want—

Why on earth would I want to leave? he says. I love it here. I want to live in Paris, near you.

He decides that he will get a refund for the tickets. It wasn't for him, this holiday, she is the one who needs to get away. Besides, somehow he knew it wouldn't be that easy.

⸺⸺⸺

RÓISÍN CHECKS IN TO A B&B near her old apartment in Bayeux, overlooking the garden where families used to camp out for the night – she's sure she remembers seeing that happen, years ago. She meets her old research group in the bar where they'd said goodbye to her, though it is different now, of course, extended into a pretty terrace with outdoor heaters where they can sit in the evening's low sun. Her old boss is greying now; colleagues show her pictures of their children in between talking about the new deep-field telescope, observations promising planets that hint at life – there could be so much life, she says, out there. She feels like the universe is filled with it.

On the way back to the B&B she finds herself standing outside the garden, a locked gate between her and the trees and what sounds like a stream. She tests the strength of the lowest bar, climbs onto it and swings her legs over to the other side. She's not sure why she's doing it, but she finds herself slipping off her shoes and socks, walking barefoot on the grass to feel the damp stems soft between her toes. And she was right – there is a stream behind the trees. The water glitters over pebbles in the moonlight and she dips her feet in, gasping at the cold, but liking it, following the flow until she comes to a clearing, lies out on the grass as water freezes on her skin and stares at the sky until she can see all the colours of the Earth in its shine.

Creeping back to her B&B in the early hours, taking the stairs two at a time to try to avoid their creak, she feels young again. A smile plays about her lips.

In the morning she goes to the university where they talk about new collaborations, sharing data across the ocean, and it feels wonderfully easy to be connected to all these people. New ideas spark as they talk: a new grant the research team could apply for, a postdoc who wants to join her in New York, a month's research they could share in Hawaii next year. Promises to be in touch are given, kisses on both cheeks exchanged. Ah, see – they joke with her, their accents strong and lilting – you are French too, you are one of us.

She calls in to the local patisserie for lunch, smiles at a display of cakes all colours of the rainbow: pineapple and blueberry, red velvet and peppermint with pure white icing. Sips her coffee and lets the flavours linger as she compares the tastes of different countries, different continents. Her favourite changes with her mood, but right now she can't imagine anything better than this.

She finds herself walking through the streets of Bayeux, reminding herself of the architecture she had loved, of the way the canals play hide-and-seek through the town, and she looks up next to a house on the outskirts that she'd forgotten about, though now she sees it again it feels familiar. There is a small fence around the front garden, a row of birds perched neatly along its top.

Inside a woman is laughing in the kitchen, while a young man leaves her side to walk to the window. She hadn't meant to stare in, but he looks back out at her. It is strange, the way his arm almost rises in a wave as if he knew her, the way she feels her smile grow.

The sound startles her as the birds take off from the fence in unison. A rush of flapping wings and synthetic notes: a mobile phone. Her mobile phone. She reaches into her pocket, doesn't know why her mum would be phoning her, or why her mum's voice sounds like it is breaking.

What's wrong?

She turns from the window.

Mum, what is it?

Liam, she says, it's Liam. I'm so sorry. He's…

Róisín is already running, away from the house that felt both foreign and familiar, and away from the man inside.

FRANÇOIS MISSES A SUNDAY LUNCH, can't face another argument. The last time he was there she barely saw him; too busy talking to thin air, only looking up to invite him to join the imaginary conversation. It took him back to when he was a child, remembering how it felt to be unnoticed by his mama, and worse, not knowing what was wrong or how to make it stop. So instead he spends the day waiting for Severine to call. She doesn't.

Hélène makes sausages with roasted tomato and rosemary, one of the recipes he has taught her; she is kind enough not to ask why he has skipped Sunday lunch with his mama.

He doesn't mention that it was his mama's recipe she has just cooked. But he phones the restaurant, offers to come in for an extra shift tonight.

When François doesn't arrive, Severine makes the ghosts wait for their lunch, and they sit impatiently around the table chattering about how she forgot to place the vegetable order this week – forgot to open the shop altogether on Thursday. Brigitte is the only one who doesn't talk all the time, and Severine has come to appreciate that. She catches her eye over the table and Brigitte looks almost kind as she asks: What's happened to your son, Severine?

Severine feels a tugging at her heart. It is strange, the way her words sink in and their meaning expands, the emotion of them suddenly binding the women together as she shakes her head and says: What happened to your son, Brigitte? And she knows she has to go looking; not for François – if he wanted to come for lunch he would come – but for the child that was stolen. She can't force her own son to understand, or to believe her, but perhaps she can find another son who is lost.

She abandons lunch – or rather serves it up to the ghosts and leaves them to it – and she starts in the shed, throwing boxes and suitcases out of the way until she finds her granny's old notes. It's not enough, so she goes straight to the church; running now, suddenly convinced that she has to find the answer. They're surprised to see her, though less so when she insists it is the parish records she wants to visit, and not the service.

Every table is loud and laughing in the restaurant and there's a queue out of the door. In this weather, what are they doing, go home – they laugh in the kitchen – but secretly they are enjoying themselves. All François can think about though is the heat and the noise and the smell and the heat, it's impossible to think about anything else and that's what he needed tonight; so it's hardly surprising he doesn't realise he's being called from the door. He's working, he can't stop; everything is perfectly timed, stepping out would ruin it. But there's that voice again.

François, it's important.

He stops what he's doing, looks up.

François!

His mama is standing in the restaurant kitchen, shouting to him.

The head chef glares at him – members of the public are not supposed to be back here, and besides, she looks a little crazy, her hair and clothes drenched from the snow, a puddle of melted ice already forming on the floor.

I've had an idea, she's smiling, I had to share it with you.

Mama – he never calls her mama, what does it mean that he's calling her mama instead of Severine? – what are you talking about?

One of the ghosts, she begins.

The embarrassment hits him unexpectedly, a rush of blood to his face; everyone will hear this.

And then she's talking to other people too, people who aren't here; she's looking over her shoulder, laughing at God knows what, arguing with an old man who isn't there. This is the worst he's ever seen it.

Severine.

There was a baby, she's saying, and he was stolen, and I think I know what happened to him.

Mama.

She looks straight up at him.

He takes her by the arm.

There's a quiet cafe, round the corner, he says. Come on. This way.

He wraps his coat around her shoulders, gently guides her out of the kitchen and towards the street, feels his back burning where every set of eyes are staring at her – and staring at him.

She lays out a family tree on the table, with little heaps of salt and pepper for people and toothpicks connecting the branches. He encourages her to drink some peppermint tea. It is quiet here, at least; that is a relief.

Do you see? she says.

He looks at the mess on the table, remembers a night when he was a boy, when she dragged him out of bed in the middle of the night and said they were running away to Paris.

Severine, he says, taking her hand, Mama, I think there's something wrong. I... I think we should talk to a doctor.

You're not listening to me. Brigitte, she had a child.

There is no Brigitte. She doesn't exist, Mama, this is nonsense.

It is *not* nonsense.

And her face is different; an expression of stubbornness he remembers from when he was a boy.

He runs his hand through his hair, tries to find the words to make her see the reality.

But just as suddenly she is back, as he knows her. I'm sorry, she says. I interrupted your evening – as if she's only just realised he was at work – you should go back to the restaurant, she smiles. I'll get the next train home. Back to Bayeux.

As she stands up, she stumbles against the table and the family tree scatters, black and white salt and pepper falling to the floor like ash.

Then she stops in mid-stride, turns back for a minute with sadness in her eyes.

You missed Sunday lunch, she says. You were missed at Sunday lunch.

François desperately wants to say he's sorry. He hadn't meant to hurt her, he'd just wanted to avoid a scene – this one, in fact – until he'd worked out how to deal with it. But then she changes again; never mind, she says, never mind, everyone else was there, and she turns and walks towards the door.

François reaches for a serviette, starts to clean up the mess then stops and rests his head in his hands. Looking up he sees Severine open the door, step outside, and rush off down the street without looking back.

He walks home that evening through the melting streets of Paris – snow turning to slush, sheets of ice into puddles – and tries to let the changing beauty of his city distract him from his thoughts. There is a comet in the sky, but tonight he will not stand outside in wonder.

They hadn't teased him when he got back to the kitchen, though he was expecting it; they had been concerned. Chefs are usually more raucous than that – all rough language and rough skin. That's how you know when something is really wrong, he thinks to himself, when people who usually prefer to goad offer kindness.

He doesn't know what is happening to his mama.

Later, Severine sits straight up in bed and puts the light on, even though Brigitte hates it.

I've had an idea, she says.

An idea about what?

What happened to your son.

There is a pause before Brigitte replies.

He is alive?

He died five hundred years ago. But he might have lived beyond that night, I think.

Brigitte is still, her face lit by the moonlight.

Great-Grandpa Paul-François begins, describing their arrival at the old chapel in Bayeux, sixty years ago. How they went to the ar-chives, down in the baptistery, found records barely legible in faded ink and misspelled scribbles.

I was the one who spotted it, chimes in her granny. There was a second marriage, to Elyn Enynimolan, 1459.

Brigitte's skin is flickering now like the embers of a fire, threatening to catch light, hissing in the breeze that shouldn't be there – you told me that before, she says.

They did, says Severine. But did you know Elyn had a son?

Severine braces herself for the rush of flame and anger that accompanies Brigitte's jealousy, but this time it doesn't come. Brigitte is staring at her, waiting.

There is no birth record for her son, Severine continues. And there's no other mention of Elyn Enynimolan here. But I looked up the name, and it's Irish – not French.

So what?

In Ireland they've started putting all their church records online, says Severine, glancing at her granny. The others couldn't travel to keep searching, but I didn't need to. I found a mention of her, Elyn, in a parish register from the west. She's down as Elyn Enynimolan *vidua*. She was a widow. And it says she had a son. Áed Enynimolan, born 1456.

Brigitte sits quietly for a moment, her hand outstretched to stop anyone else from speaking.

Her child was born before she was married?

Or it was never her child in the first place.

What did she do with my son?

Severine turns to face the ghost.

I've not been able to find out what happened to him yet. But I've thought about it, and my guess is that he stayed in Ireland. Elyn was his mother, as far as he knew, so Ireland would have become his home.

Brigitte lets the information sink in.

But we still don't really know what happened, she says.

We think he survived.

Brigitte is silent now. She had always hoped that, somehow, they would find her family – or her family would find her again. If only she had more time; another generation or two. Her silence is interrupted by the phone ringing, insistently, before going quiet again.

Oh, Severine, says Brigitte – and Severine looks up, expecting more questions about Ireland. Instead she says: What is going on with François?

Severine and her granny and Great-Grandpa Paul-François all look over to the phone that she has been ignoring since she got home from the restaurant.

He thinks I am mad, she says, laughing as if it is ridiculous, although the ghosts don't laugh with her. And then she turns serious again. It is pushing us apart.

Her granny and her mother lock eyes, move closer to one another.

So, I'll do what I have to do. I will keep him away from you, she says, and you away from him. Besides, the comet is fading – the ghosts look up to the sky, almost as if they had forgotten they needed to leave – so I'll see you next time. And in the meantime, I'll try to make things better with François.

And once they are gone, she thinks, she has to make things better with François, because soon he will be the only member of her family who is left.

- - - - - - - -

THREE DAYS AFTER LIAM'S FUNERAL Róisín boards a flight back to New York. Being at home was only making her feel worse so maybe she needs to be far away.

They have run out of wine on the plane. She swears. She is full of anger and it has nowhere else to go.

In the queue at passport control there is a family, a mother and a father, two children. The youngest is held in her mother's arms, toddler tears from before she joined the queue still patterning her face. The other, a boy, sees her staring, tugs on his father's sleeve, who puts a hand on his shoulder, pulls him forward to face straight ahead. Róisín wraps her arms around her stomach. Her bag falls to the floor. She can't stand up, she's bent double, sobs shake her body. More strangers join the queue.

Róisín doesn't want to look at the sky any more and she's given up trying to understand the Earth. She imagines going back to that day when she first left home, when she saw the whole universe between two palms and imagined it would be beautiful. What crap.

She climbs up to the roof that night, to her terraced roof garden above her new apartment, but she doesn't bother to scan the sky. She just wanted to get away from all the people crowding the streets; New York is all about the crowds, the people. She used to love that, but today it made her want to scream. She stays there all night, just sitting under the emptiness until, in the early hours of the morning, she gives a silent gasp, a dry retch, as something that was a part of her is torn away.

At coffee, the other postdocs and lecturers, students and professors all talk about galaxies, spectra, telescopes. She cannot care. She can hardly listen. What does it matter, that galaxy formation happened slower than we thought, or faster? How can she have spent her life looking at distant things too far away to hold?

We didn't think you'd be back so soon, someone says.

She looks up, disorientated. Stares at his blue eyes, his pale green shirt; she has no words any more.

There is an arm placed around her shoulder, someone trying to take her hand on the arm of the chair. She is unaware of the tears cascading down her face.

Comet Lovejoy is nearly gone, visible only through a telescope. It survived its journey through the corona, but it's not the same now as it was; its shape is distorted, its path irregular. This is a comet that will fly to the outer reaches of the solar system and never find its way back. She can't say that she blames it.

Standing in Dr Joshi's office Róisín hands over a neat white envelope containing her resignation.

Why on earth? says her boss. He is a little offended.

I can't find any answers in the sky.

That depends on your questions.

Yes.

Give it some time. I understand your cousin...

I'm sorry, she says. She needs to get out of here – she's afraid she's going to cry again.

OK. Although... well, if you're sure?

A nod; she manages that. And:

Thank you.

Do you know where you'll go?

I don't know. Somewhere remote. Isolated. I...

There is no need to explain to this man, who will have employed a replacement within the week, that finally she understands the need to be alone. It took Liam's death for her to understand his life.

I'm sorry. I just can't be here right now, she says.

As she leaves the room she blinks and rubs, desperately, at her eyes. It makes no difference.

Beyond the buildings, which are ornate and magnificent, the sun is too bright to illuminate the world; it drowns it out. Róisín holds her hand up to her face, tries to shield her eyes but can't. She needs darkness. She needs a wilderness away from people and light and hope, where the sky will get truly dark and her breath will freeze. She looks up, one more time, but she knows it is no use. There is nothing left in the sky and the ground beneath her feet is broken.

1957

Comet Arend–Roland

A brother and sister scamper around the house as their mother prepares dinner in the kitchen; frying aubergine in garlic olive oil and searing fish in butter, singing to herself, swinging her dress in time to the tune. Beside her, the ghost of her father chatters about the day she was born, reliving the story of the storm that cleared the air after a war, that left a piercing blue dawn to greet a wailing newborn into the world.

She is having so much fun she doesn't hear the door open as her children take their games outside; they are boisterous, these youngsters, never do as they're told – fearless of the world, as it should be. The sound of the traffic, still unfamiliar to her, doesn't reach inside the house. No sounds make it into the kitchen until the scream and by then it is too late.

*

Aubergine burns to black in the minutes that follow, mirrored in black fabric and black skies in the days that follow that until, one morning, Antoine appears at his mother's bed.

Why won't she play with me any more? he says, talking about his sister, and his mother kneels by the bed and tries not to let her son see her tears.

Downstairs, his sister sits, drawing swirls of dark colour in her sketch pad, and she doesn't look up when he calls her name – Ariane – doesn't notice when he does star jumps in front of her, or tries to pull off her socks. As weeks go by, their mother watches as Antoine slowly accepts that his sister will not see him, and she slowly accepts that look on her daughter's face when she hears her talking to herself.

What are you doing, Mama? she says – the first words her daughter has spoken since the accident – and when she replies that she is talking to Antoine her daughter stares at her, says simply, no you're not.

He's here, if you want to see him, she tries for one last time.

No Mama, she says, he is gone now. He is dead.

2016

Comet PanSTARRS

FRANÇOIS FINDS SEVERINE CROUCHED UNDER the desk in the old study upstairs, a finger pressed to her smiling lips, as if she is playing hide-and-seek.

Mama, I brought courgettes.

Shhh! Her hands fly about her face for a moment.

Is there a mosquito?

Ha!

He knows there is no mosquito; she is seeing the ghosts. It is happening again, just like he has been dreading it would for the past five years.

What are you doing under there?

Hiding from Antoine, she giggles, he wanted to play a game. Then, more seriously: I think he gets lonely, being the youngest.

François can't bring himself to say what needs to be said, but he thinks it – he has been thinking it since it happened before. She needs some help, and he needs help to know what kind. There is something wrong with her mind. She starts all of a sudden, noticing he is there, or re-noticing it.

You brought courgettes, she smiles, begins to stand up. He reaches forward for her arm, helps her to her feet even though she is up before he's made a difference. She's had her hair cut again, short like an actress from the sixties and it suits her.

It's good to see you, François.

And you, Severine.

She stands on tiptoe to ruffle his hair.

Such a serious man, she says with a shake of her head, reaching for the courgettes. Shall we cook together tonight?

He puts his arm around her shoulders, and they head for the kitchen.

They play music while they cook, sip wine as they slice shallots and fry courgettes in olive oil. Severine sings along to the CD, and François can stop worrying for a while. It is always like this; just as he begins to think about speaking up, insisting she see a doctor, his mama switches back to herself and he lets the moment pass. He wonders if he is a coward.

You should go out, he says. What about signing up for an evening class? Or you could try that new restaurant on Rue Saint-Malô.

Promoting the competition?

They're local.

Or maybe you're just trying to get me away from the house.

Let the past be, he says, live your life now.

My life is more full than you know.

Her smile makes it look like she has a secret boyfriend, a secret hobby, a secret identity, but it doesn't last. Her life is full, yes, but not in the way she'd imagined it would be – not in the way she has ever wished for him. She has suggested, a few times, that he take a holiday, go travelling the way he always wanted, but he hasn't gone – it's almost as if he's keeping an eye on her.

Outside, it has begun to snow. It pulls François to the window in amazement; snow in the middle of summer! But no, it is just petals from the apple tree in the courtyard. Most fall to the ground; one settles on the windowpane, gravity defied.

He turns away, returns to the kitchen to see his mama has started playing hide-and-seek again, trying to squeeze under the table while the courgettes are burning.

When he leaves she tells him to give Hélène her love, then realises her mistake – I am sorry, François, I forgot for a moment. I...

It's OK, Severine. He reaches down to kiss her on the cheek then walks to the bus stop.

His flat, when he reaches it, is not just empty of people but somehow, oddly, empty of his past as well. He's not heartbroken – they met when they were very young and young people change, he understands that – but he feels sad. Hélène was his friend, and he didn't want to lose his friend. He puts on the kettle and, looking at the phone, decides that he won't. But he does have an appointment to make in the morning, and it is not something he can put off any longer.

I'm just curious, says François, as the doctor looks at him with concern.

To generalise, early-onset dementia would be highly unlikely – *highly* unlikely – in anyone under the age of thirty. But everyone is different; every mind is different. There are tests...

Oh no, I don't think... I don't mean me.

The doctor holds out a hand, in mid-air, as if to soothe or create space for him to keep talking, François is not sure which. He stops talking, waits for more information to be offered.

It can affect people in their fifties, occasionally forties. The sooner it's diagnosed, the more chance we have to help. But, it could be other things. You could talk to a psychiatrist, if you want?

He wonders how that conversation would go with Severine.

The carnival arrives in Bayeux. The ringmaster, a younger man than before, picks a plot close to the river and where they can be viewed from the bridge – he wants the town to come to him, and he gets what he wants. There are fairground rides, a hammer that can make a bell peal, a big tent where acrobats will fly and fire-eaters swallow fire.

François laughs when he hears his mama's message, her voice so giddy, like a child: The carnival has come to town! Come this weekend, yes?

He arranges the duck à l'orange on the plate like a carnival scene, although he tells no one he has done that – they would think he was insane.

Hélène comes round to collect the rest of her stuff, some clothes she had forgotten and posters that were up on the walls. François opens a bottle of red and they talk for a while about her new place, the restaurant, their friends, then a new album that has been re-leased by a band they both love. It's friendly and they relax into their conversation; there are no hard feelings here. By the time the relationship had ended, they had both already left.

How's your mama doing? she asks, and that is when François feels the difference, the regret.

She's fine, he says, knowing that somewhere in between being together and breaking up he had kept things to himself that he should have been able to share, and that now it is too late.

Severine waits for him out in the street, the door closed and locked. She's excited and she wants to get to the carnival before dark; she's wearing her pleated skirt and lipstick. She feels young today.

François buys her a toffee apple, and one for himself, only getting halfway through before it has become too sweet and he has to drop it in the bin they pass on the way to the big top.

He watches his mama's face as she lights up, covers her eyes, laughs at the magician and the acrobats, at the old man in the top hat and tails who looks like a relic from a lost time, a less cynical generation. François can see how most of the tricks are performed, but he keeps that to himself; besides, it is beautiful to watch, the bright colours of the performers, the bold red of the ringmaster's cummerbund, the glow of the candles at the front of the stage. Severine is enjoying herself, and he hasn't seen her laugh like this for years. Then she turns away from him, seems to forget that he is there at all, and starts talking to the empty seat beside her. People turn. They stare. They avoid her as they leave the big top at the end of the show. He gives her shoulders a squeeze.

It is not to be cruel that he says it; it is because he loves her, and because he is scared of what might happen if he doesn't act now.

I made an appointment for you, for Tuesday, he says, his arm still around her shoulders. I'll come with you, and we'll see what the doctor thinks about the ghosts. OK?

Severine slumps under his arm, but she doesn't pull away and, as if realising that she has spent the last half-hour speaking to a hallucination, she silently nods her consent.

The ghosts come at a price, Severine has known that for a long time.

She has always tried to tell him her truth, she thinks, but he doubts her anyway; he is a different person to her. That is OK. Perhaps it means that he will lead a different sort of life. The thought makes her happy again, optimistic about the future. She stops, suddenly, at an old-fashioned ride, a small train for children that takes you through ghost villages in the Wild West and jungles of tigers and bears.

Shall we go on an adventure, François? she says.

He smiles, a little sadly, and buys them both a ticket.

THERE IS A LINE IN the introduction to the handbook of the British Antarctic Survey: unlocking the past, understanding the present. It goes on after that, something to do with the future and exploration, but it's not the future that Róisín's really concerned about. She's not sure which part of the sweeping statement she is drawn to but when she reads it she thinks she is doing the right thing. This is what she needs. Somewhere wild and inhospitable and brutal where she can try to understand what has happened, and what is happening, and what it is she has been searching for since she was too young to know she was searching for anything.

There will be tests, they tell her. Physical, psychological, survival. There is something appealing in that. She would like to be told that she can survive.

Róisín tries to be logical, when she thinks about her life. There are some things that she knows, and she is glad that she knows them – the orbit of Halley's comet around the sun, the tilt in the angle of the Earth's axis, the way to move from place to place, orbiting home, never resting long enough to burn. She wants to tell herself that she doesn't know why Liam chose to climb to the roof of his family's farm at dawn. The days spent trawling through that farmhouse – once where she lived, too, but not for long enough to start using the word home, for her it had remained the farm – they hadn't helped. For days she searched through drawers and cupboards, room to room, the dusty attic space empty but for a disused water tank that made her ache with its futility. There were drawings, childish drawings, of the farm, like he had drawn when he was a little boy: stick men and cartoonish animals. There were bills too, and a second mortgage she had been unaware of, followed by an hour or so of anger that he hadn't told her, that he had chosen to hide so much of himself and pretend that her arrival had made everything all right. And she does wonder – of course she does – if it would have been the same had she stayed.

But under all that, there is perhaps a part of her that knows we are too small to matter. Nothing happened, that's the thing. The universe carried on, the comets kept coming – it made no difference. A life and a death made no difference. Perhaps that is why she's frozen.

Planets are not born. What a clear-cut word that is – to imagine something is not and then, a moment later, it is. No, that is not how planets come about.

It starts with a death. A violent supernova somewhere as a star collapses under its own weight, becoming denser until it can no longer support its existence. The burst of radiation it emits can eclipse an entire galaxy, that's how loud it screams. And as it does, all those elements of iron and silicon and oxygen and carbon, the building blocks of planets and life, are thrown out into the universe to drift and search and become molecular clouds where new stars begin to burn.

But that is not the formation of a planet, that's just how to create the components that make planets possible. Now fast-forward.

Out of that debris, eventually, a star begins to burn, and under its gravity collects the leftover debris of the supernova; that which was expelled, that has been floating, meaningless, through a universe composed almost entirely of empty space. And the debris comes together, forming rocks and swirling angry gas, distant ice planets and, occasionally, an ideally placed one that is not too light and not too dark. But at the heart of it, she knows, there can be a stellar black hole where once there was a star, a nothingness from which no light can escape; the remnants of a scream at the instant of death from a star that had taken in too much, and had to let it all go.

At the doctor's she watches, passive, as the red of her blood travels, unexpectedly slowly, down the thin tube connected to a vial that will be sent away for tests. She doesn't cringe as the needle slips into her arm, as injection after injection immunise her against diphtheria, meningitis, yellow fever, tuberculosis, hepatitis A and B. So many ways to be saved against what might hurt you, but no way to be saved from what has already happened.

The conference is held at a large red sandstone country house, arched windows and a pillared courtyard and landscaped gardens – it feels as far from Antarctica as the human race gets. It is beautiful though, the sunlight striking off the tones of rose and maroon in the bricks, the windows glinting like rock pools.

Inside they watch black-and-white films of a continent a world and half a century away. Sled-dog training videos that seem to creak and slip with the ice itself, presentations about the scientific research that takes place – meteorology and biology and chemistry, atmospheric sciences and geophysics. As she listens she thinks of the comet approaching, brightening, speeding through the sky. It will be dimming when she begins her journey but another will be on its way, coming to meet it. They'll catch each other's eyes for a moment of understanding, of completeness, before PanSTARRS flees to the outer reaches of the solar system and Comet Tuttle–Giacobini–Kresák is left behind, orbiting a sun whose brightness makes its eyes sting and burn.

SEVERINE WAKES JUST BEFORE DAWN, frost creeping over her goosebumped skin as her curtains billow in the wind. It is snowing, it must be. She gets up to close the window but it is shut, the sky is clear with only a hint at the sunrise to the east. Her granny comes to stand beside her, places a hand on her temple. Severine's head has been aching badly; she always suffered from migraines but these days it seems more determined, the pain will not fade, nor will the thoughts of all the possible lives she did not lead.

What now, Granny? What happens now?

She shivers, and her granny disappears.

Where have you gone?

She knows her voice sounds desperate, that she would look desperate if anyone could see her, with her pale blue nightdress blowing in a breeze that does not exist.

She doesn't hear the door open, even though it creaks, even though to François the creak is so loud it sounds like the house is sighing.

I'm here, Mama.

What?

I heard you shouting.

She wants to say she's sorry, but he is not the family she was calling out to.

I'm here, he says, again.

He puts his arm around her and sits next to her on the bed.

I'll always be here.

It is a promise made out of kindness and it scares Severine to her core. Suddenly she is not afraid of losing her son any more, she is afraid of what he might lose.

She looks up to see her granny has returned and is smiling at her, sadly, from the end of the bed.

Shall I make you some chocolat chaud? says François, and Severine looks at him with the kind of gratitude that mingles with surprise. That is something the ghosts never do, she thinks, and she is flooded with guilt for all the ways she has been absent in all the years she has refused to leave.

François has rented out the spare room in his apartment in Paris. He has to go back on Monday, but this weekend he's decided to stay with Severine, to make sure she's OK.

He has been at Hélène's new place, though he doesn't tell Severine that. Hélène listens without offering advice; there is something about that that he finds more helpful than all the advice in the world. She's renting a two-bed over in the west of Paris, a small top-floor apartment that feels more like home than his own. Hélène could always do that, make a place feel like somewhere you'd want to spend your life. From the kitchen window, if you look hard, you can see the Seine dancing in the moonlight, flickers of silver as the stars catch the fleeting waves on an otherwise still river.

The last time he was there he stayed till past eleven, and they listened to Coeur de Pirate as they smoked and he felt the worry drain out of him. When he leant his head back he thought, for a moment, that she might do the same; that a peaceful break-up and a lasting friendship might actually be the way to find someone who loves you. But she didn't copy his gesture, just smiled kindly and offered him some peppermint tea – she never told him it was getting late but somehow he knew that it was time to be leaving. As he stood in the door she asked about his flatmate: How is it working out?

She knew him from university, their student days that already seem far away.

It's good, François said, easy, no bother.

And he kissed her cheeks, one by one, before turning to walk home across the sleepy city.

How is work? asks Severine during Sunday lunch.

His work is fine, is always fine. He is a good chef, although he'd like to change the menu more often. He feels like he is grilling sea bass in his sleep.

And Paris? Are you happy in Paris?

Why are you asking, Mama?

I don't know why you stay here, in France, she says. There's no need. When you were little you always wanted to travel. Why haven't you gone?

We'll see what happens on Tuesday, he says, and for once Severine looks him straight in the eye.

Tuesday is about why *I* haven't gone, she says, and my regrets are mine to deal with. The question I was asking was about you.

When she sleeps, he stays up, lights a cigarette in her living room even though she doesn't like smoking, pulls open the back door to the garden to let some fresh air in. He wonders what happened to that old suitcase he found in the shed as a boy, so full of another life that never was.

He's not sure why he's so nostalgic these days.

But he finds himself outside, faced with a locked padlock, a cheap thing more suited to children's toy suitcases than a shed built by his great-great-grandfather. When he pulls it comes off easily in his hand.

He holds the torch in front of him, minding his step; it is dark tonight, the clouds are dense. The case is easy to spot, lying on its side in the far corner of the shed. Pulling it to the middle of the floor he undoes the zip, noting the fabric of the case is damp, the smell slightly musty. Inside are some old clothes of his mama's, some of his from when he was a boy, and on top – though he doesn't know how it got there – is his favourite toy: a tiger, its wide eyes unblinking and shiny like buttons, parts of its fur threadbare from where he used to carry it everywhere, before the day when they had gone to the airport and the night when they had come silently back; before he had thrown it away, along with his belief they would go on an adventure, and Severine had rescued it again, in the hope that one day he still would.

Severine chats to the doctor while he takes her blood pressure, asks her to stand on some scales, checks her age; I'm not fifty-five yet, she exclaims. Asks her questions about family history – that makes her smile. She knows it's silly that she's here but François was so insistent. Maybe once she's been cleared of any mental or physical instability he'll stop worrying about her and go see the world.

You know I've only once left France, she tells him – imagine that!

He says he is going to test for pupil reaction, and that means shining a light into her eyes.

I used to want to travel, she says, when I was younger. I even tried to run away, when François was little, but you see, I would have missed them too much.

He tells her that she seems to be in excellent health, but he's going to check her reflexes, her muscle strength.

My family are all here, she says, and I was just talking to my granny and she says – you're not going to like this – she says the only times she had to see a doctor were when she was born and when she died.

The doctor has turned away from her and is making notes on a computer screen. Can you follow my finger with your eyes? he says, and so she does.

I would like to take a blood sample as well – would that be OK?

And she nods, but as the red of her blood moves, surprisingly slowly, from inside her elbow along the thin plastic tube and into the glass vial waiting to be sealed and labelled and sent away for some kind of check-up, she imagines a different version of the world. A world where blood is so thick it cannot travel, a world so desolate that a mirage can become a family. A world where she made the wrong choice.

Mrs Oquidon?

Severine.

Severine, I'm finished. You can pull your sleeve down now.

Having avoided doctors for most of my life, she tells him with a smile, though her legs are shaking, I must say you weren't too bad after all.

François calls his mama on Tuesday evening, but the phone goes to answerphone and he doesn't leave a message. If there was something to say, she would answer – she would say it to him. She doesn't keep secrets from him, he tells himself; she hasn't done that since he was a child. And even then she was no good at it.

His flatmate doesn't come home that night. François supposes he must have met a girl. He can imagine that happening; Stefan is charming and good company, more chatty than François these days.

He is feeling strange tonight because Severine has seen the doctor, but that is not a bad thing; it was the right thing to do. If there's something wrong, it can be fixed. If there is nothing wrong, he can stop worrying.

He tells himself he has no reason to fear loneliness, but it doesn't stop him from feeling suddenly, terribly alone.

François finds Severine in a pensive mood; she opens the door as if she is resigned to a fate he doesn't know about.

Is something wrong, Mama?

I know there is, when you call me that.

It is only the absence of music that makes him realise how often it is playing.

Why is the house so quiet, Mama?

She passes him the letter from the doctors.

I knew those doctors were bad news, she says, with a smile that turns into a shrug.

François feels the world dissolving.

I thought, if anything, it was my stomach, she says, I used to get these pains, occasionally...

She shakes her head, not wanting to tell him of the pain she felt when she missed the ghosts.

But they tell me I am wrong.

She takes his hand, wanting to comfort him.

I am sorry, François. They think it's in my brain.

THERE'S A MAN IN THE advanced first-aid course who seems to love it – getting to dress wounds, splint broken bones, imagine unconsciousness from carbon-monoxide poisoning and know just how to deal with it all. Róisín thinks he's been here before, and she's right; this will be his third trip to Antarctica. She wonders why he has come for the training course at all, but doesn't ask because the answer becomes clear soon enough.

Isn't it great, he addresses the room, knowing exactly what to do and when to do it?

Róisín's not the only one who finds him obnoxious; she can see others keeping quiet, balancing rolled eyes with polite smiles as they bandage a healthy arm, prepare a stretcher.

But he walks over to her, as if singling her out.

How was the psych eval? he asks.

She replies with a smile like the ones she's seen people giving him all day. The psychological evaluation was straightforward enough; she will not go crazy being alone, isolated. She is used to that now.

I'm Zach – he holds out his hand – looks like we'll be on Halley together.

She notices his badge, the same as hers. They are coded in different colours for the different research stations and durations.

You're quiet, he says. That's good – I'm loud. Anyone would think someone had planned this.

His humour is jovially delivered, and she warms to him, a little. She wouldn't want to spend time with him in life but, she thinks, perhaps he would be a good person to have around when avoiding death.

It's not just the science team at the conference, it is all base personnel. There are engineers and photographers and chefs and radio technicians; such a range of people brought together by the promise of snow.

After meeting Zach she starts checking badges more closely, wanting to know who will be at the station with her, whose faces will be the only ones she sees during the months of darkness that are the Antarctic winter.

One of the chefs for Halley finds her, joins her in the queue for coffee at the break.

You've been before? she asks Róisín.

No. No, what makes you say that?

You seem confident, and less, erm, giddy than the others.

Róisín laughs – some of the younger members of the group do seem a little overexcited. I'll take that as a compliment, she says.

Oh good! That's what I meant. I'm Tylissa – it'll be my first time too.

Róisín offers milk, pours two sugars into her coffee. Apparently we'll be out on the moors when the weather gets worse, she says, for the survival training.

Yes, I've been reading the blogs, says Tylissa. Last year's lot had to wear white-out goggles. And she grins, two coffee cups held up to her eyes to mimic them, pretending to stumble around, searching for what cannot be seen.

Róisín drives north every weekend, from the cottage she's renting to the mountains of the Lake District. She climbs to the peak with a heavy rucksack on her back and a camera, hand-held and portable, durable – like the one she will have in the snow.

She doesn't fear the dark, although mountaineers are supposed to. What does it matter, really, if the sun's rays are blocked by the shadow of half a world? It is not sinister. It's just the way it is.

Róisín knows that she has seen much of the world, so many places filled with people, and now she is going to see the remotest land on Earth. But she still wonders what would she have had, if she had chosen differently, if she had stayed on the farm. Would they have had a child of their own, as she always suspected Liam wanted? Two cousins with a child – would that have been so wrong? She did look it up once, although she never told him that. She never felt she needed children. But it would have been possible. A risk that they could have taken. If you look closely, we are all related to one another. You don't have to go back far to find it – that connection that joins every human being to another.

On the moors, they are joined by ropes as they stumble, searching for a pretend-lost member of their team in conditions meant to mimic the hostility of a snowstorm: they are wearing the white-out goggles Tylissa mentioned and filled rucksacks on their backs, and they've chosen the right day for it. The wind is howling over the land with no prospect of shelter and the rain, thrashing against their faces, is sharp enough to sting. It is brutal, thinks Róisín, as she stumbles over a rock, almost trips as her foot slides into what might have been a rabbit hole, but the snow – if this were snow it would be biting into their lips, making their fingertips too numb to hold the ropes that are supposed to lead them.

Róisín feels the rope tug but doesn't understand what has happened, the pull comes before the shout, and then she realises: Tylissa has fallen. The lack of vision means she can't tell, immediately, if it is serious – should they take off their goggles, forget the training and help now, when it is needed? Another pull on the rope, and this time the cry of pain is deeper, as Tylissa must have tried to stand up and fallen again.

She pulls off her goggles.

I fell, says Tylissa helplessly, eyes bloated with tears, the hole… my foot twisted. I think…

The first-aid team comes running as Róisín is kneeling beside her, feeling useless despite her training.

Tylissa is lifted onto a stretcher.

She is taken to hospital.

Róisín goes with her, then returns to their hostel for the evening.

Zach asks how she is coping.

She'll be OK, Róisín says. But it's a broken ankle. It'll take time to recover.

He looks down, as if checking his own legs are still in one piece, still fully operational.

She's upset that she's not going to be able to come to Antarctica, adds Róisín.

I guess that means we're going to need a new chef, he says, and Róisín can't decide if she dislikes him for his lack of empathy or for the fact that he said what she was already thinking but not wanting to say out loud.

- - - - - - - -

FRANÇOIS SAYS: I'M NOT LEAVING, Severine.

But you must.

We'll get through this. I know it's going to be hard—

I've planned your journey for you.

So we'll see the new specialist on Thursday—

Do you want to spend time in the desert?

Have you even read the latest letter?

It was addressed to me.

François lets the letter drop from his hands.

There are other things they can do now, Mama.

There are things *you* can do.

There are new drugs, and—

Foreign lands, jungles, waterfalls... You could go to Malaysia – the Bukit Lagong Forest has a canopy walkway thirty metres high in the trees.

And there's surgery, if it comes to that.

I found some information for you, she says. Here, you can travel round the Norwegian fjords in a fishing boat for six months.

But there are more things we can try first, he says. Mama?

Look at this, she says, handing him a piece of paper that he automatically takes. It says they need a chef urgently, to go to Antarctica.

For a moment François stops speaking. He is not interested in a holiday – he needs to talk to her about the possible treatments. But despite himself he looks down at the job advert that his mama has printed out. This is not tourism that she is suggesting for him, it's a whole different life.

Severine sits up, taller in the bed, realising she's on to something; tries to think of the aspects of Antarctica that would be different to any other experience he has had.

You would stay all through the winter, she says, twenty-four hours of darkness for months, but the sky, imagine what you could see in the sky – the stars would be brighter than the world!

And it would be cold, he smiles.

The kind of cold that turns the landscape into sheets of frozen satin.

He laughs. Less romantic, I think, though he's imagining it now, the way it would feel to stand alone on a plateau of snow that stretches to the horizon, to be reminded of how small we are, in a world of such extraordinary contrast.

But how could he, when his mama is ill, when she needs support?

You need me here, Mama.

No, François. What I need is for you to leave, while you still can.

She remembers her granny's words: François won't be able to see the ghosts. Not yet anyway, she'd said, he hasn't lost anyone yet. So it is now that he needs protecting from them. She will not lose her son by sending him away, she will save him. François, the world – her hands are wide, outstretched, as if holding the globe – there is so much world for you to see.

He looks at the space between her cupped hands, imagines a globe revolving between them, lit with sun on one side and dim with starlight on the other.

I'll have whatever treatment they suggest while you're away, she says. But please.

Please what?

Please go and see the world for me. Before it is too late.

*

François has been doing his research. He doesn't want to give false hope, but he doesn't want to give none either. He's been to talk to doctors he knows, friends from university who are practising now, his own GP, surgeons at the hospital; at first it was frantic, a search for information as if there was an answer he could find, some way that he could save his mama.

She's too young, he wants to scream, she needs to see the world; and that is when the guilt comes, crippling him into a ball as he hugs his knees into his chest. Perhaps she would have gone herself if it wasn't for him, he thinks, if it wasn't for having to raise a child. All these ghosts that she sees, imaginary conversations that she has had, inventing a world around her, all because she wanted to be free and couldn't be, because of a mistake she made when she was young. Her hallucinations make sense, in a way – it *was* family keeping her here. It was a baby.

Hélène cries when he tells her, making him weaken despite his resolve to be strong, to show there is hope. She holds him, but not for long enough; she doesn't know what to say. She knows she has to keep other things secret.

I'm here, she says pointlessly – of course she is here, but she can't always be, and she knows it, and he knows it too.

He sees signs around her apartment, an extra toothbrush in the bathroom where he goes to splash cold water on his face, to pull himself together. He doesn't ask her about it – what does it matter now? But it changes something nonetheless; makes him believe that he can't stay here, that this is not the place to find help.

After he leaves, Hélène allows herself to cry more, full-bodied sobs that she's glad no one is there to hear. She doesn't understand why it went wrong, she only knows that it wasn't right for her.

In the night, she holds Stefan as if he is her only connection to the world, holds him so tight she knows he will never sleep, and the guilt of having him there makes her cry harder and the gratitude of having him there eventually allows her to rest.

You can write me letters, says Severine; amazing letters, letters describing things I have never seen. Tell me about snow crystals and white cliffs stretching up beyond the clouds.

She is propped up with three pillows in a private room of the hospital, and François is by her bedside.

She looks the same, he thinks, her eyes still have their sparkle as she talks about faraway places, describes her imagining of layers of snow so thick it's hard to believe there is solid ground underneath. But when she takes his hand, he feels his body begin to shake; he will never leave her, he wants to stay, he will sleep here and she will see him as soon as she wakes, every day, until she is better.

François, she says, it is wonderful that you are here, but don't you see?

You need to get some rest, Mama. Please.

I don't want you to watch me die.

He feels a knot in his throat, cannot make his voice work to reply. The doctors moved fast, so fast there was no way to deny how serious it was. And then they stopped.

There's not much time, believe me, I know about these things – I too have sat in a hospital room, refusing to leave, and I know what followed.

He shakes his head.

The ghosts will come, François, I know you don't believe me but they will, and that will be your life.

There are no ghosts.

His voice is a whisper now.

I might even come too, though I will try not to. I don't want you waiting for me, year after year.

I'm not leaving you.

It would make me happy.

If she could lead him onto the plane she would. She knows he loves her, that is enough.

But he's not even listening now; he is bent double, his head resting on her hand over the bedclothes.

It's OK, she says.

He doesn't know why he goes to Hélène's instead of to his own apartment, but that is where his feet lead him and he doesn't have the will to disobey. And there is Stefan at the door, not even a surprise, not really. Their words glide over his head like sheets of ice and he stumbles backwards, away from the front door.

François—

Hélène calls out in a voice that is kind and sorry and wants to help, and she follows him outside, closes the door behind her, tries to apologise though there is no reason to, nor any need. She wants to explain, she says, then can't find the words to do it. She shivers in the cold.

And there are things that he doesn't say, as well. It would be pointless now to tell her that he was restless, not for a different person, but for a different kind of life.

You'll be OK? she says, at last, as he stands beyond the door.

His smile surprises her, as he steps closer again, kisses her on each cheek before stepping back from the threshold of her home.

Don't worry, he says, I'm going to be OK. And you're going to be OK.

And he turns and walks away, and doesn't look back.

It's the right thing to do, don't you see? Severine is sitting up. I don't want you here watching the end, I want you out there – in the world.

The determination is back in her voice, and for a second he allows himself to believe that she will recover, that this is not the end – that she will be home again, cooking, singing, quarrelling with her ghosts.

Then another second passes, and François knows that it is true; his mama doesn't want him to watch her die. She was always so proud, he thinks, and however much he wants to be with her, she wants him to remember her alive.

Severine sees his expression and knows what he's thinking – he is listening to her at last, and she is grateful. Perhaps she is being selfish, perhaps she should let him stay with her, for the time she has left. Perhaps it is important to be with someone at the end, but there is something more important: she wants him to have the chance of a new beginning.

They say I can go home, she says. Help me go home. And then…

OK, Mama.

So you're going to go?

They need a chef, in Antarctica, he says, just like you told me they did.

Oh, François!

I'd have to leave for the training course next week. Then fly out straight away after that.

Her smile lights up her face, and she swings her legs out of the hospital bed with the energy of a girl.

François is making dinner; slicing onions, frying aubergine in olive oil. They play music while they cook, sip red wine. What does it matter now? she says. I can have all the wine I want.

You have always had all the wine you want, he says.

Now that is true. And I don't regret it a jot.

His last days at home will always come to him in snippets of jokes, her boisterous smile, the smell and scent of the kitchen – basil and ripe tomatoes, hot lemon cordial, his mama's perfume, coffee with cinnamon and a fleeting memory of rosemary. He will travel across the world and take all this with him, share it with others. This, and not the other things he has seen – not the smell of disinfectant and hospital food and the hum of the machine that dripped clear fluids into her bloodstream. Those memories he doesn't want to keep.

She shimmers around the kitchen, dancing to music from days before she was born.

Your great-granny used to play this, she says, she taught it to me on the piano.

I've not heard you play.

It hasn't been tuned for years.

So?

Right enough, I will play for you later. From Mozart to 'Mr Moonlight'.

They sing together: Mister-er-er-er Moonlight.

He'll always remember that, too.

They set the table for family dinner, and François doesn't try to stop her. What does it matter now? If she wants the ghosts to join them for dinner, who is he to object?

Shall we put Granny at the head of the table?

Of course, he says. Great-Grandpa Paul-François beside her?

And you beside him. He is your namesake, after all.

What was he like?

Oh, he's a foolish old man, she chuckles, he's full of stories. Young though, sometimes, like when he was in the navy. He sunk a submarine, you know? He was in the papers.

And she reaches for more cutlery, more table mats, as she rings off the names he has heard so many times: Antoine and Brigitte, Ælfgifu and Henri, and Mama, his own grand-mère, whom he thinks about often.

I think we are ready, says Severine, shall I be Mama for a change?

He smiles. It is usually him that serves the food, pours the wine.

You be Mama, he says, tucking a napkin into his collar. Knowing it will make him look silly and make her laugh.

Now, she says, a little more wine. And she holds up her glass, and he follows her gesture, tipping it to clink gently with hers over the table set for a feast. But she is subdued, all of a sudden.

You are the last of our family, she says.

Probably not, he smiles – you go back far enough and you can see that everyone in the world is family.

Well then, she says, holding her glass up again. To our family.

The next morning, before he leaves, she asks him to take her to the Bayeux Tapestry.

It'll be full of tourists, he says.

Not this time of year.

They're here every time of year.

Humour an old lady, she smiles.

So he helps her out to the car and drives to the visitors' car park, parks close to the door so she won't have too far to walk.

I'm OK, she says, I can manage. But he asks for a wheelchair at the front desk anyway – just in case, he says, and she must agree with him really, because she sits down in the chair and immediately begins wheeling herself through the shop and towards the museum door.

There's something you need to see, she says.

We've been here many times, Mama, I know it well.

Look! Did you know there was a green horse?

The horses are all blue and whi—

But she is right, and he can't help laugh at her triumph as she points it out, the other-worldly green horse in a panel surrounded by foot soldiers and spears and shields and the threat of war.

Of course I'm right, she says. Now, follow me.

And she is off again, enjoying the mobility now, as she glides from wall to wall.

Halley's comet—

Looks more like a sun, doesn't it?

And see these soldiers watching? That one, there. Ælfgifu loved him, I think.

How do you know?

She showed me.

Who?

Look!

And he is standing in front of a small panel that he hasn't noticed before, despite all those visits, with school and with his grand-mére, even with Severine – she used to bring him here, but never told him what he was supposed to see.

But close to the glass now he can make out each stitch: a woman, eyes looking out from the pale background, her hair in a red shawl. Behind her, an older man clasps her face in threat: *Ubi unus clericus et Ælfgyva*. Ælfgifu. It's her. The ghost his mama always talks about; she had come from the tapestry.

But there is something about the proud look in her eyes – Ælfgifu is not cowering before this man. She is turning away, looking not at the man beside her but out, to the world, to him. There are pillars either side of where she stands, almost like a door frame she is looking out of, and that is when he remembers, for the first time in years, the day they camped out in the park to watch a comet but saw instead a sunrise. And that woman in the window, with her telescope pointed at the sky, and her eyes looking straight at him. Is that who this woman reminds him of?

And he looks away, over to Severine by his side, and he sees the same haughty eyes looking back at him, the same red shawl covering her head – though she is not young like Ælfgifu was when she was captured in thread and gold.

She looks like you, he says, eventually.

Yes.

And he kneels down beside her chair and puts his head on her shoulder.

I'm tired now, she says. Time to be going?

OK, Mama. He takes her hand. OK, Severine.

She squeezes his arm in return. Thank you. Really.

And her eyes search his as she tries to tell him now how grateful she is – that he came to see the tapestry, that he is going to see Antarctica, that he has been in her life.

Then she lets him wheel her back out to the car.

Outside, it has begun to snow. This time it is for real, he knows, as he stands in the hall, his suitcase by the door. He is finding it difficult to leave, trying not to break down, not to make things any harder for her, so he stands still for a minute and just watches the snow fall. Then he kisses Severine goodbye, gently brushes tears from her eyes and his own, and steps out into the cold.

Comet Ikeya–Seki

As the needle of the turntable lifts and returns to its starting point, Ariane stands at the window looking out towards her grandfather's old shed. She never knew her grandmother, but she remembers her grandfather from when she was a child. She remembers being shown the medal that he won during the First World War, and how he would brush away his embarrassment, preferring instead to dance around the room with her and Antoine.

She turns back to the room, more sure of herself. It isn't easy, this decision she has made, but her husband is a man who can't stay in one place. She knew this when she married him, when they dreamed as teenagers about the places they would go. But she also knows that she can't leave, that she needs to stay with her daughter, and her mother, because too many members of this family have gone and her mother's mind is breaking under the pressure.

She holds Severine in her arms, rocks her gently as she stirs from her sleep. The love she feels for her child is stronger, she knows, than any she has felt before. It makes her want to forgive her own mother, too, for being strict, for pushing her – for seeming disappointed in her, but she knows now that can't have been the case. She can't imagine ever being disappointed in her child.

I told him to go, Mama, she says, preparing herself for a scolding.

Ariane's mother will have things to say. Well, of course she will have things to say – she'll happily talk to anyone she sees and sometimes people who aren't there at all. But Ariane doesn't know what to expect now.

Have you looked at the sky? her mother says, with a look of awe on her face as she bends down to kiss her granddaughter on the forehead. It is called a sungrazer, that comet to the east. Beautiful, isn't it?

2017

Comet Giacobini

FRANÇOIS RUNS THROUGH THE SNOW as if every muscle in his body is screaming to be set free. He doesn't stop and he does not slow; he is at the furthest end of the world and his heart is clenched in a grip of guilt and loss and fleeting wonder. How could he do it, he asks himself, how could he leave? He should be at home, with Severine. His mama is dying. The others are watching him as if he's on the edge – a last-minute addition to their carefully selected team who did the shorter, intensive training and is not pacing himself, who seems to need to win. But it is not winning that he needs, it is a speed that will silence the voice in his head, that will let him live with what he has left behind. The air freezes in his lungs as he gasps, as he pushes himself harder through a vast land of silver and red.

He is sorry that they are running laps of the base, he would rather leave the red behind him and head for the endless white of the mountains in the distance, the desperate bite of the coast where the icebergs splinter in the current. But instead he goes round and round, faster and faster.

The nights have begun in Antarctica, but they are not deep; they remain in hazy colours of wine, falling for a few minutes a day like a shadow before the sun bursts out again, forcing him to see. And he remembers Severine, eyes wide, looking into the night, at constellations and galaxies and comets searing through the solar system; dancing in the kitchen while he cooked, and laughing at jokes he could not hear and dreaming of the world.

He feels untethered. Every year of his life has been spent orbiting Bayeux up until now. His skin is burning under his clothes; the cold is stabbing in his stomach, in his chest. His eyes sting. He runs. Others join him. They are a group now, racing around this strange caterpillar base, a woman is trying to keep up with him, but every time she pulls close he speeds up. His breath gasps in his ears.

In a glance sideways he sees a flash of black hair and he stumbles, catches himself before he falls, runs behind her for a moment, knowing he has seen her before, in a different world – he can't breathe – in a different life. He gets back into his rhythm, increases his pace. Some of the team, standing outside the base, are cheering now on the final lap of a marathon and he feels like his legs are going to break but he keeps going, he won't stop pushing himself until he breaks through something, until he can stand to look at the woman from the tapestry, from the window, from the hilltop in Scotland, from his home; he stumbles again, keeps going, and Severine wanted this, he did not abandon her, he is living for her, that is what she wanted; she is here.

At the end of the final lap he collapses onto his knees, then down to his chest. The nausea that has been with him for weeks is masked, briefly, by the freeze of snow on his hands, on his neck. He wants to cry, but does not. He rolls over, slowly, letting the snow melt into his hair, letting the glare of the sun and the endless sky burn his face, and he breathes. And he breathes.

He is going to be OK.

He lets himself cry out; it turns into a laugh.

He scoops some snow up in his hands, holds it to his hot face.

When he opens his eyes, the woman is looking down at him.

Maybe he is seeing things too, he thinks, maybe he has started to see ghosts like his mama and her granny before her. Then the group leader walks by and nods at her. She is not a ghost, then, this woman with wild black hair and loss in her eyes.

He must look ridiculous, he thinks, covered in snow, in sweat, lying on the ground in the midday sun on an ice shelf. In her eyes, there is something; perhaps she will smile, tell him her name. But she just keeps looking.

You should try it, he says; meaning letting go, pushing yourself to the edge of what your body can handle and screaming into the wild emptiness of Antarctica.

Maybe next time, Róisín says, meaning she wants to let go, she wants to learn how to push herself to the edge of what her body can handle and scream into the wild.

He says his name is François.

She smiles, then, in a way that makes his nausea return and his heart pound.

Róisín stands beside him while he cooks, and helps by slicing onions and passing him tins of tomatoes. She tells him about her research, about the Earth and the sky and how she came to move from one to the other.

It is amazing, out there, she says, looking up to the sky as if the ceiling of their base did not exist, as if she could see other planets in other galaxies. But if you look out for too long...

His smile is warm but he doesn't press her with questions – he knows there are things he can't talk about yet. There is something about Róisín, though, that makes him believe he might be able to. Perhaps, he thinks, she is someone who knows how to listen.

They go outside together to watch the sky, at sunset. Usually the others leave them alone, although they've never asked them to. They take one of the survival tents out and crawl inside, letting torchlight fill the space. They don't always talk, although one evening she describes the village she is from. He imagines a farm with no animals or crops, a barn with a painted For Sale sign on the wall; the emptiness of a place that used to be full of life. He tells her about his mama and his grand-mère teaching him to cook; how he used to have a special stepladder in the kitchen, a pale blue plastic one for children, to climb on so he could reach ingredients before he was able to say their names.

He pulls his bobble hat on over his windproof Antarctic one. He is not here to forget, perhaps he is here to remember who he always was. Róisín looks at it almost as if she's seen it before, smiling as she describes the places she has been to, the people she has met, from city to city as she explored, discovered, lived, until something changed and led her to a small red survival tent in the remotest continent on Earth. He asks her if she believes in ghosts. She says she believes it is possible for people to be haunted. He tells her that his mama is dying, and describes the family she is surrounded by.

Sometimes, two people and a wild expanse of snow and ice and rock can be a whole world.

It was the last thing in the world that Róisín was expecting; to find herself looking for him, wanting to be near him in the kitchen, wanting to look at the sky together. She has not wanted to spend time with anyone for so long. He is young, of course, but someone to be close to. That can be as beautiful as the stars.

She reaches out her hand, when he talks about his mama, wanting to offer compassion but not knowing what the right thing is to say.

I...

She wonders if she should talk about Liam, but doesn't want to change the subject to herself. So many years, she thinks, feeling her own grief haven't helped her know what to say to others.

Tell me something? he says. Something you wouldn't normally talk about.

Someone I knew. Someone I loved, he died.

What happened?

The wind outside is howling. It is getting late; the darkness is deeper now than it was before and nights are getting longer.

People say we are made of stardust. Ever heard that? It's not true though, not quite. All those stars we see, almost all, they're dead already. They have exploded, rejected everything that they were, and the raw components, the elements they were made of, that is where life comes from.

He likes the way she talks about the stars, sometimes, as if they are people.

So we're made from star ash?

She smiles; it is good to be able to smile. His eyes make him seem older than he is.

She begins to see him differently.

They hear on the radio that a group of sea lions have been spotted off the coast; Zach and Róisín go to investigate, and François stays behind.

He can't sleep in the night – in the darkness of his room he imagines people where there are none, reaches out to hold his mama's hand but the hospital bed cracks and breaks as if made of old parchment. On the other side he sees them, not ghosts but characters of dyed thread and stained linen, who refuse to answer his questions, whose features slip and blur into people he loves and people he has never known.

How can I know you? he says. How can this be true?

He wakes, alone. Switches on a light.

He uses the lab computer to look for pictures of the Bayeux Tapestry, of Ælfgifu and her proud stare and the cleric. He thinks he must have remembered it wrong; confused the image – what he thinks he sees, sometimes, in the dead of night, doesn't make any sense. It cannot make any sense.

And he is right, in the cold of the day, as the snow's depth thickens and he shakes off the thoughts that crowd his head – Ælfgifu has a red shawl over her hair, an expression that seems familiar, but that is all. Her features are indistinct. She doesn't look exactly like Róisín. His mind is playing tricks on him.

He goes to the kitchen, starts preparing dinner. He thinks it is Zach coming in, but when he turns, he sees Róisín, and his heart is in his throat.

She steps towards him and two halves of his life collide. He did recognise her, he knew it the first time he saw her, the day of the marathon – which was not the first time he saw her. He had seen her when he was a child. He moves towards her without even meaning to do it.

His lips taste of sweet wine and the past and home and Róisín welcomes it; she needs it. It has been too long since she allowed herself to feel like this. But his kiss is different to Liam's; she is so grateful that his kiss is different to Liam's. She closes her eyes against the tears and puts her hand on the small of his back.

When he pulls away she's left spinning, but he keeps her grounded, his eyes with their wisdom beyond his years and his hair like a boy's and his words.

Welcome home, he says.

And she puts her head on his shoulder, and they stand together listening to the distant chatter from the games room and the voices from their old lives.

They sleep with layers of clothes on; it is the only way out here, where even indoors you can see the frosty stream of your own breath. But when they wake at 4 a.m. with thunder growling like a bass drum, their fingers find their way between the layers of clothes. It is childlike, it is wondrous, to peel back a jumper, a T-shirt below that, a thermal vest, to find a warm patch of skin just north of a hip, and the need to taste something so rare.

As the nights get longer he can't stop touching her skin, as if trying to remind himself that she is real, flesh and bone, not some distant memory of a woman he once saw as a child. She laughs when he gets to her stomach; sorry, I didn't mean to tickle.

No – her hands are on his head – no, don't stop, it's good.

They compare cities, discover with laughter, and something more, how Róisín has lived in Bayeux, how François went to Scotland as a boy.

And Toronto, she says, when were you in Toronto? And New York?

He shakes his head.

I've never been.

Good, she laughs, I can show you round North America then.

I'd prefer to go to Africa I think, he says. Not so easy, perhaps, but we can discover it together.

*

It has been a long time, for Róisín, a long time since it didn't even matter; longer still since it did. François has hands like a chef. They are not unlike the hands of a farmer. Hands that work, that burn, that create. She saw Liam deliver a calf once, and he was not gentle – that would be the wrong word – it was urgent, adept, loving. He didn't hesitate, though he had the scars to prove it. François has a scar on his thumb, too. He says his knife slipped once; it is silver now, thin, almost elegant. Can a scar be beautiful? It can, she thinks.

When François thinks of Hélène it feels different now. She said, once, why are you so far away? What is it you are thinking of, chéri? Róisín doesn't use words like that, hasn't used terms of endearment, although when she pulled off his hat he found a playfulness that was short-lived but intended only for him.

Róisín feels like she is moving through the world in reverse; rewinding time to when she was young and hopeful and desperate to grow up. She tastes his skin, wondering if he'll notice, perhaps hoping he won't, as she lets her tongue-tip touch the curve where his neck meets his shoulder.

As François falls asleep, he hears voices, or thinks he does; it could be the chatter of birds or a party in the snow or a clamouring of ghosts who are lost and trying to find their way home.

Severine, he thinks, picturing his mama not as she was when he left, but when he was still a child; imagining his mama before she was a mother.

Are these the voices you heard, Severine?

Are these the whispers you chose to live with?

But even in his sleep he knows that all you can hear out here is the silence of snow and ice dust and rock.

*

Then, in the night, Róisín wakes with a start and she sees him, Liam, and she rises and begins to talk. You were the one who left, she says, so why are you here?

I didn't leave you, he says. You are being naive.

No, you are.

Perhaps we should argue.

Good, she says; for a long time I've needed to shout.

But his arm is already around her waist and she can smell the farm on him, spring grass and the musty hay from the barn, and outside there is a comet that looks like a shooting star, even though she knows it's not.

She will not ask why.

Don't fucking kiss me, she says, don't you dare.

And he smiles and says, there appears to be a man in your bed.

She turns, sees François asleep, the blond mess of his hair on her pillow.

I suppose you think this is funny, she says, but there is no one there to hear her.

She gets up before he wakes, not wanting a morning scene in bed to be the way she tells him that she's not ready for this yet. She came here looking for isolation in the Antarctic winter – for the sky, not the people.

When she returns to her room, half an hour later, the bed is made and the room is empty. She sits down on the duvet and looks at the door.

SEVERINE IS GLAD SHE IS home. They don't leave her alone for a minute, not now, and she wouldn't want them to; they keep her company always, chatter and laugh just as she imagined they would when she was a little girl and she couldn't hear them.

I'm ready, she tells her granny.

It's not time yet.

Who decides when it is time?

You always were quarrelsome.

Severine smiles; I was delightful.

That too.

They are all young now, all her family – young and full of life. They don't need to tell their stories any more; they are like giddy teenagers, wanting to play, wanting to gently tease.

Setting the table, why did you keep doing that? Brigitte asks, her gown a rich emerald now and her hair scooped up into a ponytail that makes her look like a modern girl in fancy dress.

I just wanted you to know that you were welcome.

Brigitte reaches for an apple and throws it up in the air, smiles as it floats there.

Severine watches it, not held but not falling either, hovering between two worlds and spinning, slowly, like a globe caught in the breeze. Then Brigitte shimmers away and the apple falls to the ground. Severine isn't sure why Brigitte doesn't stay for more than a minute at a time, though Brigitte knows what she's doing – she has a plan.

She hasn't told the others, but she's saving what little energy she has left to go and see François at the end. She knows it will be hard, and that she won't have long, that far from Bayeux, but their time is coming to an end anyway. And she knows she can't make him see her but that doesn't mean she can't hope. He is the last member of this branch of the family but there might be others, her descendants, that he could find one day, if she could persuade him to look; living their lives without ghosts, perhaps, or with them, somewhere, across the sea.

*

What's it like? Severine asks.

Being dead? Like running and spinning and flying as fast as the wind can carry you, laughs Antoine, holding her mother's hands and spinning her round until her feet fly off the ground.

I played that game at school.

So did we, cries her mama, mid-flight. This and handstands and stuck-in-the-mud.

So you were never here to see me? Severine asks Antoine, though she's not waiting for an answer and he's not listening. Obviously it was her mother that he was waiting for. He wanted his sister back.

I stayed here for you, says her granny. And, my darling, you are wonderful.

Even Great-Great-Grandma Bélanger is younger now, though she's shaking her head at the nonsense of the other ghosts; Henri and the sisters in lace dresses are waving to her, and her sons too, in their uniform – listen to this, Mama! They grin as they tell her jokes from centuries ago.

Ælfgifu stands in the corner, less giddy than the rest, with her daughter on one side and her soldier boy on the other; the love that started it all. Severine doesn't think she's ever felt that type of love, but it's OK – she is full to bursting with other kinds.

You can decide when it is time, she says quietly to Severine, and the others all keep playing and pretend not to hear her.

FRANÇOIS FEELS THE LOSS OF Róisín, though he tries not to show it, and in quiet moments he accepts that she has her own ghosts to contend with. He tries to be friendly. He makes her hot cocoa sometimes, when she is out in the snow, leaves cups cooling by her bed so she'll know that she doesn't have to be out there alone. But he is a little angry, too. Her grief makes her selfish.

*

Every day he tries to call Severine, via satellite, but she does not answer. He tries to get in touch with the hospital too, but they say she is home – that she is being checked on. She is comfortable. His Antarctic layers prickle with static and itch at his skin. So instead he writes to her, as he promised. He writes to her about the snow and mountains, about the furious noise of the coastline, the peace of the night; he writes to her about the centuries that have been captured within the ice.

As each snowflake falls, it carries air between its frozen crystals.

He likes the idea of frozen crystals; he thinks Severine will like it too.

Together they compress to form ice with air pockets of atmosphere trapped in bubbles.

He can imagine her, reaching out a palm for a bubble to land on, snapping her fingers to see it pop.

We're drilling into the ice, to find the layers from thousands of years ago. That's how we can learn about the worlds of the past, Mama, he writes, then thinks better of it, scribbles out the line and then scrunches up the page, begins again.

He describes the lakes and rivers beneath the ice sheets of Antarctica; how they had lain, unknown, for millennia and more: for the length of humanity. He describes what they mean, the movement of the vast ice sheets of a vast continent that they make possible.

The world is moving beneath our feet, he writes, can you feel it, too?

For days he writes, and folds the pages after they are written, places them carefully in an envelope and stores it in his suitcase. It is a one-sided conversation, but there is nothing new in that; he has been having one-sided conversations with his mama all his life.

He goes to the central pod of the base to find some company, to find someone who will listen to what he's saying and want to reply, but he finds himself standing outside Róisín's room. If she's in there, she makes no sound.

He sees her when he steps outside, a splash of colour against the snow, coat zipped up over her mouth and hood pulled down low against the cold, almost covering her eyes.

Can I just stand with you? he says, but his words are lost on the wind; it is howling tonight. The winter is settling in.

They think it's unstable, she says. The comet.

How do they know?

The way it's rotating. Unbalanced.

He looks up to the sky but it seems brighter than ever; more determined.

That means it might fracture.

What then?

She shrugs. Its trajectory would change. Might burn up in the sun. Collide with a planet. Just disintegrate.

The thought of this comet, so beautiful in the dark sky, destroying itself in such a meaningless way makes François feel hopeless.

I hope it will, she says, surprising him. I hope it will fracture into different pieces. She turns to look at him. It's been trapped on this path for millennia. Don't you think it deserves a change?

François feels something return that he thought was lost.

He reaches out a hand but thinks better of it, instead turns his eyes to the sky and lets his arm brush, softly, against hers.

Something strange happens to him every time he sees her; walking around the base, taking off her snow boots by the entrance, glancing over at him while they all have dinner together – their eyes finding one another's across the busy table, across Zach's loud voice. A subtle quickening of his pulse that brings a rush of blood to his face. The involuntary movement of his hand towards her, as if wanting to hold hers, to feel the warmth of her palm and the soft touch of her fingers. He tries to hide it; she already thinks of him as young, and this – this blushing – would only emphasise it, as if he were a teenager, giddy with first love.

He wants to tell her that this is not first love, that he has known this before, but that would be a lie. Love is different with different people, he thinks, perhaps that is why he never felt a tremble in his hands and a knot in his stomach when he was with Hélène. There was desire, certainly, and laughter, and common ground; a comfort in knowing her body and knowing that she knew his. Holding on to that simplicity meant keeping things back, though. He'd thought it was just him, but now he remembers the way she looked at Stefan and he thinks he understands.

It is not about comfort, with Róisín, it is something else; a tugging at his chest that he never asked for but that he cannot ignore, that almost makes him guilty with what he feels. It is not unlike homesickness. Perhaps that is why this rush of emotion makes him think of home every time he sees Róisín. Both are pulling at his heart. Both are out of reach.

He tries calling Severine again, wants to ask her, now that he is unable, for the stories of their ancestors.

Róisín is behind him. The phone rings out; he has not spoken to Severine since he left.

He passes the handset to Róisín, who places it down and follows him out towards the kitchen.

François? she asks, touching him gently on the arm. Why doesn't she answer?

He is surprised that she's here, showing concern for him. Perhaps it is her way of asking if his mama is still alive.

She's probably got company, he says, angry at the thought of Severine ignoring his calls to talk to her ghosts. But Róisín's silence makes him reconsider. She is being thoughtful, and he wants to think about his reply.

I think she wants me to be free, he says.

Her hand slips into his.

- - - - - - - -

SEVERINE CLIMBS THE STAIRS, PULLING François's old childhood stepladder behind her. She doesn't have the strength she used to; her arms feel frail now, although in her mind she's still young, still alive.

It's going to be a beautiful sunset tonight. She's learnt to tell from the sky, the clouds, the smell in the air. It is crisp and clear. The comet will be visible, high over the horizon, as soon as the sun starts to dip – its full name is Tuttle–Giacobini–Kresák, this comet that has been discovered and rediscovered and rediscovered again over the years as new generations of people searched the skies.

On the landing at the top of the stairs she positions the stepladder below the door to the attic, climbs to the top step and even then has to stand on tiptoes to reach the latch and push the horizontal door up and over onto the attic floor. There's another ladder now, one that pulls down from inside the gap where the trapdoor was, an ugly clanking metal thing that springs when it's least expected, threatening to trap young fingers.

Don't go up there, she always used to tell François – he was so boisterous, as a boy, always wanting to explore, to see, to know more.

He didn't listen though, he would do what she's doing now – he would pull down the metal folded steps to climb again; his head, like hers, disappearing into the darkness of the attic, feet dangling behind.

She climbs, one swaying metal step at a time, breathes in dust and silence and the smell of a place not lived in. On the final rung, she lifts herself up to kneel on the floor. She's not ready to stand yet, she needs time to rest before looking for the light switch.

She would race up after him, when she was younger and François was a child, shouting his name, trying not to let her concern sound like anger. Once, he pulled the metal steps back inside the attic, peered down at her from the darkness, a grin on his face as he refused to come back down. It was a game, to him; it was a wilderness to explore.

But in truth there is nothing much kept up here, she thinks to herself now, looking for family keepsakes to make her nostalgic but seeing only shadows of old chairs that should have been thrown away and dusty piles of games and clothes that could have gone to charity. Things, belongings, do not make her sentimental. It is the people – it is their words, their laughter – that matter. She walks into the room and trips; the further away from the hatch she moves the darker it is. She glances around, momentarily unable to remember where the light switch is. How long has it been?

But there it is, on the left-hand wall. She flicks it, and the bulb stutters to life.

François always used to bring a torch up with him.

It's like being in the tent, Mama.

Like when we went on an adventure?

Like in the park!

FRANÇOIS TESTS IT OUT, THOUGH he doesn't go far from the base. It's not seclusion he wants, just a night under the stars in a tent that glows like firelight when the torch is pressed up close to the fabric; like when they camped out in the park when he was a boy, when he forgot about the comet and watched a sunrise seep through the sky like dye into silk.

From above, the tent is red ink on a page; a single drop, curved into a perfect hemisphere under surface tension.

From inside the tent, the world is an orange glow and shadow; the torch a single beam of light that can seem like the only bright moment of a lifetime.

It is startling when, about 2 a.m., he hears the zip of the tent being pulled open. In his dream his mama had been outside, thinking he was asleep, talking to her ghosts and watching for the comet; it made him ache, to know that she had imaginary people who were more important to her than he was. He had never said that out loud, though. Perhaps he was a private child, but he'd never thought of himself that way. I'm an open book, he'd said to Hélène, three weeks in, and she'd laughed without making a sound. Is that true? she'd said with a wink, as if she knew him better after three weeks than he knew himself. Maybe she had a point; he'd never told Hélène about his mama's ghosts. She would not have understood. Not like Róisín, who knows what it is to be haunted.

Are you sleeping? she says.

Yes.

That's good.

He thinks she's smiling as she crawls inside, though he can't see her face with the torch off.

I'll just talk, she says, and you can sleep, and we'll both feel better for it.

So he closes his eyes again and gives Róisín the time and the space to talk. He listens to her descriptions of a night from her childhood, when she camped out under the stars with her cousin and taught him to watch for the speeding flight of the comet. Of how he took his toy panda with him – I had a tiger, he wants to say, but doesn't – of how they kissed, as children, an innocent kiss on his lips that changed everything as they grew into teenagers and innocence was replaced by secrets.

I think my mum knew, she says, though she never told me so, not exactly. But she was pleased when I went away; do you think that's strange? Perhaps it sounds worse than it was. She missed me, I think, she wanted to see me more often, but when I moved home, that year on the farm with Liam and . . . I'm sorry, I'm skipping ahead, but there was this look in her eye, at times, when she asked me if I was going to stay and I said I was; I think it was disappointment.

François remembers Severine's face, when he swore he would stay with her in the hospital, be there at the end.

I don't know if it was all about Liam, Róisín says, though some of it was. I think she wanted me to be free.

And he is glad of the dark; he can keep the sound of his tears silent, but he can't hold them back. Severine has never answered the phone, not once. She has chosen to be alone.

I think . . . I go round in circles, you know? Thinking I did the right things, the only possible things, thinking it would never have worked, had I stayed. I couldn't live like that, too much was missing – one person can't be enough, can they? You need more. Everyone needs more.

There is a gust of wind that makes the taut fabric of the tent resonate like a string; ripple with harmonics.

But then, on nights like this, I think . . . should I have stayed?

She curls her legs up to her chest and wraps her arms around them, rests her head on her knees.

You remind me of some things, she says, her voice muffled now through the fabric of her coat, and in other ways you are so different. Your hands – she takes his, forgetting to pretend that he is asleep, and he is glad – your hands are the same.

They're rough, from the kitchen.

His from the farm.

Why did he do it? he asks.

I don't know why. Nobody knows why, she says. I don't think you get to find out why.

He closes his fingers around hers, knowing she must have heard the break in his voice, but there is only a second of this closeness before she pulls away again.

I think I need to say goodbye, she says. I'm sorry.

François doesn't know if she's saying goodbye to him, or to Liam, or to them both. He doesn't understand why she is sorry either, not really, but he feels it; there are things that he is sorry about too, and there are times when he wishes there was someone to hear his apology.

He steps outside as she leaves, but not back to the base – he does not want to follow her, there is something else that he needs to see. He starts packing up the tent by the light of the stars, under the glow of the comet. A red survival tent is not what he needs any more.

AT THE FAR END OF the attic – there, now – beyond François's old bike and a pile of dust sheets that Severine can't ever remember using, is another ladder, the final set of steps that lead up to the roof. Their roof, with the unusual flat top, is so unlike the others in Bayeux. They're all triangles and spires, angular splashes of brown and white, whereas her own rooftop is serene as a lake but for the breeze whistling over it.

Severine climbs up and stands in the middle of the rooftop, from where she can see all the way from the canal to the hills of Normandy. Someone must have brought plant pots up, but it was so many years ago that nothing remains in them but pebbles of soil. Perhaps it was her granny, she thinks, that is the sort of thing her granny would have done. Overhead, the sun is starting to sink, but it will be a few more minutes until it reaches the horizon. She tips some of the plant pots upside down, creates a sort of bench of her granny's flowerpots in a row, and allows herself to sit down for a minute. She is tired. Her legs don't have much strength any more, but it's her lungs that are the problem; it feels like she can't get oxygen, not enough to keep her going, to fill her with wonder like she used to know, when she was a girl.

A first star appears over to the north, so bright and so alone she wonders if it is some kind of satellite. But others begin to cluster around it as the sky dips to purple fringed with terracotta. The sinking sun is like a bulb today, she thinks, its shape perfectly rounded above the horizon; a child's drawing of the way the sky should look. She stands up again, having rested enough; takes a few steps away from the flowerpots and towards the edge of the roof.

You didn't think we wouldn't notice, did you?

Her granny has arrived by her side.

I knew you would, she smiles.

Severine doesn't turn; she knows the others are here too.

Brigitte takes her right hand, and next to her Ælfgifu is peering over the edge of the roof, a silk scarf wrapped around her hair and the soldier boy beside her.

We wanted to say goodbye, Ælfgifu says, we both did. We started this, after all; the least we can do is be a part of the ending.

The soldier boy reaches for her left hand and kisses it.

Ælfgifu got my eyes wrong when she embroidered them, don't you think?

Severine looks into his eyes and tries to remember the soldier in the tapestry.

Hmmm, she smiles – he is playful, this boy, he reminds her of François when he was younger – I think, on the whole, she captured you rather well.

The twin sisters are looking in the flowerpots, lifting them up and shaking out the remnants of soil so Henri can balance them on his head; Great-Great-Grandma Bélanger looks like a little girl now and Severine's mama is here too, not young any more but middle-aged, greying and gracefully lined. And Antoine is greying now as well; her mama has stopped growing younger for him and he has grown older for her, like he would have done, had he lived. They are holding hands, and behind them, there's Great-Grandpa Paul-François, with a sailor's cap worn at a jaunty angle over his thick dark hair. They stand together on the rooftop, looking over the hills and spires of Bayeux, like in that embroidered quilt she made when she was at school; all the faces of all the family she has ever known.

François though – for a minute she stops. She sent him away to the furthest reaches of the world, the remotest continent, to a land of snow and ice so he wouldn't have to see this, wouldn't have to be the one to come home and find her, wouldn't have to answer the door to police bearing the news. He is missing from the roof, and she feels guilty for that but she hopes it will spare him some of the pain.

And it is as it should be; she knows that too. These ghosts of ancestors are not the living, and she's not either.

They stand and wait, patiently, as she thinks through what she is about to do; tries to imagine the days she has left, increasingly frail, dependent. Incarceration in hospital – that is where she'd end up, if she doesn't take control. And doesn't everyone deserve the chance to choose their own way out?

The sunset in Bayeux has been and gone, and the town now is lit from starlight and the strange ethereal glow of a comet that is brighter than the moon. On the roof Severine steps forward, her toes pointing, just, over the gutters. She looks up; holds her breath as she counts. She is waiting to see it move, wanting to see the sky change on this, her last night; wanting to witness the speed of a comet. It appears to be still.

She looks round at the faces of her ghosts, knowing each one of them, sharing a last moment of understanding.

Brigitte has gone already?

Her granny gently kisses her forehead like she used to when she was a child.

Brigitte has another goodbye she has to say, whispers Great-Grandpa Paul-François, already fading in and out of view. She's finding it hard to let go; she never found her own family, and François is the last of ours.

Severine nods; she did what she could. Then she looks down, thinks, fleetingly, of how she must have those gutters cleaned, they are blocked with leaves from last autumn, leaf mould now and grime – they'll overflow soon if she doesn't sort it out. What a practical thing, how stupid to think that, and she laughs at herself, glancing back up to the sky and that is when she understands how to see a comet flying. You cannot watch it, cannot expect it to perform while your eyes are locked on it, but look away, and while your eyes are fixed on the ground it is possible – and what a possibility it is – for the sky to change.

And then, just as quickly, she steps off the roof and all the ghosts of all her family follow her. So much company, she thinks. What a beautiful thing, to have all this family.

- - - - - - - -

FRANÇOIS POURS HIMSELF ANOTHER GLASS of red, stolen from the base supply. He is ashamed, a bit, but not enough to stop drinking it. He is on his second bottle already when he sees Róisín in the kitchen, filling a flask and a mug with what seems to be boiling water. They haven't spoken since her goodbye last night, and in a way he wants to leave it like that. She has chosen: not him. That's all he needs to know, and besides, she didn't really listen. He has listened to her; that is what he thinks as he silently lets her step out of the room. He has listened to her and she hasn't listened to him. It seems like the story of his life.

He doesn't want to blame anyone, it's not in his nature, but thoughts are crowding into his mind now he is alone, with no company and so much time to think. It is becoming too familiar, this feeling of being pushed away.

But that is not fair. His mama didn't choose to be ill, she never wanted this, she's only dealing with it in the best way she knows how. Although there were times – when he was a child, when he would be woken in the night to hear her talking; when she would run through the house laughing with family but not notice him sitting there, on the top stair, sometimes, for hours. Would life have been different, he wonders, would it have been easier for her, if she had not had a son on her own? All these stories of ghosts and staying in Bayeux and longing to travel; why did she not go?

He stands by the window in the supply room, looking out – he wishes she had seen this. Been beside him to witness the ice cloud rising from an avalanche of white on snow on white. Watched the sun rise in a sky so wide, so all-encompassing, the Earth felt as small as the tip of a needle.

All those years ago, he thinks, lying back on his bed, had she stayed in Bayeux for him? When she was supposed to be out in the world following her dreams, was she stuck at home with a baby? She never went out dancing, staying instead in the kitchen, pretending to love dancing with him; never fell in love, never explored the worlds of ice or sand or rainforest. And then, that night, when she woke him before dawn, when she stood in the airport next to a boy not understanding why his mama had tears streaming down her face. Why didn't she leave? He should have dragged her onto a plane, insisted that he wanted adventure not Bayeux, and certainly not ghosts.

It wasn't about you, François.

François sits up, head spinning from too much drink and the room spinning with him.

The battle was taking place inside her, Brigitte says. It doesn't mean she loved you any less.

François turns away, takes another gulp of wine, and lies back down.

Brigitte sits down on the end of his bed.

You don't mind if I sit here a while, do you? Then she smiles to herself. Well, of course not, you have no idea that I'm here at all.

Róisín is greeted by a blast of wind so cold it makes her eyes sting. She's not sure what she's doing out here, she only knows that she needs to be alone; perhaps she needs to push herself to the edge of what her body can handle and scream into the wild emptiness of Antarctica. She smiles at the memory, that first impression she had of François staring up at her, the wild wonder in his eyes, but too soon it is replaced by an image of Liam, eyes down, drawing the farm when she'd wanted him to admire the sky.

When she was sleeping next to François, Liam had forced his way into her dreams, into her consciousness, into her room to stand by the window and pull her back to what she wanted to leave behind. And now, having calmly packed her survival bag, having let her toes cross the threshold, peering from one world into the next, as she steps out into the blistering cold and starts to walk away from the safety of the base into wild howling evening of ice and wind, where is Liam? Not here.

Perhaps he wants her to find an isolation more complete than the one in the research base, where it will be just her and him. Perhaps that was what he always wanted.

She's walking fast now, away from the base, away from François and his second bottle of wine – she could see he was battling his own ghosts tonight. She was surprised to learn he had them too, but she wasn't able to help either of them. Although, when she told him to stay asleep, perhaps she should have asked him to wake up. But it is done. He will be OK, he doesn't know what it is like to be left behind with such spiteful finality.

Perhaps it was not spiteful. Perhaps Liam didn't think about her at all.

Her steps have turned into a run inland, towards the mountains, away from the coast and the promise of a world still revolving. She has said one goodbye, now it is time for another. Sometimes you have to leave people behind.

When François wakes from strange dreams, the room is empty, as it should be, but the feeling is so strong he can't deny it. He was not really alone before, but he knows that he is now. He knows, somehow, that a world away from here his mother has died.

He is surprised by the conviction of it – it is not logical, but undeniable nonetheless. He's been waiting for news even though the news couldn't reach him. He doesn't know what else he can do so he drinks, and cries, and lets his heart break.

But later that night, dizzy from the red wine, he finds a cup of cocoa on his shelf, half hidden behind his bobble hat. It has gone cold, developed a skin of milk that is marbled, patchy; less perfect than the snow. It is undrinkable.

He holds the cup between his hands, closes his eyes. Imagines his mama's ghost is approaching.

Róisín's running slows; her strength should be conserved if she's going to make it to the mountains.

Her backpack is heavy this time – not like when she went out with Liam, jumped the river that sloshed over rocks and old tree branches, the water soaking her feet through her trainers – and it makes her visible. It is a splash of red in the white wilderness. She is not trying to hide or to die; that is not what she wants to experience in Antarctica, miles from any other human being, on the night the comet will be at its brightest. But she needs something; wants to leave the past behind and wake up, alone, as untouched as the perfect fresh snow, and she knows that sometimes, if you hold your breath and look up at a comet for long enough, the sky can change.

She marks her way by the stars, though they disappear behind clouds soon enough and she has to trust her senses in a world that has no direction, that has lost its sense of forwards and back.

The cliffs help. Their shadow is still visible, and so she heads towards the mountain range with its tunnels of caves excavated by ice. She hasn't been there before but she's read about these mountains; she felt drawn to them, the descriptions reminding her of other caves from around the world, prehistoric homes and hidden lakes that lie undiscovered for millennia. She loves the idea of what water and ice can create when left alone, to flow, to freeze or thaw.

She gets into a rhythm. One foot after the next is all she needs to do, and she will get there.

There is something liberating about making a decision and walking straight towards it.

Cave is the wrong word for what she finds; it is a scoop into the ice, a satin-smooth concave structure, like a cupped palm, near the base of the mountain. Looking up, she can see the comet, bright and determined, and the clouds moving in from the coast. She undoes her backpack and takes out a notebook, like the one she used to carry as a child. Her sketch of the night sky is amateur at best, made worse by the difficulty of drawing in padded gloves, but this is not for publication, this is for something entirely different. She marks on the constellations she can see, flattening the dome to show the swirl of the Milky Way at the horizon, and through the upturned horseshoe of stars she marks the comet, drawn like a bigger star with a triangular tail sweeping out behind. She has seen a drawing of a comet like that before, but can't remember where. If she had colours, she would shade it in gold and red, but she only has black and white. When her eyes turn back to the sky, though, that's how she sees it – bright gold, like a child's drawing of a shooting star.

She shakes her head, irritated at her own sentimentality – shooting stars are not flying through the solar system, they are lumps of rock burning up in the Earth's atmosphere. Perhaps that's how this comet will end up.

Turning her back on the sky, she faces the ice and pulls her survival tent out of her backpack. The floor of the hollow she will use as her base camp is slippery, so she roughens it up first, gouging out chunks of the ice to create a surface that the tent can remain on. And then she crawls inside, drinks some water, turns on her torch then turns it off again, closes her eyes and begins to count. When she opens them again, the comet will have moved position, will have flown beyond the stars of the horseshoe in front of a new constellation.

When she opens her eyes again, she is not alone.

Liam is standing at the foot of her sleeping bag, a threadbare panda clasped in his right hand and a bobble hat pulled down over his ears, her own scarf draped loosely around his neck.

Why are you in the tent? he says. You need to follow me.

It's too cold, she says, we'll freeze.

He turns and pulls back the door of the tent, walks out to the soft dandelioned grass.

Róisín is met by the smell of hay and fresh morning dew.

But it's beautiful, she says, as he disappears from view beyond the edge of the tent's door, and she knows she has to be out there with him, with her hair scooped up in a ponytail and that spring breeze tickling the back of her neck.

She finds him out in the field, lying on the crisp grass and holding her old notepad high over his face, sketching something in pencil on the page.

What are you drawing?

She sits down beside him, doesn't see her snow boots but instead imagines her toes wriggling in the grass.

I'm not drawing, he says, I'm mapping the sky.

Why did you never want to do that before? she asks.

She looks up to the expanse of blue fluffy clouds so perfect they seem like a cartoon of the way a sky should be. But it hurts her neck, to keep staring up like this, so she lies down beside him, lets her whole view of the world become that sky.

You can't draw the stars though. There are no stars in the daytime.

He holds up his pencil, as if using it to measure the distance between one invisible object and the next.

Sure there are.

And he is right. When she turns her eyes back to the sky she can see them – all the stars of the universe are filling the blue sky, glittering in the sun.

Look, she gasps, as she sees the comet, brighter than any she has seen before, brighter than the sun and the moon and all the stars of the Milky Way. But when she looks back to the ground, the boy is standing up, folding his map in half and in half again and again, until it is a tiny square of paper that he lets drop from his left hand to flutter to the ground. He holds his arms out – the world is big, I think – palms outstretched as if the only way to grasp the Earth is to allow it to be infinite, a line from palm to palm that flows over oceans and continents and spans the globe. Then he turns and starts walking away.

Wait, she says, where are you going?

If you follow me you'll find out, he says, reaching out a hand towards her.

She scrambles to her feet, unable to understand why the grass has become as slippery as ice.

I can't, she says. I came to say goodbye.

He turns and starts to run away.

Wait...

Her feet seem to be sinking into the ground and her legs won't move properly, the shivering in her body won't stop.

Wait! – she is screaming now – Wait, you have to say something; you have to tell me it's OK. But her voice is drowned out by a growling, violent roar of the Earth like the ground is about to split open, like a volcano is starting to erupt and the farm is being broken in two. Her legs collapse underneath her and she falls back into the snow. She tries to cry out but her voice freezes in her throat as the avalanche of snow and rock cascades down from the mountain. The speed of it, like a waterfall as deep as the ocean, filled with shards of glass, and she rolls over, manages to crawl some distance despite her numb hands, her wrists sinking into the snow. She has never heard anything so loud; the mountain is howling, the continent breaking – it must be – nothing could survive this violence, but she forces herself to get up, to run the few metres that feel like miles separating her from the ice cave, from the survival tent, from the glow of a torch and a flask of hot water that François saw her fill; she has to do this. The last of her strength gets her back into the tent, where she collapses like the mountain around her, as the sky comes crashing to the ground.

*

While François sleeps, Brigitte talks about Severine when she was a little girl, how she would run through the house searching for the ghosts, demanding her granny repeat their conversations word for word. How once they found her, curled up under Great-Grandpa Paul-François's old desk like a tabby cat, unaware that her family was watching over her, whispering so as not to wake her even though she couldn't yet hear them. And she tells stories about how she jealously watched them make pastries, mother and son together, baking pain au raisin and brioche when he was a little boy, flour and eggshells patterning their kitchen, their hands, sugar glinting in their hair as they laughed through the mess.

And, she said goodbye, Brigitte says eventually.

She knows her time is almost up. She didn't get to say goodbye to her own child, but she is glad she can say goodbye on Severine's behalf, at least. There's no one left to see her and she is so far from home; all the others have gone and she should be with them. But she still has a moment; she still has hope.

François, Severine is proud of you, she says. She will be out there, you know, seeing the universe. I think she'll enjoy it.

He opens his eyes and he knows that it's true.

I'm glad you had your ghosts, Mama, he says to the empty room. He wishes he had said it to her before, but then he never felt so strongly that she was listening before. I'm glad you had so much family, he says, and I'm glad that I am your son. And it's OK, Mama, I promise; everything is OK.

Róisín wakes to find the avalanche has stopped, and she is not buried underneath it, although there is a metre of snow piled up outside her tent. She unzips the door and pushes the fabric down to make a steep red carpet out into the white. She has to pull herself up but there is room to crawl out, like a child leaving a toy tent that has grown too small, knowing she has to face the world.

Standing at last, she thinks she will sink but she doesn't – her feet stand firm on the fresh snow. The sky has cleared to a frightening blue, a blue that has no end, no place in her world of white, but there it is, refusing to dim. The moon is still out, in a different quadrant to the sun, and below it, to the right, is a comet bright enough to be seen in the morning sky. What a beautiful thing, she thinks, this sky, this universe; she can feel herself flying with it. She can see the continent of ice and snow, so pristine with its fresh avalanche dusting of white, a perfect expanse of nothing stretching from coast to coast, untouched by humanity.

But that is not true. Over there, on the ice shelf, a splash of red that doesn't belong in the natural world of ice and snow; one that is made by human hands. And inside, François will soon be cooking, slicing mushrooms and frying onions in oil that crackles in the heat, such contrast to the frozen world outside. François, whose mother is dying – has died, she knows now, though she's not sure how. François, who thinks the sky is beautiful, who listened and did not talk. She wants him to talk now. She wants to be the one to listen.

Róisín looks down to realise that her feet have sunk into the snow. It is time to move forwards. She is ready.

She packs up the tent and collects her backpack and begins the long walk back to Halley VI, over the ice and through the snow and back to the human world.

When the sun is high over the Halley VI research base, François is woken up by steps outside his bedroom door. He knows her footsteps, understands that it's Róisín before the door opens and she steps inside, her hair wet and still frosted with snow, her skin raw, almost transparent from the ice. For a second he thinks she almost looks like a ghost. But there's no such things as ghosts. Róisín – she is real.

He stands up.

Róisín hadn't realised that François had a mirror in his room, but he must have, because out of the corner of her eye she sees her own reflection as she steps inside; her dark hair looks wild, her eyes full of loss and hope and her snowsuit, once a bright red, is darker from the ice, almost clinging to her skin like a dress blowing against her body in the breeze.

You're back, he says quietly, almost a whisper, almost a question, and she walks towards him and they meet in the middle of the room, neither of them sure what words to use. Perhaps she could say hello, she thinks. I missed you. I have come home. But she doesn't speak.

Brigitte looks at this woman who looks just like her, and she knows her family. She reaches out but stops herself – this is enough. She doesn't need to be seen, she only needs to know that through generations and centuries her family has survived. Goodbye, she says, unheard, before slipping away from the Earth at last.

You're back, he says again, his voice finding its strength now that Róisín is here, his palms touching the melted snow on her clothes.

Yes.

I was hopeful.

Her smile turns into a laugh, and his does too, a laugh of finally understanding one another and knowing there is no need to ask for explanations.

She pulls her hood back from her head; she breathes, forgetting how there had been no hood in her reflection, just long, dark hair.

Is it still snowing outside? François asks.

Róisín doesn't know, but she takes his hand and they move to the window together to watch the outside.

It is snowing, lightly, but well enough to cover her footprints leading from the wilderness back to the base. It is as if no one has ever walked there before.

It's beautiful, he says.

Yes.

And peaceful.

She smiles; I think it is miraculous.

They stand together in the kitchen, taking turns to make the food that reminds them of the people in their lives. François makes pain au chocolat; Róisín makes boiled eggs and soldiers; together they make a tagine, cracking cinnamon sticks before throwing them into the pot, filling the base with the spiced sweet smell of lamb and apricots – food to share. And then they start to invent; new dishes made of ingredients they take turns to pick from the cupboards, combinations they would never have thought of on their own but, in this kitchen, as the snow falls, everything seems possible.

And then in the night, they are woken by silence. The snow-storm has passed and the world is quiet.

Wrap up warm, he says, looping a scarf around her shoulders, we could freeze to death out there.

We won't freeze, she says, pulling his bobble hat down over his ears. The comet will protect us.

And she is right, in a way; they don't feel the cold as they step outside and gasp at the sky, filled with hundreds of shooting stars, golden in the moonlight.

What's happening? he asks.

Her hands are held out as if she is trying to catch the stars, as if they will fall to the ground like dancing confetti to rest on her palms and in her hair, and he understands that the comet has broken under the pull of gravity, after all the distance it has travelled, it has burst apart to shower the world in light and settle in the winter's ice.

I thought it would go on forever, she says, orbiting the sun, glancing at the Earth, never getting to rest.

There are plenty of other comets to do that, François says, because he thinks that she will miss the endlessness of a comet's journey. He looks over to her, to see if he's said the right thing, but Róisín just smiles, because the sky is filled with sparkling pieces of light and she knows that now, given some time, they will find a way home.

Acknowledgements

A HUGE AND HEARTFELT thank you goes to: Terry Karten, Gregg Kulick, Christina Polizoto, Jillian Verrillo, Katie O'Callaghan, Allyssa Kasoff, the sales reps and everyone at Harper; Alison Hennessey, Kathy Fry, Sarah-Jane Forder and everyone at Harvill Secker; Cathryn Summerhayes, Siobhan O'Neill and the team at WME; Caitrin Armstrong, Claire Marchant-Collier and Scottish Book Trust; all the people who offered feedback and encouragement while I wrote this book, including Margaret Callaghan, Kirsty Logan, Nick Brooks, Katy McAulay, Jane Alexander, Viccy Adams, Maria Di Mario, Gill Tasker and Anna Power; my family, Mum, Dad, Ally, Steve and Granny, for their unconditional support; the ghosts, of course; and finally, to Michael, with love.

About the Author

HELEN SEDGWICK is a writer, editor, and former research physicist. She won a Scottish Book Trust New Writers Award, and her writing has been published internationally and broadcast on BBC Radio 4. She has performed at the Edinburgh International Book Festival, the Edinburgh Festival Fringe, and Glasgow's Aye Write. She grew up in London, but now lives in the Scottish highlands with her partner, photographer Michael Gallacher.